Jane Gordon lives in London with her family. She writes regularly for a number of national newspapers including *The Times*, *The Daily Mail*, *The Sunday Mirror* and *The Mail on Sunday*'s You magazine. She is also the author of *Hard Pressed*, *The Stepford Husbands* and *My Fair Man*.

JANE GORDON

Misconceptions

HarperCollins*Publishers*

HarperCollins*Publishers*
77–85 Fulham Palace Road,
Hammersmith, London w6 8jb

www.fireandwater.com

A Paperback Original
1 3 5 7 9 8 6 4 2

Copyright © Jane Gordon 2002

Jane Gordon asserts the moral right to
be identified as the author of this work

A catalogue record for this book
is available from the British Library

ISBN 0 00 651101 5

Set in Sabon by Palimpsest Book Production Limited,
Polmont, Stirlingshire

Printed and bound in Great Britain by
Clays Ltd, St Ives plc

I would like to thank Nino Mulabegovic for all his help, support and inspiration. He is that rare thing, a real life hero.

Thank you, too, to The Coven.

Thanks are also due to John Rush at Sheil Land for his unstinting support during the long drawn-out creation of this book. And to Maxine Hitchcock, my editor, who handled my manuscript with such sensitivity and provided me with inspiration and, among other things, the title *Misconceptions*.

For my own three perfect conceptions – Bryony,
Naomi and Rufus – with so much love . . .

Misconceptions

Chapter 1

ᘒ

It's difficult to explain exactly how the whole idea came about. We didn't cook it up along with one of the quick pasta suppers that the three of us would share one night a week. It wasn't one of those notions that occurred to Joanna or Carole or me – after two bottles of red wine – that promised, at the time, to be the answer to all our problems but which, in the cold light of the next day, would be revealed to be ridiculous and unworkable. Like the time that Joanna came up with a plan to heighten our spirituality by trekking to Nepal. Or the evening when Carole talked about her dream of creating a women's cable channel with links through to the worldwide web. It wasn't some fanciful fantasy given life by alcohol and the passion of our friendship.

No, this big idea happened one Sunday afternoon in late spring when we were all more or less sober. I had, of course, brought along to our picnic a bottle of cheap champagne which we had consumed from plastic cups along with our sandwiches and salads.

We were lying on the grass in Chiswick Park watching Carole's husband Goran play with their son Sasha and Joanna's daughter Emma. Carole was about seven and a half months pregnant with their second child, her stomach so swollen that you could see her extended tummy button through the thin, floaty dress she was wearing.

'Christ!' she said moving herself awkwardly in an attempt to ease the weight. 'Did you see that brute kick?'

And I had. A ripple, a rapid movement – like that moment in *Alien* before the creature emerges from John Hurt's stomach – that indicated a foot, or maybe a tiny clenched fist, hitting out from within Carole's womb.

'This time next year I want a baby,' I said with a long, deep sigh as I held my hand against her tight stomach and felt the fluttering motions of her unborn child.

'No ya don't,' said Carole opening one sleepy eye and glancing across at her husband and son, 'your life's perfect. You're in control, you're earning a fortune, you've got your beautiful minimalist flat, your Persian cat and a rich, attentive, married lover. Why on earth would you risk losing all that for a baby?'

'It might look like perfection to you but it's shallow, it's empty, it doesn't mean anything. I'd give up everything I've got for a little of what you have. What's more if John doesn't want to go along with it then I'll go it alone,' I said, my eyes still following Goran and the two children.

I have always found the sight of an attractive man gently interacting with young children profoundly moving. From time to time I have even indulged in wild fantasies involving strange men I have seen pushing baby buggies in public places. Once when I was wheeling my trolley (forlornly full of Sheba tins, half bottles of champagne and low-calorie ready meals) round Sainsbury's I fell madly in love with a father of two. The electric charge between us, as I bent down to pick up his baby girl's shoe, was so tremendous that we ended up having a coffee together, eyeing each other lasciviously over the heads of his children right there in the rather horrid supermarket café. But when, a week later, we met up one night for a secret assignation, I discovered that without his children his allure had gone and I realised what he was – a rather ordinary, weak man looking for an extramarital affair.

Watching Goran, a man I knew to be strong, sensitive, clever and charming, carefully lifting Emma onto his shoulders didn't, I hasten to add, excite me sexually but it did contribute, I suppose, to the way I felt that day. And, along with the sensation I experienced when I held my hand against Carole's straining stomach, it contrived to make my ovaries spin and my hormones scream.

I could tell that Joanna, too, was aroused in some profoundly biological way by the sight of Goran being a sort of surrogate father to her daughter.

'I never believed that the perfect man existed,' she said at some point 'but Goran makes me wonder if I was wrong. If I were with him, Carole, I'd have six, eight, ten babies . . .'

'I'd just settle for one,' I said as I noted the tender way in which Goran diffused his son's apparent jealousy of the attention he was giving to Emma.

'You're all talk you two,' said Carole with one of her throaty laughs. 'You're probably just trying to make me feel OK about looking so awful. Like some grotesque blow-up doll that's been over-pumped with air until she's fit to bloody burst. Your problem is that you both think yourselves into relationships and then think yourselves out again. If you left it to lust or instinct or whatever it was that drew me to Goran you'd be fine. Natural selection, that's the answer. Let ya body do the thinking.'

'Your body and your brain were both engaged when

you found Goran. A girl could go on looking for a lifetime and never find a man like him – user-friendly without being useless, good-looking, clever, sensitive . . .' Joanna continued in an unusually forceful tone.

'Don't forget his beautiful DNA,' said Carole smoothing her stomach and looking adoringly at her stunning son and his equally attractive father. 'I am lucky, aren't I?'

Goran was the only man in any of our lives – I had been divorced for five years and stuck in a relationship with a married man for the last three – who had been able to accept our friendship. The only man, in fact, who had ever managed to get on with the three of us.

Joanna's ex-husband Harry had been as antagonistic towards us as my almost-ex-lover John currently was – 'Bloody witches you three, unnatural' – he'd rant whenever I refused to cancel one of our meetings for a quick tryst with him.

All the men that we had individually been involved with over the twelve years of our friendship had resented our bond. It was my belief – aired so often that the other two would boo when I brought it up – that in the twenty first century it was no longer women who couldn't cope with their partner's involvements in same sex activities (football, boys' nights out and so on) but men who could not and would not tolerate their girlfriends maintaining their female friendships. Dismissing us as witches was a modern day manifestation of an ancient male hatred of female to female friendships (except when it involved them in a sexy lesbian love triangle).

Of course it's true to say that our closeness could have seemed rather cloying to other people. But then we weren't *just* friends, our relationship was deeper and more important than that and I suppose that in order to understand what was to subsequently happen I need to explain the link between us.

It wasn't one of those friendships that evolve through school, university or work. Where close proximity at an important time of life forges relationships between women in which mutual experience glues them together. We didn't come together like that and the mutual experience that was to bind us was unknown to us when we first met. In fact we didn't even meet each other at the same time. Joanna had known Carole on and off for a couple of years through a mutual male friend who, some time later, became my lover. It's odd that I can't remember the exact circumstances of our first meeting as a threesome – I daresay we met at some party or other – but I do recall, with total clarity, the night on which we discovered that we were, well, sisters under the skin.

It was at the end of a long and drunken Halloween dinner at my then lover's flat when everyone else had left and he had fallen into a sleepy stupor. The three of us began to tell scary stories, in rather the way you do at adolescent sleep-overs, each of us attempting to outdo each other with tales that became gradually more spooky, bloody and absurd. It was Joanna who first mentioned that she was adopted – her story was about a changeling child with supernatural powers – and within seconds we realised that this was our unique link. Not the supernatural powers but the fact that all three of us were changelings of a sort. Although our separate childhood histories were very different, each of us had been adopted and each of us had grown up within difficult and dysfunctional families.

It's difficult to explain how it feels, when you are a child of six or seven, to realise that you are not a part of a real family, that your siblings and your parents are biological strangers to you. It isn't just that you feel an outsider amongst your peers – the other girls at school, the children who live in the same street – it's a sense of loneliness that grows stronger and stronger as you grow older and older. That blood connection shouldn't be important, I know, but as you mature – as your body begins to take shape and your facial features change – you start to wonder more and more about your real mother, your real father, your real relations.

As a baby, from the evidence taken from the albums my parents carefully kept rather than from my own vague memories, I had no doubts and no worries. The photographs of my adopted mother holding me in her arms suggest that we were, at that time, the centre of each other's worlds. But by the time I was a fully formed child, and my own recollections took over from the posed images presented to me by my parents, it had changed and the predominant emotion that I aroused in my mother was anger. From the age of seven my main preoccupation was my hidden past, my lost true identity.

Which is why the changeling fantasy was such a powerful one for me – and Carole and Joanna – as children. That night, the night we found each other, we all admitted that we had, during that awkward pre-pubescent stage, indulged in a series of fantasies in which we would discover that we were really the daughter of a nobleman or a famous film star or the richest man in the whole wide world.

I can't adequately describe the emotions I felt when I was able, after all those years, to talk openly about my childhood and those feelings of being an outsider within a faux family. The stream of anecdotes that we

shared that nigh~~t, th~~ ~~m~~ ~~s~~
similar reminiscences ~~from~~ ~~a~~
feel like suddenly dis~~covere~~
three of us were chan~~g~~
even entertained fantasi~~es~~
did) that maybe we had al~~l been well~~
It was the closest I had go~~t~~ ~~to my~~
belonged, to feeling I had kin.

What might have been a mere~~l~~
transformed by the discovery of o~~ur~~ ~~into~~
a powerful alliance that, we solem~~nly~~ ~~vowed, w~~ould last
forever. Nothing would or could co~~me betw~~een us, least
of all a man. Certainly not that first man, that ex-lover
whose name I can no longer readily remember. Nor indeed
the succession of other men who drifted in and out of our
lives in the years that followed.

Which is what made Goran so remarkable. His ability
to not just accept our closeness but to understand and
encourage it had amazed us all. But then Goran, too,
knew what it was to be an outsider, leastways here
in Britain. Goran had been born and raised in Bosnia
where he had become, like his father before him, a
respected surgeon. The great tragedy of his current life,
although he never showed any outward resentment, was
that he was unable to work as a doctor in this country.
Discovering that he would have to start again from the
beginning, pushing his way through the hostile British
medical establishment and taking endless exams that he
felt were beneath him in order to be at the very bottom
rung of his chosen field, had defeated him. Instead of
performing intricate micro-surgery he was now working
for a friend of his – another Bosnian exile – who had a
small lock-up garage where they serviced cars. Perhaps the

...bout Goran was his apparent ...nyone else would have viewed as a ...edown. And the fact that he didn't seem ...at Carole, Joanna and myself all earned more ...e did in professions that were, when compared with his real calling, trivial and shallow (I work in a production company producing TV commercials, Joanna is a graphic designer and Carole was in corporate PR).

What made Goran even more unusual was that, despite growing up in a culture in which males were masters and females walked five paces behind them, he really enjoyed the company of women. Which is not to say that he was some cheap Lothario. He was very good-looking with dark, dark glossy hair and distinctive eyes – almost black but here and there flecked with yellow – but he didn't seem to realise his own physical appeal and he didn't flirt. He loved Carole and he therefore loved the people she loved. He understood women, he listened to women, he was affectionate and caring. He didn't mind when we all banged on about our work and he could even stand it when we bitched about other women. So that we would be quite happy, on our regular all-female evenings together, to allow him to occasionally join us.

Carole used to say that he had a strong feminine side that was often misinterpreted by other people (John still insisted he was a 'bloody poof'). But there was nothing effeminate about him. Rather he was extraordinarily masculine in the way in which he protected and nurtured Carole. Man enough, whatsmore, to get on with the three of us and in the process turn us into a sort of foursome.

It had been Goran who had suggested our getting together that afternoon and Goran who had made the picnic. But then of course Goran could do anything. He was a great cook, he was willing and able to care for Sasha when Carole was late home from work and at the same time he was adept at all those stereotypically male jobs around the home – anything from rewiring their run down house to plumbing in a power shower.

'Is there anything that Goran couldn't do if he put his mind to it?' Joanna asked as the three of us lay back and watched him entertaining the children by deftly juggling three apples in the air.

'I doubt it,' Carole responded with a low chuckle. 'But I tell you what he does best – he makes beautiful babies, beautifully.'

It was certainly true that Sasha shared his father's beauty – he had the same black, flecked eyes, glossy hair and strong muscular build – and that he had also inherited a keen intelligence and sensitivity. I didn't let myself think too much about the physical reality of Goran impregnating Carole with his super sperm but I think that both Joanna and I at that moment acknowledged that he was a perfect specimen of manhood.

'That's the thing isn't it, though?' I said after a moment or two. 'Even if everything worked out with John and we got together properly I'm not sure I'd want to jump into the gene pool with him. I'd be frightened of having a child with allergies and mild autism like his poor son.'

Voicing this truth – that however desperate I was for a child and no matter how often I had dreamed of John leaving his wife I had never felt comfortable about the idea of him as a potential father – was the turning point for me that day.

I knew, even before Joanna inadvertently led us to our big idea, that the father of the child I longed for would have to be stronger – emotionally and intellectually, anyway – than John.

I suppose it was my comments about John's genetic deficiencies that provoked Joanna to start talking about her theories on the future of mankind that afternoon. She began telling us how we would soon be living in a world in which men would be graded as prospective partners by the strength and genetic perfection of their sperm. She believed (but then it's important to understand that Joanna had good reasons for her hatred of the male of the species) that scientific advances would lead us to a society in which the survival of the fittest – at least as far as men were concerned – would become a reality. She had this theory, backed up by a string of strange statistics, that men without declining sperm counts would be prized and valued by society and kept in fertility centres as sperm kings who would professionally impregnate women. Meanwhile the physical rejects, with weak, weedy, imperfect seeds, would be emasculated (mind you, the voicing of Joanna's theory was enough to do that to most men anyway).

Carole and I had heard all this, or something pretty close to it, before but on this particular day we came up with a new game – a Fantasy Fertility League – in which each of us would list our top ten perfect men. Mine were, needless to say, predictable (Ewan MacGregor and Brad Pitt were one and two) but when it was Joanna's turn she just looked across at Goran and inclined her head. And it was then, out of the blue sky on that late May afternoon, that the idea was, well, born. We all three looked at Goran as he tumbled with the children and then we all three looked at each other.

It was Carole who gave voice to our thoughts. In fact,

when I look back more closely at the hazy events of that day it seems to me now that of the three of us it was Carole who conceived – and I realise what a terrible pun that might seem – the whole turkeybasting business.

'Goran the sperm king,' she said.

Chapter 2

&

Of course it didn't happen just like that. We didn't shake hands on it in the park, it wasn't a done and dusted deal. But the idea had lodged in all our heads even though we didn't actually refer to it again for several months.

I suppose that, subconsciously, during the time between the picnic in the park and the birth of Carole's baby seven weeks or so later, I was sorting my life out in preparation for what was to come.

I had resolved, on that day, to make the final break with John but it proved more difficult and taxing than I had expected. By which I don't mean that I had a change of heart, but that he did. Which, as Joanna said at the time, was bloody typical male behaviour.

Throughout our three-year affair it had always been me that had wanted to establish a real relationship. It had always been me that had put the pressure on John to leave his wife and live with me.

We had met through work and it's easy to see now that the affair had always been more important to me than it was, at that time, to him. John was the client on an account I was working on and in the heady, initial months of our liaison we were able to use business as an excuse to get away together. If we were making a commercial – and in the first year of our relationship John put more and more work my company's way – we could go on location and stay together. But as time wore on, John's passion wore off and my patience wore out, and we saw less and less of each other, managing at most one evening a week tucked up in my flat. I think that affairs with married men almost always follow the same pattern, well they have done for me. They start on a glorious, clandestine high and they end on a desperate low with me, inevitably, turning into exactly the kind of clinging, whingeing, dependent woman he was initially trying to escape from.

Mind you, looking back, I think that John could have written the Married Man's Manual. Such was his experience of extramarital affairs and how to conduct them that he could have made a fortune penning a guide to running a long-term affair within a long-term marriage. Because he knew every cliché that has ever been uttered by a married man to the woman who wants to be his second, or, in this case, third, wife. He could have compiled a dictionary of excuses, endearments and useful phrases that could be listed and looked up by muddled married men eager to know how to keep two women happy at the same time.

When I think back over some of the conversations we had and the awful corny triteness of some of his statements, I could cringe.

'Of course I love you darling, of course I want to be with you, of course we will be together forever. Just give me a little time to sort things out/If only I were the kind of man who could put my own happiness before my responsibilities I would have walked out on my wife the day I met you./Darling, you have to realise that my wife is emotionally unstable. And I just couldn't forgive myself if my leaving caused her to do something stupid / We haven't had sex for five years – since Joe was born.

We are like two strangers living under the same roof'
and so on.

John had so many pat excuses for not ending his
marriage and so many neat little phrases that summed
up his own unhappiness (he once actually said to me
that he was 'trapped in a loveless union'), all of which
I swallowed like some big pill that would make me feel
better. But which never quite did.

So you might have thought that my bringing down
the final curtain on our act (post-coitally, as it happens)
would have been something of a relief for John. That he
would have thought to himself that he could now move
on to some other 'other' woman and further extend
his repertoire of extramarital experience. But no, John
suddenly decided that I was 'the love of his life'. He
would leave his wife, he would consult a divorce lawyer,
he would find us a rose-covered cottage somewhere where
we could live together happily ever after.

The awful 'I want what I can't have' game that I had
been playing (and losing) for the last three years had
now reversed. He would ring me at all times of the day
and night telling me how much he needed me, loved
me, wanted me to have his baby. And of course, such
is human nature, that the very idea of committing to him
repulsed me.

When he realised that there was no going back he
turned nasty. He was so convinced I had someone else that
he put a private detective on me. There were terrible scenes
outside my flat late at night and early in the morning. At
the weekends he took to turning up wherever I went –
shopping, to lunch with Joanna and Carole, whatever.

By the time I did extricate John from my life, a week before

Carole gave birth, I was finished with men for ever. My hormones were still singing the Hallelujah Chorus in my head, but now they weren't connecting through to my heart. I wanted a baby more than ever but the experience with John had confirmed so many of my old prejudices about men – or perhaps I should say so many of Joanna's old prejudices about men – that the idea of being a single mother seemed infinitely more attractive than the more conventional alternative.

So that a couple of weeks later, as Joanna and I sat in Carole's kitchen watching her nursing her mewling newborn baby, the conversation turned, totally naturally, to our own maternal ambitions.

'Here,' Carole said, holding out her son to me.

'He's so, so beautiful,' I said in awed tones as I held the tiny boy.

'I told you before, didn't I, Goran makes beautiful babies beautifully,' Carole almost whispered as she watched me.

The infant Nino was so perfect that he turned my sense of broodiness into a kind of dull ache. The very smell of him, that baby-sweet scent touched with a drop of posited sick, was like a narcotic to me. I was thirty-five, time was running out. Pushkin, my Persian cat, was no longer a good enough surrogate child. I wanted what I was holding here, flesh of my own flesh, blood of my own blood.

'God, he's perfect – look at his little fingernails, look at them, Chrissie,' Joanna said as she took Nino from me, carefully cradling his head as she did so. It was obvious that she was as hormonally crazed as me.

'Are you still determined to have a baby in the next year?' Carole asked, looking at us with a piercing intensity that made me feel slightly self-conscious.

'More than ever,' I said.

'So am I,' said Joanna with a hard edge to her voice. 'Emma's five now and she wants a brother or sister. I don't think I can wait any longer.'

Joanna's problem, as she freely and frequently admitted to Carole and me, was that she wasn't that interested in men or sex. I sometimes think, to my shame, that one of the reasons why I could bear to be friends with her was her lack of sensuality. Joanna was so beautiful, so naturally and irritatingly physically perfect that it would have been impossible, had she used her looks, not to be jealous of her. While Carole made no pretence of being anything other than a 'bottle blonde' (in fact she often claimed that she had no idea what her hair colour might now be, she had been streaking and tinting it for so long), Joanna was the real thing. She had this lovely flaxen hair and very pale blue eyes that dominated her face in a childlike way giving her the look, clichéd though I know it might sound, of an angel. Well, an angel with a very full, sensuous mouth.

Joanna always used to say that she had the world's lowest libido, and we went along with this even though we all knew that her problems were deeper and darker. Her relationships with men had always been complex and I suspected emotionally, if not physically, S & M (with Joanna very much the 'M'). I never understood why she married Harry who was fifteen years older than her, arrogant, unattractive and chauvinistic. Even his money, inherited rather than earned, couldn't have persuaded me to spend more than five minutes with him, never mind contemplate the idea of a lifetime.

Although Joanna spent a great deal of time talking about her opinions of men in general, she very rarely spoke personally about her own experiences. I have always assumed that she was drawn to Harry because in some awful way he conformed to her idea of male normality. Her adopted father had been very controlling of her as a child. Playing on her vulnerability by following periods of intense and inappropriate interest in her with times when he would affect a total emotional withdrawal, much as Harry seemed to do. Harry's behavioural characteristics, even his looks, certainly echoed those of her adopted father. And although Joanna never confirmed this theory the manner in which both men treated her suggested to me that I was right.

They had this astonishingly wonderful wedding at the chapel in Harry's uncle's country pile at which Carole and I were both bridesmaids. The reception was like something out of a lavish period drama on television. The grand hall was draped in thousands of full-blown perfect bridal roses and illuminated by church candles set in crystal chandeliers. There were frock-coated footmen serving vintage Krug, a famous string quartet playing the most beautiful music and a guest list that could have walked out of the society columns of *Tatler* (and naturally enough eventually appeared in them). Carole and I were so overawed by the whole thing that we began to rethink Harry. Perhaps their union would be a happy one.

But later, when Joanna asked me to help her to go to the loo (her dress was so vast she needed someone to hold it up while she sat down to wee), she began to weep and told me she had made a terrible mistake. By that point I was too drunk to offer her any good counsel and instead reassured her that no one was ever sure that they had done the 'right thing'. I still regret the fact that I wasn't more alert that night and that I didn't connect the livid purple bruise on her thigh – revealed as I helped pull up her tights – with her tearful outburst.

Carole and I hardly saw her during her marriage. Harry clearly didn't approve of us and even our phone calls seemed to be stilted and awkward as if they were being censored by him. She has never really opened up about the full horrors of that time but I know enough to understand why, subsequently, Joanna has shut herself off from men. Harry was an unfaithful, brutal bully who mistreated, neglected and finally abandoned her when she was seven months pregnant with Emma.

Joanna's talent as a graphic designer and a little bit of Harry's money made it possible for her to work from home and base her life around her baby. They were a tight and devoted little family unit. She was absolutely adamant that she would never bring a new man into the equation because she knew that it would destroy the balance of her relationship with her daughter. Since her experience with Harry had confirmed all her misgivings about men, rooted so cruelly in her childhood, it was no hardship for her to remain celibate.

The only man that Joanna could tolerate was Goran. He had, in the years since he had become involved with Carole, very gradually won her round and made her believe that he had, as she would often say with a rueful smile, 'broken the mould'. Her initial dismissal of him in the early days of his relationship with Carole had been oddly reversed after the birth of Emma. It was then, during the difficult moments in her daughter's infancy when Joanna was a neurotic and fearful single mother, that Goran had proved himself to be the exception to her rule that all men ARE bastards. During one frenzied health scare in the midst of a meningitis epidemic, Carole's husband (rather as he was to do later with me in a very different crisis) sat by her side one whole frightening, feverish night, proving himself to be sensitive, caring and trustworthy, no mean feat for a man with Joanna.

The last few years of Joanna's life had, I think, been the happiest since I had known her. Indeed I wonder if watching how she handled her life and seeing how much satisfaction and love she gained from her child might not have had a profound effect on my thinking – she was a very satisfactory role model for single motherhood. She had, if you like, proved to me that it was not necessary to find the 'right' relationship before you had a child, she had shown me that it was possible, maybe even preferable, to have a baby without also having a man in your life. The only thing that she wanted, the only thing missing from her current life wasn't a man but another baby, a sibling for Emma.

The sight and the smell of baby Nino that day in Carole's kitchen was the final impetus for Joanna and me. It was the only time, apart from the afternoon on which the idea originally occurred to us, that the three of us talked about what we were about to do.

'So,' Carole said with a slow smile as she took Nino from Joanna, 'you are both certain that you want what I've got.'

I remember a slight chill went through me at that moment because I thought she had changed her mind. Or at any rate that she was attempting to change ours.

'How would it be possible,' I said, tears slipping from my eyes, 'to hold Nino and not want what you've got?'

'I know, I know,' she replied in a gentler tone, 'but

I need to know that you both understand what this all means.'

'That we would finally be real blood sisters,' Joanna said emotionally.

'It will be the final culmination of all the feelings we have had for each other since we met. Don't you remember, Carole, that night we found each other? Don't you remember that moment when the three of us discovered that we – oh God, this sounds so over-dramatic and I don't mean it to – belonged together?'

I think both Joanna and I sensed, then, that Carole was hesitating, that she was withdrawing a little from us. For some reason, she wouldn't meet our eyes, her face focused away from us towards a pinboard in her kitchen on which dozens of family pictures were displayed.

'Of course I remember how wonderful it was to find kindred spirits, to find you and Joanna. But Goran? He wasn't part of us, he was part of me,' she said.

'But because he is part of you he has become part of us, don't you see? If you don't want this to happen, it won't. I don't think Chrissie or I could bear to do anything that might change our relationship with you, you do see that don't you, Carole?' Joanna said.

'It's incredibly generous of you to even consider what we want, what we need,' I added, aware that maybe it was some suddenly surfacing jealousy that was holding Carole back.

'Goran isn't, he isn't always what he seems . . . He isn't necessarily the one-dimensional version of the perfect man that you think he is, he has his frailties, his faults,' she said cautiously.

'He's the closest to perfection in a male that I have

ever encountered but that doesn't mean that I harbour anything other than respect and admiration for him. He's your husband, Carole, and that's, that's – well sacred,' I said softly.

'I am just saying that you mustn't idealise Goran. He is human,' Carole replied.

There was an awkward silence then and we are so close that awkward silences only happen when we are too drunk to speak or one of us has confessed some terrible misdemeanour.

'Aren't we all,' I said, somehow managing to break the spell and produce from Carole and Joanna, a peal of laughter.

I went over to Carole then and put my arms round her, the two of us standing for a few seconds clinging to each other.

'OK then, darlings, we'd better get on with our plan,' she said as she moved away from us to check the softly sleeping Nino.

Chapter 3

❧

I have been trying, as I relate this story, to analyse my own motivations, to understand why I allowed this whole thing to happen. Why, I keep thinking, was I so desperate to have a baby? What had brought me to this point – this desperate state of primal need – at this time? And why was Joanna so similarly obsessed that she, too, entered into our strange covenant without a backward – or perhaps that should be a forward – glance?

I can't attempt to explain Joanna's feelings and motivations during this period of our lives because, close friend though she always has been, she doesn't talk much about her inner emotions. I have to accept that, as she claimed, Emma's need for a sibling, along with her own biological needs, were her primary reasons for wanting another child but I did sometimes wonder if she had some other, hidden agenda.

My own crazed mental state at this stage of my life is far easier to explain and understand, but then I would think that, wouldn't I?

Most people make the decision to have children, rather like everything else in their lives, because of a mix of hormonal confusion and peer group pressure. Just as, when I was twelve or thirteen, the actions of the other girls in my class had an effect on my own sudden need to wear make-up, dress in outlandish clothes and kiss 'with tongues' so, in my late twenties, the experiences of my friends impacted on my own behaviour. I mean of course there was an element of hormones kicking in when I snogged James Standbridge behind a tree at the old recreation ground, but it wasn't just pubescent lust. It had an awful lot to do with what my best friend of the time, and every other girl worth looking up to, was doing. It's a pretty appalling admission, but I guess that throughout my life my actions have been influenced as much by what I thought everyone else was doing, as by what I actually wanted to do myself. I think that my need to follow what all the other girls did was probably linked to my desperate desire to belong. I spent most of those turbulent teen years trying not to let the world see that my adoption had made me an outsider in the suburban community in which I was living. However hard I tried to be like all the other girls, I would always be the odd one out.

Alongside all those fantasies – that Joanna and Carole shared as children too – in which I was dramatically revealed as a princess or an heiress, there were other deeper and much darker thoughts in my head. I was not, as my parents' mantra to me throughout my early years insisted I was, 'special' because they had chosen me. In truth, no matter how sensitively it was put, I had been given away by my birth mother. I was a reject, not 'good' special but 'bad' special. And my need to compensate for that and my desire to appear like all the other girls led me to follow them blindly – if Jill and Caro had lost their virginity/learned to drive/had their ears pierced then so should I. I didn't want to be special, I wanted to be the norm. That's probably why I got married to David when I was twenty-seven and three quarters, three months short, I was to discover, of the national average age.

The fact that I knew it wasn't 'true love' didn't particularly worry me – but then I was pretty convinced that no one ever really 'loved' their life partner in that fairy tale, happy ever after way. Nor was I bothered by the fact that we didn't share each other's interests, humour or life ambitions.

What made me walk away from him, five years later, was a combination of boredom, sexual incompatibility and the fact that so many of my friends and colleagues, and Christ, society in general, had divorced or split up from *their* long-term partners.

And now, three years on, with time running out, I was under a new form of peer pressure – to have a baby. Again I found myself in a situation where I didn't want to miss out on what my friends had done. I was thirty-five for God's sake, and once more I didn't want to be the odd one out.

Add to that the fact that my hormones were kicking in like they hadn't since the days when I snogged James Standbridge (I swear I could feel my womb move and tremble whenever I saw a baby) and you have some idea of the internal pressure I was feeling. But that's not the whole of it. Perhaps I am just seeking to justify my actions, but I like to think that for me, this time, it was more than a combination of hormones and peer pressure.

Something else had come into play in the last few years. I had discovered during the infancy of Sasha and Emma that I was actually rather good with children. Worse, I discovered that I really, really liked them. Watching them evolve from these tiny scraps of shrivelled skin into beguiling and beautiful beings was just the best thing ever.

To the outside world, even to Carole and Joanna, I remained the same selfish, career-crazed, man-mad Chrissie. Everyone joked about how nothing was going to change me, I would always be the same skinny, boyish Chrissie with her unconventional taste in clothes, her married menfriends and her wild, extrovert personality – the girl (OK, woman) whose only real commitment was her Persian cat.

And while Joanna and Carole were very happy to let me see their babies – and in Emma's case, particularly, I was pretty involved in subsidiary childcare – they were never really aware of how deeply I had bonded with their children.

I was just mad Auntie Chrissie who would come into the house laden down with outrageous clothes and unsuitable, i.e. non-educational, toys. They didn't think me responsible enough to have sole care of their infants, except on the odd occasion when they were desperate for a baby-sitter, but they liked me being around as a second pair of hands.

They certainly never saw me as some potential earth mother and I think their opinions meant so much to me that they probably influenced my own external view of myself and the way I behaved. By which I mean that I didn't dare display too many outward signs of my true feelings, I accepted their preconceived view of my character. I didn't go in for any emotional slobbering and slathering over Emma or Sasha. I didn't show any interest in the practical side of parenting, things like feeding them and bathing them. And I certainly never offered to change a nappy. But inside I had this sneaking suspicion that me and babies might be a good combination.

I will never forget the first time that Joanna, who had

flu at the time, allowed me to take Emma out in her buggy to the park. I can remember hoping, as I pushed her round the big pond and over to the swings, that people would think she was mine. I can remember too, probably for the first time in my life, secretly experiencing a pang of envy and regret when I took her home and handed her back to Joanna. This feeling, this maternal side of me which I had carefully contained from everyone else, had been growing at about the same pace as Emma and Sasha who were now both a little over five. And I believe that this knowledge of just how rewarding children can be played its part in my madness. A madness that was further heightened by my lifelong need to be part of a real family.

Playing Auntie Chrissie with Emma and Sasha had, in some way, made me feel as if I belonged in their family units, but now I wanted more. I wanted, craved, needed, yearned, longed for my *own* baby.

Maybe too, the sense of sisterhood, of kinship, that I shared with Carole and Joanna played a part in the whole business. This feeling that I wanted to extend our bond, establish a proper blood link, may well have influenced my thinking at that time, making me less cynical, less realistic about what I was getting into.

Achieving my goal, the conception of my own baby, in the weeks following Nino's birth, became a total preoccupation for me. I could think of little else but when and how we would put our plan into action. Joanna, I discovered in numerous phone calls, was finding it equally difficult to concentrate on anything other than her ovaries. But we were both nervous of bothering Carole because we knew how busy she was with her newly extended family.

We longed to move forward but we were frightened of being too direct. What we wanted to find out, more than anything, was whether Carole had talked to Goran about our curious plan.

It wasn't until my birthday dinner, around two months after the birth of Nino, that the subject was finally raised in his presence.

Birthdays were an important part of the friendship ritual we had evolved over the years. As children all three of us had experienced pangs of regret mingled with the excitement of the celebration of our 'birth' days. As we grew up, those anniversaries became more and more significant reminders of the fact that we were different. They were less a cause of joy than of rueful introspection and soul-searching of the 'what if my mother had kept me' kind.

It was only after the three of us had met and established our powerful friendship that our birth date became something to look forward to. Just as other people regard their birthdays as family occasions, so now could we. Along with Christmas (which with its attendant stories of virgin births and babies in mangers became, during my own late childhood, another period for introspection and separation), our birthdays became special again because we spent them with each other.

We took it in turns to host our celebrations and on this particular evening it was held at Joanna's cottage. Goran, as the only man we had ever allowed to infiltrate our inner circle, had become a vital component on these occasions, helping with everything from the food preparation to the washing-up.

Our parties might have had a small and exclusive guest list, but they were big in every other sense. Champagne flowed, fairy lights and decorations were brought out and the food was expensive and extensive.

There was, I think, something a little special about this particular evening. Not, heaven forbid, because it was any major milestone for me age wise, but because there was this atmosphere, this sense that we were on the verge of something that would change all our lives.

Part of the evolved routine of our birthday celebrations was the present giving. Usually there would be three or four joke presents – most often presented by the children – and then a special combined 'big' gift. I opened my parcels with the usual excitement, exclaiming over them in the appropriate manner. A lot of thought had gone into the main present – delivered in the distinctive carrier bag of my favourite designer – and as I pulled the Westwood rose-print silk dress out of its tissue paper I didn't have to feign my pleasure.

When we had finished our dinner, cleared the table and thrown away all the beautiful wrapping paper, Carole said that she had a special extra present for me this year. And, no, Goran didn't jump out of a giant cake wearing nothing but a big ribbon round his neck. It wasn't like that, there wasn't anything physical.

Right from the start I am absolutely certain that there was never any question – certainly in my mind – of our coming between Carole and Goran. The idea of his being our perfect man was always a biological notion. In fact I would go as far as to say that I never, ever thought of Goran as a man with whom I might have a sexual relationship. Carole had, as we had established over Nino's cot shortly after his birth, no need to feel any jealousy towards Joanna and myself and her husband.

When we first met him I suppose there must have been

some kind of physical appraisal. I know that I felt very threatened by his sudden presence in Carole's life – they had met in circumstances that she thought highly romantic but that I, protective of my friend, regarded as highly suspicious. In the course of her work Carole had organised a weekend conference at a grand London hotel in which Goran happened to be working illegally as a washer-up. At the end of the big dinner on the Saturday night Carole had gone into the kitchens to thank the chef and had slipped over and badly sprained her ankle. Goran had responded to that old clichéd cry of 'is there a doctor in the house' and had gently examined Carole's finely turned ankle, placed several bags of ice over it and reassured her that it wasn't broken. Those big, black eyes, that caring, sensitive touch and his poignant personal history – a doctor reduced to washing up in a hotel – amounted, for Carole, to love at first sight.

He hadn't been in Britain more than a few months, his English was fractured and Joanna and I were dubious of his motives. We had this notion that he had become involved with her not out of any genuine attraction but out of his desperate need to be allowed to stay in this country. He was so unlike anyone she had previously been involved with. Carole was so glamorous – she had this remarkable hour-glass figure which was almost permanently encased in hour-glass frocks – and her lovers had always matched her successful, dynamic image. They were confident, achievers, usually a few years her senior (and, as often as not, married). Goran was four years younger than Carole and, in the early days, dependent on her for everything – his passport into Britain, the food he ate, the roof over his head.

It took about eighteen months for me to accept Goran.

At the beginning of their relationship I found their passionate intimacy irritating and unsettling. But by the time they married, when Carole was three months pregnant with Sasha, I was convinced Goran was the best thing that had ever happened to her. I am not sure how he achieved this turnaround, with slow, stealthy charm, I suppose, but anyway eventually he wooed us as surely as he had wooed his wife.

I have been trying to remember exactly when it was that I began to trust him. I think that women, however sexist this might sound, first begin to rethink their response to a man in a moment of crisis. And for me the drama that promoted Goran from Carole's doubtful consort into a knight in shining armour occurred when I was involved in a frightening car accident. Not frightening in the sense that it, in any way, threatened my or anyone else's life. But disturbing because it happened in the middle of the night on a remote road on the outskirts of London. Driving home from a shoot, having shamefully consumed slightly more alcohol than was probably legal, I suddenly picked up in my headlights the shape of what looked like a young deer and, in order to avoid hitting it, I swerved off the road. Although I didn't think there was much damage to the car, my head had slammed against the steering wheel and I was trembling with shock. I had landed in a small but deep ditch at the side of the road into which one of my wheels had wedged so that try as I might, I could not move the car. I couldn't ring the AA because I thought that somehow the police might get involved and I daren't risk being breathalysed. And in the end, despite the fact that it was now the early hours of the morning, I rang Carole.

Goran turned up, driving his work van, about half an

hour later. He was so strong, so kind, so supportive that all the reservations I might previously have had about him dissolved into the misty pre-dawn air. He examined the cut to my chin, deciding that he could close it – I had been steadily bleeding since the car had left the road – with some butterfly stitches he had in a first aid box in his van. He wrapped me in a blanket, sat me in his van and kept saying to me, in oh such comforting tones, 'Don't worry, Chrissie, I look after everything.' He gently cleansed and covered my cut, and I can still recall the extraordinarily soft yet sure touch of his hands as he held my face up to the light and pronounced that there would 'be no scar to your beauty'. (His English, at that time, was still heavily accented and his grasp of grammar poor, albeit often charmingly so.) He managed to get my car out of the ditch and attached to the tow bar of his van and then he drove me home where he made me some sweet tea and reexamined my wound. In all my life only one other man – and I hadn't then met him – was to ever care for me in that way and when Goran left, sometime after dawn, I had totally taken him to my heart.

But however much I admired and respected him I never entertained even the wildest, secret fantasy about him. I never consciously felt jealous of Carole, except in a very abstract way, and I never wished that he were my partner, rather than hers. He was the natural choice for our unnatural plan because, as he proved again and again after that first breakthrough moment, he was an intelligent, caring and sensitive human being whom I knew through my observations of him with small children to be the ideal biological father.

I think too, although I know it might sound preposterous to people who come from more ordinary family setups than those of Carole, Joanna and myself, that I saw him as *kin* – perhaps in the way that some people relate and bond with their brothers- or fathers-in-law. Carole may have tried to deny it but Goran *was* a part of us, and therefore part of my imagined ideal family. Any suggestion of sexual contact with him would have been as shocking and unimaginable to me as an incestuous union. Goran was always Carole's man. We were too close to her – and subsequently too close to him – for there ever to have been even the slightest hint off a flirtation between us. I would have staked my life on the fact that Goran shared this view – in all the years that I had known him I had never seen him do anything in the least bit inappropriate. I had never seen him, as would have been possible bearing in mind her extraordinary beauty, let his eyes linger too long on Joanna. He didn't give off any of those signals that, occasionally, even your most platonic of male friends might suddenly emit.

There was no question Goran himself viewed either Joanna or myself as potential sexual partners. We were beyond that as the events of that birthday evening confirmed. Carole's special present to me was her husband, but not in a sexual sense. She reached her arm across the table to grasp Goran's hand smiling first at me and then at Joanna.

'Goran knows, it's OK. He regards you as family anyway, don't you, darling?' she said looking lovingly at her husband.

'I think it's the most incredible compliment to me. And it will make the three of you into a proper family. Real blood ties,' Goran replied, his distinctive black, flecked eyes, in the soft candlelight, taking on a strange almost otherworldly glow.

'Not what you might call a traditional family,' I said, in slightly slurred tones, 'but better than that. I mean for us – for Joanna, for Carole, for me – it will be like one of our childhood dreams come true. It's like turning our changeling fantasies into a proper reality, taking control of our futures and really belonging together. We are family.'

At which point all three of us simultaneously broke into a loud chorus of Sister Sledge's song.

We had, of course, had a bit to drink that night. The women, that is, not Goran. I probably should have said that Goran was a Muslim, although it never really seemed important. In the part of Bosnia from which he came the rules were rather more relaxed and the only really obvious difference between his lifestyle and ours was that he didn't eat pork and he tried his best not to drink alcohol. But he never – well he had never – been remotely censorious of our drinking and on this celebratory night we had consumed more than was usual even for us. It was obvious to us all, despite our state, that Goran was a more than willing partner to our plan.

'So, where do we go from here?' I said casting a quick bashful glance at him but directing my question at his wife.

'Definitely not up to the bedroom with Goran,' said Carole with one of her long infectious dirty laughs.

When Joanna disappeared and came back with a big birthday cake and they all sang *Happy Birthday Dear Chrissie* I felt as if the year ahead really was going to be a turning point in my life.

As I blew out the symbolic candle, I made my wish. So confident was I, and so inebriated, that it didn't enter my head to think of the complications that the granting of that wish would bring with it.

Chapter 4

It was Joanna who did most of the research into the whys and wherefores of turkeybasting. She was the kind of person who, having made a decision, will then systematically, perhaps even slightly obsessively, find out everything there is to know about the subject in question. And in this case that involved her in an extensive multi-media sortie. She trawled through some of the strangest sites in cyberspace – www.womb.com, for example – in her bid to find out the facts. She accessed lists of experts in the field and traced the history of the whole business back to a now somewhat disgraced female doctor who had helped childless couples back in the 1950s, to conceive babies spawned from the sperm of strangers. She spent ages at her local library sifting through back issues of newspapers containing stories of women who had, in the past, artificially impregnated themselves, often in circumstances that the mass media found morally offensive ('THE VIRGIN BIRTH – lesbian couple have IVF baby on NHS').

Joanna and I spent several evenings together going through all this odd and disturbing information, marvelling at the lengths to which women will go in order to procreate. We were incredibly judgmental about what other females had been through and yet, curiously, we never attempted any rational analysis of our own actions.

Rather it was Joanna's belief, which she subsequently instilled in me, that what she and I were doing was the equivalent of a revolutionary act. Her confirmed conviction that in the future more and more women would free themselves from the constraints of the traditional relationship enabled her to view our plans as 'one small sperm sample from man, one giant leap forward for womankind'. I wasn't quite as convinced of the obsolescence of the male but my experiences with David, John and every other man who had come into my life made me fairly certain that I would never find myself as a part of a traditional family unit. So that while I went along with Joanna's contention that what we were doing was tantamount to a radical social experiment, I also believed that for me it was a practical solution to an impossible problem; finding the perfect man, falling in love and creating a baby together before it was physically too late for me to conceive.

Since Carole was so absorbed in her domestic life during this period, Joanna and I found ourselves meeting up without her, sitting, for hours on end, in restaurants or in each other's homes, feverishly talking about insemination. There was something of a Girl's Own adventure feeling about our attitude at this point. It was as if we were planning some hugely exciting new sport or foreign holiday – white water rafting down the Orinoco or abseiling down a rock face in the Pyrenees. And I suppose, although I know the parallel is both crass and corny, we *were* embarking on a dangerous journey into the unknown.

Joanna finally found the most comprehensive guide to the subject in an obscure lesbian and gay bookshop on the Charing Cross Road. It was American (needless to say) and it had what struck me as the most hysterical title ever, *Self-Fertilisation – A Beginners' Guide*. I laughed 'til I cried when I saw it.

'It's the ultimate self-help book,' I screamed as I thumbed through the pages of what appeared, due to the amount of anatomical drawings, to be a step-by-step instruction manual on one-woman-and-a-donor pregnancy.

Joanna drew up a table – she is a great list and table person – with a kind of countdown to conception. Preparation, if we wanted to do the whole thing according to the book, was vital. Joanna was very strict with me, forcing me to give up smoking and insisting on my taking a bit more exercise, getting earlier nights and swallowing various vitamin supplements. I didn't mind walking to the tube station each morning, or slurping down Sanatogen Gold tablets but phasing out the fags was so difficult for me – I had been a confirmed smoker since I was fourteen – that I was unable to stick to the rigid alcohol programme of no more than two units per week. Not, you understand, that drink was a problem for me. It was more of an aid to relaxation really, my first glass of wine of the evening signalling to me that my working day was over. Joanna, herself not exactly an alcoholic but none the less attracted to the feeling of wellbeing that the odd glass could induce, went along with this one vice, indulging alongside me in rather the way that she always had done.

But in every other sense I really did try to be more sensible about the way I lived my life and making those changes made me feel I was on my way to achieving my goal, making a perfect baby.

The handbook wasn't, of course, just packed with advice on how to get your body balanced in preparation for pregnancy, it also taught us how to work out our menstrual cycles and to know when we would be at our most fertile.

Now all we needed, at different times of the month thank goodness, was a sample of Goran's super sperm. And although we both knew that Carole was more than willing, in fact since Nino's arrival she had become increasingly keen for us to turn our sisterhood into a motherhood, and despite the fact that Goran was complicit in our plans, it was nevertheless difficult to, er, raise the subject.

We managed, though, one Wednesday night at her place. It was the first of our meetings in ages that had taken place in Carole's crowded, chaotic kitchen. Holding Nino in my arms made me ache with a kind of maternal lust. He had reached that stage when the first windy facial expressions are transformed into really responsive smiles and the sight of his old man's face, with its distinctive black and yellow flecked eyes, wreathed in grins impacted on my hormones like a fork of lightning on a metal umbrella.

When Sasha and the baby had finally been put to bed and the three of us were sitting drinking wine and relaxing, I summoned up the courage to talk about Goran's sperm count.

'Carole,' I said cautiously, glancing across at Joanna to make sure that she was with me, 'this business of the babies. We've bought a book, we know what we've got to do. I've given up smoking and we've even started to take folic acid. We've done everything we can but there's something we can't do and it's really a little awkward . . .'

Carole, who had for once failed to cook us one of her splendid meals and had instead sent out for a takeaway

Chinese, looked up and gave us one of her enigmatic smiles, followed by a short, throaty laugh.

'Oh, I know what you need and I'll organise it for you.'

'The thing is,' Joanna went on nervously, 'there is this thing about timing. It has to be, er, fresh . . .'

'How fresh?' said Carole with another bright smile that suggested that she was completely unfazed by the idea.

'Forty-five minutes fresh,' I replied, quoting page seventy-three of *'Self-Fertilisation – A Beginners' Guide'*.

'Then Goran will just have to come, so to speak, to you when you're ready, won't he?' Carole said with a short – perhaps a little too sharp – laugh.

We laughed along with her but perhaps there was something a little hollow about it and something a bit sinister about Carole's slightly desperate need to share her *sperm king* with her two best female friends. Looking back I can see that all our decisions, so momentous and life changing, were taken not just under the influence of our hormones but also under the influence of alcohol. I think that maybe we didn't really want to think too hard about the consequences. Joanna and I were, by that time, so biologically driven that we went in blindly, not wanting to see the flaws in our actions. But then I think that a lot of people do that, really, they want a baby in a very *simplistic* way. They don't let themselves ponder too much on what happens when that baby becomes a child or, more disturbingly when that child becomes a teenager and finally a judging adult.

In the time between our kitchen conversation and the moment at which I was, according to my calculations, at my ripest, I justified what I was about to do in all sorts of ways. I would find myself, last thing at night, going through all the men I had ever slept with and working out how often I had risked a pregnancy since I was sixteen. They say that women are impregnated much more often than they think but that as many as one in two conceptions is naturally aborted within a couple of days.

There had been times, in my late teens, when I had endured nightmarish moments when I thought that I was pregnant. I can remember vividly the joy I felt once when, after three weeks of agonising, I went to the loos at school and saw the first drops of dark blood on my regulation green knickers. What I am trying to say is that there are probably as many women who have babies accidentally as there are women who have them by design. When I was married to David I remember one particular holiday when I had forgotten to take my pill – the mini-pill that doesn't cover you if you fail to take it for even one night. And in the final stages of my relationship with John I had depended on withdrawal because sex became so rare and irregular. I reckoned that there had been about twelve occasions in my fertile life when I might, just, have conceived. But not one of those men, would be as fit a biological father as I imagined Goran to be. Not one of those men, and not all of them were that well known to me, would have stood up to the kind of scrutiny that I had given the father of my prospective child.

What I was about to do was, I reckoned, far more sensible than the accidental conceptions I might have mistakenly made in the past. The fact that despite all those furtive unprotected fumblings I had never become pregnant didn't worry me. I wasn't concerned about my own fertility. I reckoned that my hormones were telling me that now was the time, and this was the man.

I didn't talk to Joanna about how she went about enacting the single-woman-in-the-twenty-first-century version of the birds and the bees, but I decided – on *the* day – to make it special. I wanted to create a feeling of romance despite the cold and calculating way in which I was making a baby (well, I can tell you that the steel edge of the turkey baster is far colder and more calculating than any man I have ever come across). I had rung Carole that morning and told her that I was ready and she had rung me back in the afternoon to arrange a time when Goran was available. I had taken a day off work and I spent the rest of that afternoon physically and psychologically preparing myself for the momentous task ahead of me.

I reasoned – perhaps 'reasoned' is the wrong word – that it was important to somehow have a memory of this day. You hear women talk about the moment at which they conceived their child – some highly charged and meaningful sexual exchange with their partner that they claim was the time that his sperm met their egg and fused. Public curiosity about the offspring of the rich, the royal and the merely famous has caused all sorts of speculation about conception – didn't the tabloids work out from Cherie Blair's due date the exact night and place at which Leo was first mooted? Printing, in the papers, pictures of the exterior windows of the very bedroom at Balmoral in which it was thought that the Blairs did the business.

The solo circumstances of my own planned conception didn't affect my need to have a mental snapshot of the fusion of my own egg with Goran's sperm. Absurd though it might seem, I wanted it to be 'special'.

So that afternoon I went about creating the right atmosphere and the right emotional state for the occasion. Oh,

I know it sounds silly but I went through exactly the kind of preparations you might if you were planning a magical first night with a new lover. First of all I made my flat look and smell wonderful. I cleaned up and threw out the build-up of the last few weeks, pushing everything I didn't like or couldn't face, like credit card bills and bank statements, into cupboards and drawers. Then I went out and bought some extravagant props for my beautiful home; my taste in clothes might be wild and over the top but my living space is a minimalist shrine. New candles, an environmental oil infuser, stacks of polished autumn fruits and armfuls of the pink lilies that, ordinarily, offer the only colour in my big cream and beige open-plan living area. Shopping has always been my favourite form of therapy and that day I indulged myself in my favourite department store, buying a very convincing fake fur throw for my bed and, most excruciating of all, bearing in mind the task at hand, an exquisite new set of Barbie pink La Perla underwear.

I stocked the fridge with a variety of special treats, including a bottle of good champagne and, that done, began my laborious personal preparations. I spent an hour soaking my body in a bath filled with my favourite Jo Malone oils. I exfoliated, I creamed, I soothed and caressed my skin, I even did my bikini line. I washed my short, spiky dark hair and gently blowdried it so that it softly framed my face. I even made up my face with extra care and subtlety noting, as I looked in the mirror, an unusually lustrous quality in my green-grey eyes.

I timed everything so that I would be ready when Goran and Carole were due to arrive at nine. At eight-thirty I took off my bathrobe and put on the new underwear slipping over the top of it a cashmere jumper and a pair of jeans (I resisted the urge to put on a long silk negligee because I didn't want Goran and Carole to misinterpret my motives). Then I took the champagne and a single fluted glass upstairs to my bedroom in order to make everything ready. I lit the two dozen church candles that I had dotted around the room and then I put on my favourite Samuel Barber CD.

When the door bell rang at five to nine I felt like a nervous young virgin, jumpy, excited and bashful. I think that I blushed for the first time in fifteen years when Goran kissed me on both cheeks as was his custom and made his way into my flat. It was Carole who somehow diffused the awkward nature of our assignation, gently whispering instructions to her husband who, without any apparent reluctance or embarrassment, disappeared discreetly into my bathroom, which doubtless still harboured the heady scent of all my oils, creams and cosmetics.

Carole sat with me, chatting away about the children and the latest renovation plans that she and Goran had drawn up for their huge, ugly Victorian home. I poured her a drink and listened passively as we waited. I suppose he was only gone for about ten minutes but it seemed like an eternity and when he crept back down the stairs I found myself unable to meet his eyes or look closely at what it was he was holding in his right hand. Carole, again, made everything less awkward by gulping down her drink, getting up and indicating that it was time for the two of them to, er, leave me to it.

Our goodbyes were quick and perfunctory. No mention was made of what was to happen next, they both just hugged me and went, leaving me staring at the Tiptree jam jar Goran had left on my kitchen worktop. I went straight upstairs aware that the biological clock I could hear ticking now was the one counting down the forty-five minutes I had to do the deed. My bedroom looked stunning in the collective glow of all those candles. I opened the champagne – I couldn't manage this thing without a little alcohol – poured myself a glass and drank it. Then I stood in front of the mirror and slowly removed my jeans and jumper, gyrating my hips like a lonely lap dancer in a deserted club.

Solo sex is, I think, generally regarded as much more normal, necessary and acceptable for men than it is for women. Perhaps that's because we can't – well I can't anyway – just slip into a state of sexual autopilot at the mere sight of a centrefold or the sound of the man-made panting of a soft porn video.

Women – in my experience (which is, I hasten to add, limited to me) – have to work harder in order to arouse themselves and achieve any kind of sensual satisfaction. So, yes, I did caress my near-naked body in the mirror, running my hands across my breasts and then down between my thighs, in order to seduce myself. Heavens, however strange and unnatural this act I had to perform was, I still needed a little foreplay.

When it was over I didn't light a cigarette or talk about how the earth had moved. I didn't even ask myself 'how was it for you?' I just went to sleep, waking up at about four in the morning to find my metal and plastic partner digging uncomfortably into my spine. Momentarily horrified by what I had done, I got up, went to the loo, put the turkey baster in the dishwasher and turned it onto the boil programme.

Chapter 5

❧

Joanna rang me a couple of days later to confide that she, too, had made love – and hopefully a baby – with a kitchen implement she had bought in Divertimenti. We were both rather appalled at our equal eagerness to turn our mad plan into a fruitful reality.

I suppose it was naive of me to expect to conceive on that first occasion. For two weeks afterwards I walked around in a glow, convinced that inside me cells were dividing and multiplying to form a tiny perfect foetus. I knew the date that my next period was due, and I am rarely late, so when it came, and went, I mentally punched the air, jubilant that it had all happened so easily. What on earth, I thought, was all this fuss about? All that business about infertility that was said to be the curse of my generation? Such was my stupendous arrogance and self-satisfaction that I actually thought, and voiced aloud to Joanna, that perhaps other women had problems because they went about getting pregnant in the wrong way.

On the same afternoon on which I went out and bought a Predictor pregnancy test, three days after my due date, I found myself, in the loos at my office, weeping at the sight of the blood on my pure white M & S high-legs. It was probably just as well that the first attempt failed because

I did manage to gain a little humility. And I did, finally, understand something of the pain that infertile women go through. The feelings that swept over me, as I stumbled out of the cubicle and got a Tampax from the machine, were the exact opposite of the ones I had experienced all those years before as a sixteen-year-old schoolgirl. In place of joy there was sorrow, instead of relief I felt a feeling of regret. I began to relate to a woman in accounts at work. I didn't know her that well but I had heard, as you do in small companies, of the agonies she had suffered during her four unsuccessful attempts at IVF. I hadn't previously been able to appreciate why this woman – Jean – would put her whole life on hold, taking no interest in her career or the usual social banter of office life, because of her desire to conceive. But now I realised that being barren, being unable to have a baby, was probably one of the most terrible things that could happen to a woman. Leaving her feeling, as Jean confided to me a couple of weeks later, that in the most profound sense she was a failure, a dud, a reject of nature, someone apart from other women, resigned to a future as the eternal maiden aunt.

In my case, of course, it was too soon to experience such intense feelings – I had, after all, only had one try. But nevertheless I found myself, last thing at night, again going through all the men I had ever slept with and counting the times when I might have conceived and then coming to a quite different conclusion from that I had reached a few weeks before. But who knows, until they actually try, whether or not they are infertile?

Meanwhile Joanna, who in any case already had proof of her own fertility, became pregnant from the contents of her very first Tiptree jam jar. So sensitive was she to my own feelings – I had rung her tearfully on the afternoon my period had started – that she couldn't bring herself to tell me that her own impregnation had been successful. It was Carole who broke the news to me and Carole who, very gently, suggested that I try again in the middle of my next cycle.

Both Joanna and Carole, not to mention Jean in whom I had half confided, (although I hadn't mentioned to her the strange circumstances of my botched attempt at conception) counselled and comforted me, reassuring me that it took most couples an average of six months to 'get lucky'. Bolstered by this, and more determined than ever to have a baby, I waited for the right time of the following month and then tried again. More pragmatic this time I decided, as Joanna advised, to have two shots that month, three days apart.

I didn't go to the same, rather sad I think now, lengths to create the right romantic atmosphere for conception. Instead I decided to jettison all the pretty props, the soft music, lighting and underwear, and spend the entire day following each insemination in bed. If I didn't move, I reasoned, the millions of little sperm that were wriggling their way through my vaginal canal would have a greater chance of successfully reaching their goal.

In the weeks following the second – and third – attempts, I was not nearly as confident of my condition as I had been the last time. Rather I walked around as if any slight movement could cause me to spontaneously abort. I wore flat, sensible shoes, which raised a few eyebrows in an office used to seeing me teetering around on stilettos or, at my most tame, in kitten heels, and refused to do any sudden reaching or lifting. I told everyone, apart from Jean, that this was because I had done some damage to my back but I am not sure anyone really believed me.

I was at home at the weekend, mercifully, when I discovered that my period had come on, this time two days early. I rang Joanna who came round with Emma in tow and attempted to comfort me. It was a little awkward because she hadn't yet told her daughter of her own pregnancy – she wanted to wait until she had safely reached three months – and I wanted to moan and groan about the cruelty of fate, although 'fate' hadn't really played much of a part in our plans. But we did manage, while Emma watched a video, to talk a little about my feelings and Joanna repeatedly attempted to reassure me that it was perfectly normal for the human body to take a little time to conceive (although, again, 'normal' had little to do with our big idea).

'But I did it twice this time – I mean there must have been a trillion of Goran's super sperm coursing through me and not one made it. And I mean we know that he's fertile – look at you and Carole – so it might be me,' I whined.

Joanna suggested that maybe I wasn't reading my menstrual cycle right and we sat down and studied my calculations written at the back of my diary. There was always, she said, a margin for error and next time she would supervise me, take my temperature and make sure that I was ovulating when I thought I was. I was torn between gratitude and irritation at Joanna's intervention. Part of me found her attitude a little patronising; she was, after all, nearly six weeks 'gone'. But another, very telling, part of me wanted someone else to share the responsibility of my own conception.

But by now I was very neurotic and extremely anxious to fulfil my biological imperative. My entire life, I see now, has been ruled by the anxiety I experience when

I can't have what I want. The spectre of infertility now made me even more crazed to have a baby. The idea that I would never become pregnant now haunted me in much the same way as, a year or so previously, the thought that John would never leave his wife had done. If I was biologically crazed when we went into this whole mad turkeybasting plan I was now mentally obsessed as well – I didn't just want a baby, I would die if I couldn't have one.

During the time at which I reckoned I would next be at my most fertile, Joanna went into full state-registered nurse mode, turning up to check my temperature morning and evening until she deemed I was, well, properly ripe. Most disturbing of all, though, was her suggestion that she might help me to do the deed. I was outraged by this idea for two reasons: The first, obviously enough, because close though we were, I felt the idea of Joanna wielding the baster was just that little bit too intimate a step to take. And second, because inherent in her premise was the idea that I was incapable of completing what was, after all, quite a straightforward task without making some mistake. Did Joanna think that I had been, as it were, journeying down the wrong path? Did she imagine that I was so dizzy and incompetent that I didn't actually know where babies came from (and how they got there)?

I did, though, agree that she should be there for the delicate task of moving the contents of the next Tiptree jam jar (actually I think Carole must have run out – or gone on an economy drive – because the next samples came in Sainsbury's own brand jam jars) into the baster. That far, but absolutely no further, I would let Joanna go.

There was, on the next occasion, something a little

farcical about our situation. Joanna, Carole and myself sitting together sipping our wine and chatting as if we were at one of our regular get-togethers, while upstairs Goran got it together. I felt rather dejected when he came down this time. This was getting, rather like the sexual act itself, a little repetitive.

The difference between this time and the previous dates with a jam jar, though, was that this was very much a group effort. Goran who had, perhaps, become used to this odd procedure, moving into the kitchen to cook us up a pasta supper while we women went upstairs to baste up a baby.

Carole and Joanna, I hasten to add, were not actually in my bedroom with me when my baby was conceived. But they had painstakingly explained to me, as if they were *Blue Peter* presenters telling an audience of small children how to make a doll out of a bit of cardboard and some Blu-tak, exactly what I was supposed to do, Joanna tapping her tummy to indicate 'one she had made earlier'. They left me alone for about twenty minutes which was about eighteen and a half minutes longer than they needed; if the average sex act lasts 5.6 minutes then turkeybasting isn't just a more efficient alternative, it's also a speedier one.

It sounds appalling now but afterwards we all sat round my kitchen table and ate the penne with a quick sausage sauce that Goran had prepared. We gossiped and giggled as we did on any other, more normal, evening the whole thing coming to an end when Joanna realised she had to be back to relieve her babysitter by eleven-fifteen. We parted, as always, with hugs and kisses. And no, Goran didn't say 'thank you for having me' as he left. Well I hadn't had him, had I? At least not in the accepted sense.

I knew that very night that I had conceived although I still went through the process of insemination three days later and again three days after that. I have always been sceptical about women who say that they know, at the moment of union, that they had 'made love and a baby'. But that night I felt the same. Not, you understand, that I had looked lovingly at the instrument of my pleasure (it wasn't, anyway, pleasurable) and felt some psychic connection. No, I just felt somewhere inside me, deeper than any man – or kitchen implement – had ever penetrated, that something had biologically clicked. I went ahead with the two follow-up jam jars (and the same strange supper routines) but I knew they were unnecessary, I knew the deed had been done the evening that Goran had cooked his favourite River Café recipe.

I didn't say anything to anyone, though, and I consciously tried to put the whole thing out of my mind as I waited for my due date to come round. When it came and went I didn't, this time, mentally punch the air but I did cross my fingers. I didn't get the Predictor out – the one I had bought two months before – until I was nearly two weeks overdue and not once during that time did I share my growing confidence in my physical state with either Carole or Joanna.

I did the test on a Saturday morning and the colour on the indicator changed within seconds of my placing it into the small sample of my urine. Even then, safe in the knowledge that I had, indeed, conceived, I was unusually circumspect. I didn't tell anyone. Of course Carole and Joanna kept asking me and I kept changing the subject which wasn't that difficult as it was by then Christmas time and everyone was madly busy and distracted.

I had this fear, common amongst women, that I wouldn't

be 'safe' until I had missed at least three periods. But of course I couldn't wait that long to tell my friends. I told them on Christmas Day which, over the years, we had chosen to spend together rather than with our variously estranged families.

Carole hosted our little celebration that year because Joanna, who was nearly twelve weeks pregnant by then, was suffering terribly from morning sickness and my flat was deemed an unsuitable and dangerous place for small children. Goran and Carole's home was the antithesis of my own fashionable living space. It was, I thought, a particularly ugly, old Victorian villa, vast and cold, in Acton that Carole had inherited from her adoptive grandmother. The four-floored house had previously been divided into bedsits and was still home to three sitting tenants; her grandmother, as far as I could make out, had been a clever and somewhat sinister exploitative absentee landlady making money out of a series of run-down cheap properties. Very slowly, as the old people living in their squalid rooms died or moved on, Carole and Goran were renovating the house. But since Goran was doing all the work and they lived on a strict budget it wasn't exactly World of Interiors.

But that Christmas Day, covered in bunting and illuminated by multicoloured fairy lights, it was as good a place to be as anywhere else I can think of. The cold, damp and slightly eerie atmosphere (it could have been the set of one of those black and white gothic horror films – it was a cross between the big house in *Psycho* and 10 Rillington Place) lightened and brightened by the warmth and laughter of friends and family.

It was when Carole carried in the big, golden turkey

and Goran was carefully carving it, that I told them my news. That I was now four weeks overdue and had tested positive. Everyone was thrilled, everyone raised their glasses to the future, even the children who could have no real idea of how their own family would soon be strangely extended, and toasted each other.

I can remember that day so clearly. Indeed if anything it was that day rather than the day of the conception that comes first to mind when I think back to that period of my life. I can see us all sitting, apparently so happy, so close, around that table. We had all dressed up. Carole, whose figure had gone back to its pre-baby perfection, was wearing a long dark frock which, uncharacteristically for her, did little to show off her hour-glass shape. Joanna, sickly rather than glowing, was already showing signs of her condition – the waistband of her black taffeta skirt stretched so that the top button had popped off. Emma, beside her, looked as if she might have wandered off the top of the Christmas tree – a dainty fairy in her glittering white and silver party dress. I was clamped into my prized Voyage slip dress with a matching ribboned cardigan, complemented, now that I was confident of my pregnancy, by a pair of high t-barred purple shoes that clashed perfectly with my yellow and red outfit.

At the head of the table sat Goran, resplendent in an antique dinner jacket and bow tie, a look of pride and contentment on his handsome face. Sasha and Nino, also wearing bow ties, were positioned on either side of their father. Perhaps the memory of that day is so clear because I have a photograph of that Christmas Day dinner – an Instamatic snap taken by remote control so that everyone's faces could be captured.

Much, much later – far, far into our future lives – I was to look at that picture, from a quite different perspective. If I had studied the face of the man at the top of the table more closely at the time would things have turned out differently? If I had paid closer attention to the way Goran held his head, the triumph in those dark eyes, the arrogance with which he looked towards the camera, might I have been able to change the course of our shared history? And if, when I examined that picture on the day it was taken, I had taken notice of the way in which Carole's smile, usually so bright and luminous, somehow did not reach her eyes, would I have acted differently? If I had realised then what I saw later in those eyes which, even taking into account the poor quality of the picture, were so clearly hiding something, some doubt, some fear, some discomfort, would my life have taken a different turn? Because I can see now that she, and she alone amongst the three women, had some idea of the enormity of what we had done. Carole, and Carole alone, had doubts about the eventual outcome of our plan, she had seen the spectre at our feast.

But that day neither Joanna nor I could see past our own excited anticipation of our pregnancies. Even when we were clearing the table, carrying loads of piled plates, pulled crackers, sauce bowls, glasses and empty bottles into the kitchen, we didn't have a moment's doubt about what we had done. We were so sure of ourselves that we made some silly joke when we saw the baster filled with the congealed fat from the turkey, lying in the sink. How we laughed, fools that we were.

Chapter 6

It was at this point in our story that the old cliché 'the best laid plans' took on a special meaning for me. I returned to work after the New Year feeling fit and healthy. As yet I had none of the usual unpleasant side-effects of early pregnancy – I wasn't tired and I wasn't nauseous.

I felt that I was as able to perform the essential tasks of my job as I ever had been. My work has always been quite physical. As a producer of television commercials, I was expected to muck in and do anything from planting a field of fake flowers in mid-winter to creating a snow storm in midsummer. And I was determined that nothing would change because it was very important that I hold on to my job.

I have never been a very practical person and despite all my anxieties about conceiving a child, I had never really considered how I was going to be able to support it. I just assumed, as I think a lot of people do, that I would carry on as ever. I was good at what I did and I enjoyed it. I had worked hard and, despite the problems provoked by my split with John, who was still an occasional client of my company, I had done well. At this point in my pregnancy it never occurred to me that I might ever want to give up my work which had, until then, largely provided the greatest pleasure and fulfilment in my life. It never entered my head that, actually, I might like to become a full-time, rather than a part-time evenings and weekends only, mother.

I reasoned that the best thing to do was to keep my condition under wraps for a while in order to prove that nothing had changed in regard to my work and that nothing was likely to change. I was very careful about confiding in anyone I didn't trust. In the end, my need to share my news with someone other than Carole and Joanna forced me to tell Jean. The look on her face when I told her that I had succeeded where she had continuously failed – she was about to embark on her fifth IVF programme – will never leave me. Her lips quivered, her eyes filled with tears and, although she bravely insisted that she was 'so happy' for me, her face told a quite different story.

Whatever her real feelings were, though, I knew I could rely on her not to say anything to anyone else at work. It was important to me to keep my news secret for as long as I possibly could, simply because I worked in an industry in which women really were equal to men. If I wasn't prepared to shift scenery, pick up props and work eighteen-hour days during an important shoot, then I couldn't hope to hold on to my job.

And it was in the course of keeping up appearances in my professional life that the impossible happened. Just at the moment when I wasn't looking for Mr Right, and certainly didn't need him, what happened? I met him. Well, I met Rob Rider.

At the end of a week-long shoot for a coffee commercial, a variation on the standard boy-meets-girl over a delicious cup of Red Mountain Reserve theme, I found myself along with my colleagues at a celebration party. During that whole week on location in a small village in the New Forest, I had been aware of him, something about him stirred something in me although I didn't consciously accept it as a physical attraction. He had been working as one of a team of landscape gardeners called in to transform a barren stretch of land behind a picturesque, but derelict, thatched cottage into a manicured, mature suburban garden. Now and again during the working day I had noticed him looking at me in a way that disturbed me – not as if he wanted to ravage me but as if he wanted to look after me, help me, ease my workload.

Everytime I went to move some prop in that garden he would be there before me, picking up whatever it was – once a small piece of statuary, another time a hanging basket – and carrying it wherever I directed. And although when our eyes met and we shared a smile something shot through me, I dismissed it because I wasn't looking for a romantic entanglement and anyway he was so not my type. I liked dynamic, dark, difficult men – clichéd though I know it sounds – with so much testosterone that they had a five-o'clock shadow at three in the afternoon. I had never in all my life been drawn to the kind of man I imagined Rob to be. He had natural flaxen hair that was a little too long and a little too curly so that, with his pale face, he was almost girlish. And although I hadn't taken in every detail of his appearance at that point, I had the impression of a blue-eyed, baby-faced angelic man whose gentleness probably covered an inherent weakness (how wrong I was).

It wasn't until the end of shoot party at the village pub that I really spoke to him and began to question my initial reaction. Perhaps my opinion of him was coloured by the effects of two glasses of white wine, the first I had drunk since I discovered I was pregnant, but, anyway, he suddenly seemed so my type.

It might, too, have had something to do with the fact that he wasn't wearing the regulation green uniform of the company he worked for but was instead wearing mufti – just jeans and a shirt but infinitely more flattering than his work clothes had been. It didn't transform him into an approximation of my usual man, the dark, swarthy success stories I usually paired up with, but it did make him look much more masculine. The combination of his muscular physique and his soft touch (those nurturing green fingers) suddenly seemed extraordinarily appealing.

I dare say that my own transformed appearance that night might have changed the way Rob looked at me, too. During shoots, I tend not to take too much care with my appearance, particularly when it's an outdoor location in midwinter. I hadn't worn any make-up that week and had spent my days bundled up in thick baggy fleece trousers, layers of jumpers and my big working boots. So the sight of me with make-up, a sequinned cardigan and a shortish skirt (in the absence of a bosom a girl has to do the best with what she's got and in my case that's my legs) probably surprised Rob as much as his did me.

But I think now that it was chiefly my hormones that drew me to Rob that night. By which I don't mean that the feelings were purely sexual but that the hormonal imbalance in me which had been brought on by my pregnancy somehow affected my mental as well as my physical state. I even think, but perhaps I am just attempting to justify all that subsequently happened, that had I not been already pregnant when I met Rob Rider I would not have looked at him twice, never mind fallen madly, madly, madly in love with him.

It is, after all, a well-known fact that pregnant women have lapses of taste. In every sense of that word. They can find the most unpleasant and unpalatable things – like pickled onion and honey sandwiches – absolutely delicious. And it is said that a pregnant woman should never be responsible for any redecoration because her usual innate good taste will have suddenly disappeared. Joanna is proof of this – when she was carrying Emma she redecorated her bedroom in a dreadful dull, dark red colour that she thought absolutely wonderful at the time. Every accessory in the room, from the duvet covers to the thick velvet drapes, had been carefully chosen and in some cases hand-dyed, to match the ox-blood red paint. Carole, who is much more direct than I am, did try to say something about the womb-like qualities of the decor and its Freudian connection to her condition, but she didn't listen. It was only after Emma had been born that she realised that her bedroom was startlingly reminiscent of one of those inside-the-human-body documentaries in which a camera travels down the oesophagus until it reaches the aorta and, ultimately, the anus. Truly, truly gruesome.

Then again pregnancy can have the most peculiar effect on your normal critical faculties so that films that you simply could not have sat through, a few months earlier, can move you to a terrible, tearful mush.

What I am trying to say is that if the hormonal confusion of pregnancy can make you eat things you would never normally dream of touching, never mind swallowing, if it can make you cry at mawkish movies and if it can cause you to pick colours, patterns and even floral curtains that you would never in a million years have chosen previously, then it stands to reason that it can have an effect on your choice of partner. Men whom, at any other time of your life, you simply wouldn't have noticed can become suddenly very alluring. But the big difference between the way in which my hormones affected my choice of men, and the way in which Joanna's hormones influenced her choice of decor, films or sandwiches, is that in my case the distortion had a positive, rather than a negative, effect.

And although this might sound far-fetched and even a little bit mad, I am actually trying to say something quite deep here. I mean we are all influenced by all sorts of things in our choice of partner. All my adult life I had been searching for the man who would be all things to me. The trouble was I had been looking at the wrong men in the wrong places. It was only now, when I was already with child, that I was able to see other more important qualities in men. Nowadays I like to think that it was my unborn baby that chose Rob. And perhaps that is not such a fanciful and absurd idea.

Anyway, I suppose I should cut short the philosophy and get on with the story. Me and Rob. I can't remember what we talked about in that first conversation probably because it was so noisy. After a few minutes of trying to say something meaningful against a soundtrack of the Goo Goo Dolls, we decided to just dance, a slow dance which involved his arms enclosing my body. I didn't want the music to stop, I didn't want Rob to have to take his arms away from me, I didn't want the moment to end.

When, inevitably, it did we stayed where we were just looking at each other. Love, I think, makes idiots of us all. It's impossible to describe how you fell in love with someone without resorting to the kind of hackneyed phrases that belong in the torrid pages of those cheap soft porn novels written by and for women. You know the kind of thing – 'we didn't need words, the connection between us was beyond that. Some deep primeval force in both of us communicated through our eyes to our souls'. But honestly it really was like that for Rob and me that night. At least it was when we danced that first long, slow dance.

It might have gone on like that if the music and the dancing hadn't got faster and louder. I don't know if it was the wine or the heat or the close proximity of Rob, but I suddenly felt very, very ill. A great wave of nausea had overwhelmed me and fearful that I would throw up, I headed for the door. He told me later that at first he thought I had simply run away from him, that I had rejected him. Half an hour later, when I hadn't returned, he decided that he might as well go home.

He found me, lying face down on a little stretch of grass that bordered the pub's car park. When he knelt down to help me I came out of my comatose state long enough to tell him, between retches, that I loved him. And the wonderful thing is that the sight of me – mascara spread across my pale face, my clothes and hair clotted with vomit – didn't put him off. Nothing seemed to put him off. Not even the fine layer of sick and snot that covered the front of his shirt where I had lain my head could come between me and him.

'There, there,' he said gently as he stroked my head, his hand pausing on my forehead long enough for him to gauge that I had a fever. 'We'd better get you home.'

I remember thinking, before I threw up yet again, that I was home. That with him anywhere would be home. He helped me up and led me over to his van. Inside it smelt of earth and manure which only served to make me sick again, which only served to add to the awful smell in his van.

I kept apologising in the way you do when you are out of control. 'Sorry – retch – sorry – retch – sorry, oh god! I'm going to be sick again . . .' And through it all I kept wondering if this was morning sickness or love sickness.

I'm not sure how long we were driving but we eventually came to a long dirt drive at the end of which was an old farmhouse. It was, he told me as he carefully carried me to the door and over the threshold, his brother's house. It had been their childhood home but his brother, who ran the landscaping company contracted for our commercial, lived there with his wife and children.

'God,' I muttered. 'What will they think of me?'

'It's alright, Chrissie,' he said, 'they're away. That's why I was here this week. To keep things going while he and the family had a break.'

He took me upstairs – I was too confused and sickly to take in the details of my surroundings – and into a bathroom where he proceeded to fill a tub with hot, scented, bubbling water. When he had checked the temperature of the water, he turned to me and asked me if I would be alright undressing myself. I nodded and indicated that he could leave. It took me an age to remove my clothes and summon enough energy to sink into the bath. I sensed, guessed, that Rob was sitting outside the door just in case anything might go wrong.

I washed my face, dunking my head briefly beneath the water and feeling, as it removed the last traces of sickness from me, much, much better. Not exactly well, but definitely better than I had felt when I had lain down to die in that grass outside the pub.

When I had pulled myself out of the bath and dried my body on the thick, white bathsheet, I felt almost human again.

'There's a clean nightshirt and a bathrobe out here,' Rob shouted from the other side of the door.

Pulling the towel up to cover my modesty, I opened the door and snatched the nightshirt and robe before darting back into the bathroom. I stood for a while looking at my reflection in the mirror as I buttoned up what appeared to be an original Victorian nightie.

I must have been sick some ten or twelve times in the period between my leaving the pub and my arriving at Rob's brother's house. I felt purged but very, very weak, when I emerged from the bathroom, my hair smoothed down and my face scrubbed clean.

Rob showed me into what had been his own child-hood bedroom. The decorative theme was aeroplanes. There were models of planes on every available surface, the wallpaper was printed with tiny Messerschmitts and above the bed, a hanging mobile of different models of early aircraft hovered in the air.

I must have fallen asleep in seconds, tucked beneath the crisp white sheets and blankets of the single bed that Rob slept in as a child.

I woke briefly several times in the night, aware that he was sitting, snatching what sleep he could, in a nursing chair placed by the door as he watched over me. I drifted in and out of sleep, deliciously aware of the fact that I had finally found what I had always, always wanted. The man of my dreams. Dreams, that night, that featured his face, his form, and the wonderful promise of his presence in my life forever.

Chapter 7

❧

The sight of five different planes, in formation over my head, slightly startled me the next morning. It took me a while to work out where I was and why I was there. I don't think that I had ever felt quite as ill as I had the previous evening. It was the kind of sickness that transported you back to your childhood which was quite fitting really since I now found myself in the shrine of my new love's boyhood.

The man himself was slumped across the chair he had sat in all night as fast asleep as it is possible to be. He looked, I thought, quite beautiful. Right from the start, well from the moment he found me lying dying on the grass outside that pub, I knew that Rob wasn't the kind of man who would pull out when the going got tough. A man who can fall in love with a woman – and I knew he had – who has just emptied the contents of her stomach all over his jeans is not the kind of man who gives up easily.

And a man who can love you when you look your very worst and not dressed in your party best is not the kind of man who is going to run out on you when your belly is swollen in the final stages of pregnancy. Even then, at the very outset of our relationship, I was mentally fitting Rob into my life, pushing away any mental objections I might have had – should have had – about embarking on a love affair with a foetus already growing inside me. It never occurred to me, then or later, to regret the baby that I was carrying. It wasn't, after all, as if it was the product of a relationship with another man, it was, I thought then, my baby so, in an odd sort of way, although the timing was terrible, there was no question of infidelity.

Very carefully, concerned lest I wake Rob, I edged my way out of the bed and crept towards the door. I felt light-headed and slightly faint but I managed to find the bathroom. The sickness had gone but my stomach churned alarmingly and my head was still burning. I guessed that I had contracted some kind of flu – it had been a bad winter for viruses – and although I knew that there was nothing seriously wrong with me I was nonetheless worried in case it might have affected my baby.

I was not, though, bleeding and I was certain that I hadn't eaten any of the forbidden foods of pregnancy, soft cheeses or pre-cooked chicken that might harbour listeria. I made my way cautiously back to the bedroom and lay down on the bed. Rob woke with a start, the expression on his face indicating that he, too, wondered where he was and how he got there.

'Chrissie? Are you alright?' he asked as he came over and settled me beneath the sheets and ran his hand across my forehead. 'I really think that we ought to call a doctor.'

I was alarmed by this suggestion. I really didn't want Rob to know that I was pregnant. For the first time in my life, melodramatic though it sounds bearing in mind the fact we had only really met the night before, I knew I was in love, and I knew that love was returned. I didn't want anything to come between us and even in my fevered state,

I was aware that the circumstances of the conception were going to be difficult to explain. In time I would tell him. But I wasn't ready yet and I certainly didn't want some doctor to discover my condition and reveal it to Rob. So I shook my head and reassured Rob that it was just the flu, adding that half the office had come down with it in the last couple of weeks.

'Then I'll nurse you through it,' he said gently. 'I don't think you should eat anything yet but we must get some liquids down you.'

He went away and came back a few minutes later with a glass of water and a sachet of Dioralyte that he had found in his sister-in-law's first aid box.

'It puts back the essential vitamins and minerals that you lose when you are sick,' he said earnestly, clearly repeating what he had read on the back of the pack, as he handed me the glass.

I sipped the drink and put it back on the table by the side of the bed. Weak though I was, I didn't want him to think, well, *ill* of me. I wanted him to know that I was ordinarily a very robust person, that he hadn't got some sickly neurotic on his hands. To that end I kept telling him how sorry I was, how I was, never, ever unwell and protesting that I really should go home. But he wouldn't hear of it.

'I've nothing else to do this weekend and my brother doesn't come back till Monday so it won't put me out at all,' he said.

Most couples get to know each other during courtships that take place in romantic settings over a protracted period of time. Ours was conducted round my sickbed in his boyhood bedroom during one weekend. I slept off and on that first day, but when I woke Rob would be sitting there, on the end of the bed, and we would talk, our conversations becoming more probing and wide ranging as I began to feel better.

'So,' I said at one point as I glanced round his room, 'your first ambition was to be a pilot?'

He smiled and shook his head.

'No I think my father's first ambition was for me to be a pilot. And his first ambition for Paul was for him to be a lawyer. It's funny how parents impose their own dreams on their children isn't it? Maybe I did love planes when I was a toddler. My mother says that my first word was "plane" and that I used to stand in the garden staring up at the sky pointing excitedly everytime I saw one. My favourite toy, she says, was a small metal Boeing 747 that went everywhere with me. And from that came all this,' he said indicating the mobiles, the models, the wallpaper and the curtains. 'My father inherited this place – we have a vineyard as well as the landscaping business – from his own father. It had been in the Rider family for over one hundred and fifty years and he resented having to devote his whole working life to something that didn't interest him. He didn't want that to happen to Paul and me. He was determined we would escape from what he thought of as the family curse. But the thing was both of us loved the land. I don't remember having any interest at all in Boeing 747s or Messerschmitts but I do remember being passionately interested in nature. I think my parents were bitterly disappointed in both of us. My father used to rant on about what a waste of money our education had been. Paul tried much harder to live up to my father's dreams. He went to university, studied law for two years and then had a breakdown. I didn't even get that far – I flunked out in the middle of A'levels.'

Their father had suffered a stroke in the late eighties, a year after his beloved wife and their adored mother had died of cancer. He lived on for a further six months during which time he finally accepted the idea of Paul and Rob taking over the business. They had changed the name to Green Piece and expanded the company in order that it might fit more comfortably, and hopefully profitably, with the times. A year ago they had opened a London nursery in Barnes, having discovered that small urban backyards were much more lucrative and cost effective than vast country gardens. Rob ran the London part of the business and lived in a tiny flat over the Green Piece shop which left Paul and his wife Anna the run of Glebe House with their children.

'They've kept my bedroom exactly as it was when I was six and I come down as often as I can at the weekends because Paul's workload is much bigger than mine and anyway I can see the children,' he said.

What other important things – apart from his love of children – did I learn about Rob that day? That he got ten O'levels, that he played piano up to grade six, that he swam for his school and had his appendix out when he was eleven. That his brother was thirty-six – the same age as me – and that he was thirty-two. This last piece of information was the most alarming as it was the first time I had ever gone out with anyone younger than me. Not that we had gone out yet. All we had done was stay in and talk.

It wasn't just Rob talking. I told him as much as I could bear to about my own family background. That I had been adopted, that my parents had divorced when I was nine, that I had grown up in an ugly town in Surrey and that I was an only, unhappy lonely child. I told him a little about Joanna and Carole, explaining the closeness of our friendship and the bond of adoption that linked us. I didn't mention Goran or how the bond between us would shortly make us more than friends, it would make us family.

By late afternoon that first day I was beginning to feel much better. My temperature had gone down and my stomach had settled. Rob ran me a bath, found me another crisp, clean white nightgown, presumably one of Anna's, and then left me alone whilst he went downstairs to cook me my first solid meal.

I wanted to go down to eat but he was very firm about my staying in bed. Locked in the bathroom, though, and reunited with my handbag (isn't it incredible the way that women hang on to their bags even when they think they are dying – apparently when Rob had found me my left hand was clenched round the strap of my bag and even when I was throwing up I didn't let go of it), I spent a little time on my appearance. I sprayed myself with Arpège – I couldn't quite shake off the lingering smell of sick – I combed my hair and put on some very discreet make-up. A little eye pencil, some concealer to cover the black shadows beneath my eyes and a touch of Clinique's natural Air Kiss lipgloss.

I was quite struck by the way I looked that evening. The white cotton nightie with its full sleeves and buttoned fastening was strangely flattering. A world away from my usual extrovert style of dressing, it gave me the look of a Victorian waif. I thought I looked a bit like Anna Friel (people often said that I reminded them of her) and I went back to Rob's bedroom feeling rather pleased with myself.

In my absence he had not only changed the sheets, he had also pulled the curtains, put on the novelty lamp, shaped, needless to say, like an airliner, and tidied up the room. He served me supper on a tray laid with a cloth. It was a simple meal. Not, he said a little defensively, because he could only cook simple meals but because he didn't think I should eat anything too rich. He had prepared a fine soup, sprinkled with croutons, and plates of scrambled eggs laid on thick fresh bread.

I told him that I hated eating in bed and he spread a blanket over the floor and we ate the food as if it were an indoor picnic. When we had finished he put everything back on the tray and took it downstairs.

I knew that I would have to make the first move that night. It was obvious that Rob was too well-mannered and too considerate to take advantage of me. I would have to take advantage of him.

I got back into bed and waited for him to return. He looked at me a little sheepishly and then asked if I wanted to go to sleep.

'Yes,' I said, pulling the sheets back and indicating that there was, just about, room for him in the little single bed.

He told me later that he was disturbed, at first, by the idea of having sex beneath the Messerschmitt mobile that had hovered over his head when he was a child. Which might explain the gentle and rather tentative way in which we made love that first time. It wasn't the usual explosion of passion you get when two people who have been circling each other for ages finally come together. But then we had only really known each other for twenty-four hours and for eighteen of those, I had been so ill that there had been no time to build the tension between us.

I cried when it was over and Rob rocked me in his arms until I slept.

Someone once told me that it isn't sexual compatibility that is important in long-term relationships but the ability to sleep peacefully together. And although, in the weeks to come our lovemaking became more urgent, erotic and exciting, it was sleeping next to Rob that I loved the most. I had never had a partner whom I felt so comfortable nestled against during the night. We slept locked in each other's arms (although it has to be said there wasn't enough room to stretch out) and we woke up still together, smiling into each other's faces.

We made love with more energy and less inhibition in the morning, winter sunlight creeping through the crack in the curtains. And then we got up and had a bath together, something that, again, felt very dangerous to Rob in his childhood home.

Afterwards we went downstairs and cooked a big breakfast. I felt born again, if that doesn't sound too fanciful. I even managed that morning, as I watched Rob eating in the unfitted country kitchen, not an MFI or a Shaker country kitchen but the real thing with a big old dresser painted, and slightly peeling, and battered Windsor chairs, to blot out all my concerns about my pregnancy and how it would affect this fledgling relationship. I just wanted to enjoy the moment, to do all those things that new lovers do without worrying about the problems we might encounter in the future.

Rob had all sorts of plans for that day. He had carefully washed the clothes that I had been wearing on Friday night and although it might probably have been better had I borrowed a pair of Anna's jeans (although perhaps she only wore white Victorian nighties), I was so touched by his thoughtfulness that I pulled on the crumpled but clean finery I had worn the night we met. A sequinned cardigan that had shrunk a little, a short skirt, and a pair of t-bar high heels wasn't the right look for a winter walk in the country, but Rob found me a long waxed Barbour and a woolly cloche so that I wouldn't freeze, even if I did look like a freak, and then he took me on a tour of the land he loved so much . . . Although he kept describing it as a 'small holding', it seemed huge to me. It was, he explained as he led me round, the quietest time of their working year. The nurseries looked bare and barren in the bright, cold January light and the vineyards looked like nothing so much as wilted bushes in furrowed land.

But the big wild back garden of Glebe House – acres and acres stretching down to a little copse with a stream – was beautiful. My delight at his childhood haunts seemed to further fuel Rob's lust because suddenly, as I sat on a little home-made swing that had been hung from the branch of a huge old oak tree, he fell on me, pulling off the woolly hat, (just as well, really) and easing the Barbour off my shoulders and laying it down as a groundsheet for our lovemaking. Suddenly the sequinned cardigan, short skirt and high heels seemed much more sensible clothing for the occasion.

Rob ground, in every sense of the word, into me like a man possessed and I thought, as I came, that perhaps there was something particularly symbolic for him to have made such passionate love to me on his home turf. This time, when it was over, Rob cried and I rocked him in my arms. He was full of remorse for what he called his 'selfish greed' in making love to me like that. Was I cold? Did I feel alright? Could I forgive him?

We walked back to the house with our arms round each other, his stretching over my shoulder, mine tucked round his waist. I had never, ever felt so happy, so complete, so full of hope for my future. When we got back we went straight back up to the little single bed and made love again, giggling and fooling around in the way you do when you are intoxicated by mad, romantic love. By now I had begun to mercilessly tease him about his plane-filled bedroom and when I found, in his cupboard, a stack of his old toys which he claimed he was saving to give to his nephew and niece, I emptied them on the floor and we sat, for ages, building a Lego house. Perhaps love doesn't turn us into fools, but into children. Perhaps it releases us back into a childish state in which we can believe in magic, miracles and a golden, happy future.

By midafternoon the pressures of the outside world began to break up our idyllic day and big grey clouds closed in around us. I went upstairs and tidied up Rob's bedroom while he made a few phone calls and cleared up the kitchen. At five he drove me back to the village pub where I had left my car on Friday. The atmosphere between us became tense and awkward.

'Can I see you again?' Rob asked as we parted.

It was a strange question to ask given the unguarded intimacy we had enjoyed over the last two days. It had never occurred to me that we wouldn't see each other again. But perhaps I had misinterpreted him, perhaps he didn't see any future for us.

'Why wouldn't we see each other again?' I replied eventually in a slightly anxious voice.

'I wondered if you were married or something,' he said looking away from me and out of the car window towards the pub where we had met. 'I sensed that you were holding something back, not being totally honest with me . . .'

I hadn't, I realized overestimated Rob Rider, I had underestimated him.

'No I'm not married and no I'm not holding back any secret lover or anything. I'm just a bit wary of men I suppose,' I said, looking up at him. He kissed me then. One of those long, long movie kisses. Not just tongues but mouths and lips and full-on arms wrapped round each other. Then we exchanged phone numbers, office, mobiles, even e-mail addresses, and arranged, in principle, to meet the following evening when Rob came back to town. This wasn't like any love I had ever experienced before, I thought as I drove back to London that evening, this was something more. I turned on the radio as I hit the M3 and, as if by some magical intervention across the airwaves, they were playing the song that Rob and I had danced to on that Friday evening. A beautiful, melancholic love song the lyrics of which, I realised as I drove home that night, were poignantly relevant to our relationship. I can't remember all the words – and I tried to find the track the other day in my scramble of old CDs so I could listen to it again – but I can recall a few of the most prophetic words: 'And I don't want the world to see me/ because I don't think that they'd understand. When everything's made to be broken/ I just want you to know who I am . . .'

Chapter 8

❧

The first couple of months of my relationship with Rob, before my pregnancy became a heavy physical and mental weight, were so wonderful that I almost began to believe that everything would be alright. That we could live happily ever after together in uncomplicated bliss.

We weren't able to see each other as much as we would like because we both had such demanding jobs. I was away a fair deal – shooting commercials everywhere from run-down inner city estates to Mediterranean beaches – and Rob's responsibilities at the Barnes nursery and at the vineyards in Hampshire weren't the kind you could put away at five in the evening or ignore over entire weekends.

We tried to spend at least two nights during the week together, one at my flat and one in the little studio over the ramshackle Green Piece shop in Barnes. I didn't try to hide Rob's presence in my life from the people I worked with because, after all, quite a few of my colleagues had been witness to the first night of our romance at that end of shoot party. I suppose at some level, although I didn't consciously admit it, I thought it was a good idea for them to see that I was madly in love because, when eventually the news of my pregnancy emerged, they would just accept Rob as my partner.

But away from work, with my two closest friends, I kept my relationship secret. It was the first time in our long and mutually dependent friendship that I had kept something from them. I told myself that I would tell them in time but that the time was not now. I wasn't ready to face up to the practicalities of my situation – I wasn't ready to tell my friends that I had fallen in love and I certainly wasn't ready to tell my love that I was pregnant with another man's child. Particularly since the 'other' man was the husband of one of my two closest friends. The moral implications of what I had done were only just starting to impact on me and for now I didn't want to grapple. I just wanted to enjoy the moment with Rob.

We continued to meet, during this period, for our regular meals together and although both Carole and Joanna made remarks about how quiet and withdrawn I was, I deflected their suspicions by claiming that I was suffering from morning sickness.

Joanna, meanwhile, had begun to show signs of her pregnancy and was sufficiently distracted by her own plans for the future to take too much notice of what would, at any other time, have been uncharacteristic behaviour from me. She did ring me a couple of times and quiz me about how I was feeling but I think in the end she put my quiet reserve down to my hormones, or at any rate, my coming to terms with the idea of impending motherhood.

I think, though, that no matter how favourable the circumstances of a new relationship are most people are a little reluctant to share their new man or woman with their old friends or their family. You wait, don't you, until you have got to know everything about your new lover before you think of exposing him to the scrutiny of those who have previously been closest to you?

So it didn't seem that odd to Rob that I wasn't in a rush for him to meet Carole and Joanna. I had, on that first weekend, talked a fair deal about them and told him how important they were in my life – more vital to my emotional security than my family had ever been. I carefully avoided the subject of their partners – or I suppose that now should be partner – because I didn't want to think about the consequences of what I had done at that point. Anyway, I couldn't even say the name 'Goran' in front of Rob. But he didn't push me on the issue of when and where he would meet my two best friends, never mind their partner/s.

I suppose we had been seeing each other for about five weeks before he brought up the subject of my meeting his brother. We were lying in bed at his studio flat late one Thursday night when he mentioned that he had told Paul about me.

'What did you tell him? You didn't say anything about my being ill and staying in Glebe House that weekend did you?' I said anxiously.

'No, I didn't say anything, he did,' Rob replied, smiling at my reaction. 'We are very close and he just guessed I had someone new in my life.'

It might sound stupid – oh God I suppose the whole bloody story sounds stupid – but I hadn't thought about Rob and other women until this moment in our relationship. I mean, I suppose I had vaguely accepted that he must have had other lovers but suddenly I became disturbed by the notion that I was just 'someone new' in his life and not *the* love of his life.

And so began our first row. Me suddenly coming over all jealous and questioning Rob about just how many women he had taken home to his brother's house, just how many women had laid in that little single bed beneath the Messerschmitt mobile. Or, for that matter, how many women he had slept with in the rather more spacious double divan in which we were now lying. My anger was further roused when, instead of gently reassuring me, as I had come to expect from Rob, he just laughed. The more he laughed the angrier I got until I was so furious I got out of bed, pulling the duvet off him and wrapping it around me to allow me a little dignity, and stomped off to the bathroom where I locked the door and screamed.

Eventually I had to come out which made me feel even more foolish. Looking back I think that perhaps I do tend to idealise Rob when I talk about him because, in fact, he was quite manipulative. His strategy, to just ignore me when I lost my temper, worked in his favour. I crept back to the bed and threw my arms around him and we made love again, this time with me taking a more assertive and active role.

Later he told me about his first love, an older divorced woman (my heart sunk a bit at that) who lived in the same village. The affair lasted for three years and he still saw her from time to time although she had remarried. There had been other lovers, closer to his own age, and he had lived with a girl for a year when he was at agricultural college but there had never been anyone, until now, with whom he could see a future (my heart soared a bit at that).

It seemed that Anna, who had been Paul's first girl-friend, had always taken a rather proprietorial role in Rob's affairs. She was, he said with a fond smile, like a second mother to him particularly since the birth of the twins, a boy and a girl. Protective and sometimes a little hostile towards women she deemed unsuitable. And now, he added, she wanted to meet me.

'When?' I said, fearful that I would not be able to live up to the expectations of a woman who wore crisp, starched Victorian nighties.

'This weekend. I've got to help Paul with the stock-taking so I need to go down to Glebe House. Come with me?'

I spent the following day preparing myself for what I knew would be quite an ordeal. I was well aware how important it was to Rob that his family like me. And I sensed, from what he told me and what I had gathered from my first weekend in the old farmhouse, that Anna was not necessarily my sort of woman. Nor I hers. Just packing was a nightmare because I had this instinct that my taste in clothes – which was as extreme as my personality, being either stark jeans and t-shirts or dresses and skirts of impossible girliness – would not meet with Anna's approval. In the end I rushed out and bought a simple skirt from M & S and one of those fake waxed Barbours, reasoning as I paid for them, that if I was going to embrace Rob and the country life, I had better dress for the part.

We got down to Hampshire in time for a delicious dinner prepared by a smiling and apparently sweet Anna Rider.

'Thank goodness you're here,' she said kissing Rob fondly and giving me a quick, cold appraisal. 'Five minutes longer and the meal would have been spoiled.'

In other words, we were late. She was exactly as I had imagined her. By which I do not mean that she was wearing a Victorian nightie, but that she had the slightly prim and scrubbed appearance of a middle class, middle England mother. Just the merest hint of lipstick on her set mouth, no jewellery apart from her wedding band and hair that was cut – no doubt because it was practical – in a blunt mousey bob.

Paul Rider was a little taller and darker than Rob and rather more warm towards me than his wife, taking my coat and leading me up to the room in which I was going to stay – not Rob's bedroom but a little spare room with rose-covered wallpaper and a pink candlewick bedspread.

Downstairs in the drawing room, a place I hadn't seen on my previous visit, the furniture was rather fine and antique and the big bulbous sofa and chairs were covered in a floral-printed linen. Working in the film industry – yes, commercials are part of the film industry – I am the kind of person who always likes to slot interiors, and exteriors sometimes, into famous movies. Paul and Anna's home looked as if it might be the set for one of those classic black and white movies made in the forties in which everyone still dressed for dinner and the flowers in the vases were full-bloomed roses plucked from the garden. A little like the house in which Celia Johnson lived in *Brief Encounter*. It was quite a surprise, then, when Anna handed me some champagne because I had rather expected sherry.

The dinner was fantastic, as I must have told Anna at least ten times. I sensed straight away that she wasn't prepared to like *anyone* that Rob brought home. I felt that I had intruded on her relationship with the two brothers, Anna as the little mother that had replaced the one they had lost too early in their lives. I knew that winning her approval would be a long and hard task. Helped, that night, by the tearful wakening of one of the twins.

When Anna brought Camilla downstairs the baby, who was seventeen months old then, took an instant liking to me. Children, I decided, would be the common link between Anna and myself. I had bought both babies presents – a stuffed Miss Tiggywinkle for Camilla and a brightly painted pull-a-long wooden plane for George – and I could feel the frozen gaze of Anna melting a little at the sight of my obvious interest in her children. Indeed I spent most of that weekend building on the spark I had noticed when I had taken Camilla from Anna's arms and cuddled her. While Paul and Rob spent all day Saturday stocktaking in the office at the vineyard, I helped Anna with the children bonding as quickly and effectively with George as I had with Camilla.

I felt throughout the two day period as if I was playing a part in a rather old-fashioned play. It was quite a strain trying to carry off the role of the kind of woman that I imagined Anna would like – solid, dependable, god-fearing and sensible. I wore my flat work shoes all weekend, kept the make-up to a minimum and – a wonderful touch this, if I do say so myself – I put a black velvet headband in my hair. I even went to church with them all on the Sunday morning and found myself, when we got back, rolling out the pastry for the apple pie that Anna was preparing as the inevitable, conventional accompaniment to the roast beef and Yorkshire puddings (hand-made, not Aunt Bessie's best) she was serving.

But while my ploy seemed to work rather well with Anna and Paul – the latter exclaiming, as we left that evening, that I was 'perfect' – it didn't go down as well with Rob. We had our second row in the car that night when he asked me what I had been playing at all weekend.

'The sort of woman that would fit in with the whole Rider family image,' I snapped back at him.

'Why are you so sure that Paul and Anna wouldn't like the real you?' he asked.

'Because it's obvious that Anna is in control in that house. She's an old-fashioned – and please don't get me wrong here, Rob, I am sure she is very wonderful and well meaning – plodding, narrow-minded housewife. Do you really think she would have anything in common with the wild, irresponsible Chrissie?'

'Why not? It would have been better than that phoney performance I watched this weekend. You were mocking her, Chrissie, and through her you were mocking Paul and me. Everything about you was false from that bloody hairband to that waxed coat. Did you get the wardrobe girls at work to call in the uniform for "boring, country housewife"?'

I had never seen him so angry. I told him that I had only done it for him, that I knew how important it was that his family accept me. But I couldn't get through to him at all and when he dropped me off outside my flat he didn't even kiss me. He just told me that the most important thing to him in a relationship was honesty. That the one thing he could never forgive was the kind of deception he had seen me pull off that weekend. That my behaviour had caused him to question whether or not he knew me at all. Perhaps, he said ominously, I was someone other than the person he had fallen in love with. Then he leaned across me and opened the door as if to dismiss me. I got out feeling stunned and humiliated. But also as if I had been found out. I burst into tears when I got into my flat and waited about half an hour, the time I thought it would take him to get back to Barnes, before I rang him. He had the answerphone on.

I didn't hear from Rob for four days. I left messages on his mobile, his answerphone and I even e-mailed him. I was terrified that I had lost him. I had been so sure that Rob was right for me. It had been the first relationship in my life in which I hadn't played games. I had been myself. But I had, all along, kept a dark and dangerous secret and I now knew I had to tell him the truth. If, that is, he ever talked to me again. When he did, finally, ring me I told him that I needed to tell him something. He said he was rather busy and for the first time in our six week relationship, he was uncertain as to when he could see me again.

He couldn't, he told me in cold tones that reminded me of those that Anna had used on my arrival in her house, see me for at least a week. Eventually I persuaded him to come over to my flat for dinner the following Friday evening, but I was left with the worrying feeling that, between then and now, he might ring to cancel.

I was tempted, during the following few days, to ring Joanna and ask her advice. But I resisted calling her because I knew that she would not be able to understand how I felt. How could she when, as she had admitted to me so often, she believed that men were dispensable? She would see my hopeless state as a kind of weakness, a giving in to the old traditions that have bound women for centuries and she would no doubt counsel me to put Rob out of my life.

Every night I would get myself to sleep by indulging in wild fantasies in which I had met Rob before I had got involved with the whole mad, fantastic turkeybasting scheme. In my dreams it was Rob Rider, not a kitchen implement, that had impregnated me. I even began to question the fact that I had been successful in my last attempt at insemination. If only, I thought, I had failed again and then met Rob and everything had happened naturally. But at the same time I knew that, as I have said before, I could not have met and responded to Rob as I did had I not already been 'with child'. To think otherwise would be to betray my baby, and I could never, ever do that.

As it got closer to the day on which we were set to meet I became more and more nervous. I found myself rehearsing the speech I would make when I finally told Rob about my condition. I even wrote it down and memorised it so that I could be sure, when the moment came, that I wouldn't be lost for words.

I arranged to have the day off, that Friday, so that I could make sure that everything was perfect that night. I bought all the foods I knew Rob liked and I made the flat look as beautiful as it could – and me, too. I had my hair trimmed (Rob had made some comment about long hair and I was determined, for the first time in about ten years, to grow my own spiky crop into something fuller and more feminine) and bought some new more natural make-up, if that isn't a contradiction in terms. At about five, Rob rang to say that he might be a bit late. Instead of telling him not to bother to come at all, which was what I really felt, I came on like Mary Poppins and told him, in the sugar sweet tones of some sub-Anna character, that it didn't matter what time he turned up. By the time he did arrive – at nine-thirty – I had drunk three glasses of wine, the most I had drunk since discovering my pregnancy, and was rather the worse for wear. More than that, I was really, really angry. My carefully nurtured belief that Rob was different was beginning to crumble. I was starting to think that he was exactly the sort of bastard that John had been.

I didn't bother to serve the dinner I had so carefully prepared. I was so tense about telling him the truth and possibly losing him forever that I blurted out what I had intended to say before he had even had time to sit down.

'The thing is Rob, I'm pregnant,' I said as soon as I had let him into my flat.

He looked at me for a moment with an incredulous expression on his face. And then he threw his arms around me and held me tight.

'So that's it, Chrissie, darling, why didn't you tell me?' he said.

'Because I was too frightened by how you would react,' I spluttered.

'Is that why you were so odd that weekend?' he asked.

'Partly, I suppose. I really did love George and Camilla you know and I really do like children,' I said, too weary and too fearful to care what he thought any longer.

'Oh darling, darling, darling,' Rob exclaimed. 'I know exactly when it was. It was that Sunday, wasn't it, when we made love in the garden of the house? I knew that something had changed then, I just didn't really know what. That's the first seed I have ever sown with all my heart.'

I realised, straight away, that my plan had backfired. I had meant to tell him about Carole, Joanna, Goran and me. I had meant to tell him what he had claimed he wanted more than anything else – the truth. But he had misinterpreted my message and assumed that I was telling him that I was expecting his child. Not that I had already been pregnant, albeit only by four or five weeks, when we had met. And the look of joy and wonder on his face made it impossible for me to correct my – his – mistake.

I never intended to deceive Rob. I never wanted to trick him into believing that the child I was carrying was his. But it had happened and I was too much of a coward – and too much in love with him – to disillusion him. If he loved me enough, I thought as I sank into his arms, he would eventually be able to come to terms with the truth I had been trying to tell him. And not the lie he now believed.

Chapter 9

❦

Life, rather like our story, is cyclical. And a few months later in the brilliant late spring sunshine I found myself, along with Carole, Joanna and Goran, sitting in the same park in which – a year previously – we had hit on our brilliant idea.

Joanna looked like Mr Blobby that day. Same high pink colour, same spotty complexion (the hormones had brought on a sudden bout of teenage acne) and similarly bloated limbs and body. Her beauty, and normally Joanna is as dazzlingly beautiful as the young Grace Kelly, had been so totally obliterated by her pregnancy that it was almost as if she had mutated. She was about a month from her due date and it was as if all her energy had been sapped by her baby.

I, by contrast, at five and a half months was still glowing and hardly showing. In fact, if anything love and pregnancy had conspired to improve my looks. It had filled out my angular, boyish frame and face and given me, well there is no other word for it really, a real 'bloom'. Even my hair seemed thicker and the colour richer, more russet than plain dark brown, and I think I looked more glamorous and feminine than I ever had in my life. Why, I even had bosoms.

The biggest problem in my life was Rob. Not my relationship with him, which was growing and strengthening like the bedding plants in his nursery, but his belief that the child I was expecting was his. I was now in an impossible situation. If I told Carole and Joanna about Rob they would want to meet him and somehow or other they might let slip that the conception of my baby had not taken place on a Barbour laid out in the garden of his brother's house. I was torn between telling the truth to my two dearest friends and telling the truth to the man I loved. And, coward that I was, the easiest course open to me was to keep on deceiving everyone and leading a double life.

I have always been the kind of person that can convince themselves that problems will eventually sort themselves out. I have always had the facility, at least in the daylight hours, to put things out of my head and believe that everything will turn out for the best. Rob was a little curious about the fact that I was reluctant to introduce him to Carole and Joanna but whenever the subject was raised I had managed to deflect his concern with some suitable excuse – that Joanna wasn't feeling too well, that Carole was too busy with work and children – and put off any possible social occasions on which he might have expected to meet them.

On this particular day I had been saved from any confrontation by the fact that Rob, at the busiest time of his working year, had been forced to go down to Hampshire to help Paul with a huge contract. I even used his work commitment to my advantage by giving Rob the impression, that day, that I felt a bit let down by his failure to be with me. Before he had left my flat, early that morning, we had rowed over the way that he was 'always working' at weekends and never able to give time to me. I had snapped at him that on the one day when

I had finally managed to get my two friends together for a celebration picnic he wasn't going to be able to be there. I managed to gloss over the minor point that I had not told him about the arrangement until the day before (and that I would be horrified if he had been able to come).

I felt a bit guilty about the way I had manipulated the situation. And, as we sat as we had all those months ago watching Goran playing with the children (Nino was now a little crawling butterball with the same brilliant black eyes as his father and brother), I almost wished that Rob was here with me even if it meant confronting things – like the paternity of my baby – that I didn't want to address.

There had been moments, in the last couple of months, when I had almost weakened and told him the truth – perhaps that should be 'strengthened', not 'weakened' because it was cowardice that stopped me.

The most testing time had come on the day of my first scan which Rob had noticed marked on my wall planner in my kitchen. He was desperate to come with me and upset that I hadn't given him warning. Just for a minute I was so paralysed by fear that I couldn't come up with any excuse as to why he couldn't be with me and why I hadn't forewarned him of the date. I didn't know exactly what they did at the scan but I knew they took measurements of the baby and calculated the due date with a high degree of accuracy. The idea of Rob discovering that my pregnancy was more advanced than he thought possible (or imaginable) in such a cold and clinical setting as the antenatal clinic, was so awful that I experienced an adrenaline rush that enabled me to come up with a convincing reason why he couldn't be there. I told him that it wasn't the real scan because it was too early and that partners weren't encouraged to attend.

But even without the presence of Rob that day in the park, the dynamics of our friendship had changed. Had been changing, in truth, over the previous few months. I got the impression that Joanna was holding back on something in rather the way that I was, although I hadn't given much thought as to what it might be. Carole's role was changing, too. It was as if, because of her greater experience of babies and birth, she had decided to take on a kind of matriarchal role in my life. Our meetings and phone calls of late had come to involve more and more advice and warnings about everything from my diet to my pelvic floor exercises. Sometimes I would come home from work to find messages on my answerphone reminding me not to forget my clinic appointment or offering me some handy hint on early pregnancy such as how to overcome flatulence.

At first I found her interest touching, perhaps because my relationship with my mother was non-existent; she suffered from Alzheimer's and even if I had told her of my pregnancy, it's doubtful she would have understood or remembered. It's nice to feel that there is someone out there worrying about whether you are wearing a vest and eating your greens. But it began to irritate me after a while because it was almost as if Carole didn't believe I could look after myself. And while, I suppose, I had generally encouraged this image of wild irresponsibility throughout my adult life, I did find the level of concern directed at me from Carole patronising and maybe even a little intrusive. I mean she knew how much I wanted a baby, did she really think I would be stupid enough, now that I was finally pregnant, to do anything that might harm it? And really some of her advice was so infuriatingly obvious that sometimes she made me feel like a mentally challenged child.

I had tried to hide my irritation by turning it into a joke, referring to her as 'the midwife' because of the way that she had begun to treat me like a patient, rather than as a friend. The way in which Carole had, since the birth of her second child, embraced the role of 'earth mother' was, I couldn't help but notice, totally at odds with the way she used to be. The outrageous, funny Carole that I knew and loved was becoming more and more heavy-going (in more senses than one – she seemed to have put on, not taken off, weight in the last few months). And while I could understand that with two young children it was difficult to find time to do things like have your roots done or take an interest in life outside the home, I had this sense that Carole had let herself go in a way that wasn't quite healthy. And her habit of ringing me several times a day 'just to check up on you, Chrissie' had begun to become a serious threat to my sanity and I had begun to avoid her calls, leaving my answerphone on even when I was at home. Not just because I wanted to scream when she said things like 'Chrissie, I think you should take some iron tablets because you looked sooo pale when I saw you last' but also because I was frightened of the Rob thing. We weren't living together and we hadn't got to the stage when you pick up the phone in each other's flats but I was nonetheless tense about the idea of Carole discovering about Rob during one of her calls. Or, perhaps worse, the possibility of Rob finding out about the complicated circumstances of the conception through his having inadvertently picked up the telephone in my flat. Until the day of our picnic, though, there had only been the merest hint of a change in Goran. Whilst he was still sweet, protective and pretty near-perfect, his attitude had become a little, well, proprietorial. Not, you understand, that this seemed so terribly strange or even worrying at the time. I think that I imagined his concern about my pregnancy to be prompted by his sensitive and caring natural tendencies.

I didn't realise quite how proprietorial he was becoming, though, until part way through the picnic when he began to talk about Joanna's delivery. To my amazement it emerged that Goran had attended antenatal classes with Joanna (against her wishes, I discovered later) and that he was planning to be present at the birth.

'It's a mother's duty, Joanna,' he said at some point, 'to give their baby the best possible start in life. And that doesn't just mean giving up alcohol and keeping yourself fit and healthy during pregnancy – which Chrissie should be addressing now – it means ensuring that she has a natural delivery. The more medical intervention a woman has the more complications arise. Epidurals are like cosmetic surgery – only used out of vanity and cowardice by women who are preoccupied with their own part in the birthing experience and oblivious of the needs of their child. We'll have a natural delivery, Joanna.'

An awkward silence followed this pronouncement and, as usual at such moments, it was up to me to lighten the mood a little.

'Well, all I can say is that when it comes to my turn I'll have everything that's going. Preferably a general anaesthetic and intravenous morphine,' I said glibly, alarmed though I was by Goran's odd and somewhat dictatorial comments about childbirth.

'Statements like that just confirm to me how ignorant and immature you are. Motherhood is about more than your needs and your comfort. It's time that you faced up to what you have got yourself into, Christine,' he said in a stern voice, using my full name in the way my father had done when I was in trouble as a child.

'I think, Goran, that you can be certain that I will do what I think is best for my child,' I said a little defensively.

'*Our* child,' Goran corrected me in such a cold and commanding tone that a chill ran down my spine. For the rest of the picnic, as I tried as hard as I could to keep the subject off childbirth, those words kept echoing in my head; 'Our child', 'our child', 'our child', and I was filled with a terrible disquiet.

I caught Joanna's eye several times and was aware of a kind of mental fusion. It suddenly hit me that Goran's new interfering behaviour might have something to do with Joanna's evident unhappiness. I had been so caught up in my relationship with Rob in the last few months – and so desperate to keep it secret – that I had neglected Joanna. When Goran took the children off to buy ice creams and Carole was lying soaking up a sudden burst of sun, I managed to get five minutes alone with Joanna and it all came out.

In the last few weeks both Carole and Goran had tried to become more and more involved in Joanna's pregnancy. She told me then about the antenatal classes and how humiliating she had found having Goran as her birthing partner particularly since he had insisted, on several occasions, on addressing the NCT teacher and the other couples present in rather the way he had addressed her that afternoon. She began to cry as she told me about other instances of interference – lists of names that Goran had sent through the post, books on ante and postnatal nutrition that he had given her, articles about child development that he had cut out and kept for her.

'I got into this whole thing because I believed that it was the most sensible, practical and safe way of my having another baby. I am very happy as a single mother, Chrissie, I never expected him – well, them really – to want to have any direct input into this child,' she said, her face filling with fear when she noticed Goran walking back towards us.

The atmosphere that day was the most strained it had ever been between the three, or should I say four, of us. The picnic that Carole had prepared had hardly been touched and the children had spent most of the afternoon fighting. Midafternoon, the sun disappeared behind a mass of granite grey clouds and it became quite cold.

Big drops of rain began to fall and we started to scurry around getting everything together. Within minutes it had become a huge downpour and we heard the first threatening sounds of rumbling thunder. We started to run, then, back through the wooded pathway to the car park and as we neared the clearing Emma, riding her bicycle in and out of the bushes, accidentally crashed into her mother causing Joanna to stumble and trip onto the hard concrete path.

We were all screaming and crying then because Joanna seemed to have knocked herself out and was lying so awkwardly that we thought she might have broken something. Goran put her in the recovery position while Carole ran back to the car for the mobile phone. When the ambulance finally arrived – some fifteen minutes later – she had regained consciousness and I went with her, holding her hand and trying to comfort her even though I was frightened for her life, and the life of her baby. When they lifted her on to the stretcher there was – on the rain-soaked path – a quite distinct pool of blood.

Chapter 10

❧

I am not sure now how I managed to convince the ambulance men that I should go with Joanna to the hospital. Or why Goran didn't push me aside and make a greater claim to be close to her. After all, as he had so firmly reinforced that afternoon, he *was* the father of her child. But for some reason, inhibited perhaps by the presence of Emma, he instead stayed with Carole and the children and let me go. Joanna clung to me all the way to the Chelsea and Westminster Hospital. The pain of her fall seemed to be forgotten as she began, in the twenty minute journey, to experience the greater agony of a suddenly induced labour.

'Oh God, Chrissie, this is my punishment,' she said.

I tried to dismiss this notion, pointing out again and again that it was nothing more than an unfortunate accident. Everything, I said with as bright a smile as I could muster, would be alright.

'It is a punishment, Chrissie, I know it is. I've done a terrible thing. Oh poor, poor Emma,' she said, weeping uncontrollably until she was overcome by another sharp contraction.

There was something rather surreal about our situation. It was like finding yourself in one of those fly on the wall documentaries set in an A and E department or in a particularly gory episode of *Casualty*. The moment we arrived at the hospital, and Joanna had been transferred to a trolley, everything and everyone seemed to go into overdrive.

Within minutes, they had discovered that her leg was sprained not broken and that, thankfully, the blood had come from a deep, but not serious, cut on Joanna's knee. But they were very concerned about the fact that she had gone into premature labour and decided, when they detected signs of distress on the foetal monitor, to give Joanna a caesarean.

Joanna seemed infinitely more frightened of Goran arriving than she was of having an emergency c-section. She clung to me right up to the moment that they took her into the theatre and such was her distress that the medical staff agreed to let me, dressed in gown, hat, mask and surgical boots, be with her.

'Goran's not here, is he?' she kept repeating as the anaesthetist prepared her for the epidural.

'Don't let him in will you?' she entreated when they dropped water onto her naked belly in order to check that the area they were to operate on was free of any physical sensation.

It probably wasn't the best experience for me to have witnessed. Particularly as I was only three months or so from the delivery of my own first child. They put up a screen so that Joanna couldn't see but I couldn't help but let my eyes glance down to the surgeon's scalpel and the bloody mess into which his hands disappeared.

Getting the baby out was very quick, I think it took no more than fifteen minutes from the moment at which they knew the epidural was working. It was a healthy six pound baby boy (although to be honest it was difficult, from my vantage point, to acknowledge that the thing covered in all that white mess was even human let alone attempt to decide its gender) and it gave a cough and a cry which seemed to please everyone in the crowded room, except for Joanna and me who, overcome at the sight of her son, sponged down a little and wrapped in a towel, both burst into tears. Not the mournful kind that Joanna had been shedding as she went into theatre, but the lump-in-your-throat moved-to-tears variety. It was a strangely binding experience, watching this woman who meant so much to me holding her newborn child. It had an almost religious impact on me. Although, to be honest, Joanna – beautiful though she is – and her newborn baby didn't look anything like the usual representations of mother and child that are imprinted on our brains from the famous paintings of Mary and Jesus. Her hair was a matted mess, there were mascara scars running down her face, she was trembling from the cold (apparently a common reaction to the epidural) and the infant in her arms resembled nothing so much as one of those cats they breed without fur.

It took them far longer to put everything back and sew her up than it had to snatch the baby from her womb. And just as they were finishing, the door to the theatre opened and Goran, also in gown and boots, was shown in.

'You can't come in, she's feeling terrible,' I said, moving towards him in an attempt to shield Joanna.

'I just want to know that everything is all right, Chrissie,' he said, moving over to look in the little plastic cot in which his son had been placed.

'A boy,' Joanna managed to say.

It wasn't until much later that I thought that perhaps the expression on Goran's face that day was one of triumph rather than of natural paternal pride. You can, of course, rewrite history in your head and maybe my recollections have become confused, but I seem to remember questioning his response to the newborn child even then. The situation he found himself in, mind you, wasn't an easy one. No one, to my knowledge, has written an etiquette book that deals with complicated issues such as whether or not it is acceptable for a sperm donor to show any pride in his progeny. He may well have felt just plain awkward standing in a delivery room looking down on the first result of our big plan.

'Can I hold him?' he eventually asked the houseman who had delivered his son.

'There's nothing wrong with him, he's a fine healthy infant,' the doctor replied.

Goran glanced across at Joanna and she looked away as if to say that she couldn't stop him but that she wasn't going to watch him pick up her baby. He carefully held the little boy up and peered at him as if he were searching for some hidden flaw (it was rather like the way that those experts on *Antiques Roadshow* look at rare and very valuable Ming vases). He didn't cuddle the baby, or kiss him, he just looked him over and then carefully laid him back in the cot. Clinical, I can remember thinking at the time, a clinical examination devoid of emotion.

Something, it struck me for the first time, that was entirely at odds with the man I thought I knew.

When he had finished he came over to Joanna and told her, in polite but detached tones, that he had brought Emma with him and that she was waiting to see her brother.

While Joanna was moved to a side ward I went and found Emma. She was in the hospital crèche, surrounded by a few other children but somehow terribly apart from them. She flew into my arms when she saw me and began to sob and I held her and rocked her until she stopped. She was frightened and confused. It took me sometime to convince her that her Mummy was OK, that she wasn't going to die and that it wasn't Emma's fault. I was angry, then, with Carole for not explaining to Emma what had happened. The little girl, only five-years-old, after all, was distraught. Carole should have come to the hospital with her, even if it meant dragging her boys along too. She should have explained to Emma that her mother was all right, that the injuries she suffered when she fell were minor. To have allowed the girl to come to the hospital with Goran under the childish misconception that her mother was fatally wounded struck me as cruel and irresponsible and I remember thinking at that moment that in some way her actions that day had prompted a further rift between Carole, Joanna and me.

When I had calmed Emma down, cleaned her up and got her a drink and some crisps, I took her in to see her mother. Exhausted though she was, Joanna threw open her arms and embraced her daughter. There was such an extraordinary bond between Joanna and Emma – I think there often is in family units of two – that I felt awkward witnessing this scene and I left them alone for a while and withdrew into the corridor outside the ward.

Goran was sitting in a chair waiting for Emma.

'Chrissie, I'm worried about Joanna,' he said, his voice full of its usual solicitous concern.

'I think she is in shock, Goran, and you know how fragile she is, I am sure she will be fine when she has rested a little,' I said.

'It was the worst possible circumstances for her delivery

– that fall and then an emergency caesarean. I am worried about how she will cope now. And Chrissie, why is she so hostile to me?' he said, his handsome face contorted with what looked almost like pain.

'She's just confused, Goran. And you know how suspicious she always has been of men – apart, of course, from you. Perhaps she's just reverting to type or maybe it's hormonal. She seems to think you want to control her.'

He looked shocked by my words and it took him several moments to regain his composure and respond.

'Chrissie, in all the years you have known me have I ever given you or Joanna any reason to doubt me?' he eventually asked with such sweet directness that I found myself blushing.

'Of course you haven't. If you had would we have got into this whole thing with you?' I replied.

'I can't help it, you know, if I sometimes express my concern for these babies. I am human, Chrissie, and although being a father, in the accepted sense, was never part of our deal, I can't not care. It's not in my nature to turn away when I see something that concerns me. And even though I suppose I should have thought about it long before today, I am concerned about Joanna's mental stability. Is that unfair, Chrissie?'

It wasn't unfair. In fact it was very fair comment. But for me to agree, to even nod my assent, would have been a betrayal of my friend. Although the memory of Goran's odd and controlling comments at our picnic was still fresh in my mind, I was also aware of how irrational Joanna could be and I had suspected, all along, that she had exaggerated her reasons for doubting his motives.

The strangest thing about Goran from the beginning to the end of our story was the way in which his very presence could somehow dispel your doubts. Whenever you were with him you were utterly convinced by him. His manner, his presence was very compelling, charismatic even, and reassuring. And now, regardless of the first stirrings of doubt about what we had done, I found myself turning to him for comfort. I was, of course, exhausted and Goran was, after all, a doctor so perhaps it was not so odd or recalcitrant of me to, as I did moments later, burst into tears when he put an arm cautiously around me.

'There, there, Chrissie, it will be all right. You have been through a terrible experience this afternoon and in your condition it was bound to have upset you,' he said. 'I'll take Emma home with us, you mustn't worry about her she will be fine with the other children. And you, you must go home now and get some rest. You must look after yourself now, Chrissie.'

It seemed sensible for Carole and Goran to look after Emma, despite Joanna's misgivings. Joanna no longer had contact with her family so there was no loving granny to step in and help. And I had to be in work the following morning so I couldn't be responsible for looking after Emma.

Comforted by Goran's return to his normal role in our lives – sweet and supportive – I crept back into Joanna's room and found mother and daughter sleeping in each other's arms. I gently took Emma from Joanna and carried her out to Goran. Then I helped Goran to get her to the car and to strap her, still sleeping, into a child seat.

When they had driven off, I went back into the hospital with a heavy heart and sat by Joanna's bed watching her sleep. I must have fallen asleep myself for a while because

I remember being brought out of some fearful dream by the awful sound of a baby's cry.

Joanna didn't wake and I walked over to the little cot and touched her son in a rather pathetic attempt to calm him.

'He should go on the breast,' Joanna said a moment later.

I lifted the baby carefully out of his cot – his fragility was truly frightening – and laid him on his mother's chest. He looked even more like a little pink-skinned furless cat when, with his eyes still shut, he began to sniff around in search of whatever it was that was seeping out of Joanna's breasts at that point (the milk, I already knew, doesn't come through until the third day after delivery).

Eventually mother and child made some sort of contact, the infant clamping on to the mother's nipple for a few minutes before it fell back to sleep.

'What are you going to call him?' I asked gently.

'Tom,' she said.

'Nice,' I muttered 'Any particular reason?'

'Emma chose it. She wanted to call him Tom if he was a boy,' she said.

'But it wasn't high up on Goran's list of chosen names,' I said in flippant tones.

Joanna's big, blue eyes began to spill tears again. Tears that spattered off her face and threatened to splash onto the tiny, sleeping body of her son.

Very gently I took the baby from her and put him back in his cot. He didn't stir and I was oddly pleased with myself for having completed this feat so successfully.

'What am I going to do, Chrissie?' Joanna said as I sat back down on the chair next to her bed.

'You're going to be as good a mother to Tom as you are to Emma,' I said in light, bright tones.

'But what am I going to tell Emma?' she asked.

Joanna was absolutely terrified that Emma might find out that Goran was her baby brother's father. I tried to soothe her by telling her that Emma wasn't old enough to understand the birds and the bees any way you told it – with a stork or a turkey-baster. It would be years, I said with a smile, before she had to explain anything to Emma.

Joanna wasn't easily calmed that night. She began to confide in me as she hadn't for ages – well forever really. She told me how frightened she was by Goran and Carole and how stupid she now thought it was to have become a part of their family. It was as if the complications of Emma's half-brother also being Sasha's half-brother had not properly occurred to her before.

I told her, as gently as I could, that I thought it was a little too late to start thinking about that now. And then she burst into tears again and said that she hadn't really thought about the implications of what we had done. She had just allowed herself to think about the end product, the baby. It had been a case of the end justifying the means. Her worry now was that Carole or Goran would tell Emma.

Worse, she said through her tears, she didn't know what name to put on the birth certificate. Until I had met Rob I had always thought that I would put 'father unknown' when it came to my turn but I suddenly realised that the father was very much *known*. And that, in a world in which a father's rights were becoming as important as those of a mother's, it was feasible that Goran could use the law to get visitation rights or custody or some say in the way in which we raised his children. It sounds stupid to say that we hadn't thought about this before but honestly we hadn't. At no point during the previous months had we talked openly about our expectations of Goran as father to our children. I think we thought, unrealistically I now understand, that he would just be a positive presence in the lives of our little families. A kind, benign influence in their childhoods. A godfather, not an involved, demanding biological father.

That hadn't been part of the game plan I had imagined when we had come up with our big idea. Because we had trusted him, hadn't we? We had no qualms, no question marks, no doubts about his motives. We had cast him in the role of the passive, perfect physical father for our children. It was the reality of sitting there – with the transparent cot containing a living, breathing being beside us – that made me begin to think about the moral implications of a blood link between our babies.

Joanna couldn't stop her sobbing. She said that she wanted to run away, that she felt trapped, that she realised it had all been a terrible mistake. I tried to calm her, telling her it was the baby blues, a hormonal imbalance that was making her illogical, that was causing her imagination to race. Joanna was by far the most emotionally fragile and introspective of the three of us and she was often a bit obsessive about the kind of problems that most people, and certainly Carole and myself, would quickly dismiss. But that night, even after my reassuring talk with Goran, I couldn't just dismiss what she was saying as the ramblings of a woman temporarily unbalanced by the trauma of childbirth. Perhaps because of my own fatigue – and the shock of witnessing emergency surgery – I began to feel unnerved by the way she was talking.

What should have been a joyous time for her – after all hadn't she wanted this baby more than anything else? – was turning into a ghastly vision of a future in which Goran and Carole hovered over her like gruesome, twisted co-parents to her child.

It was only then, as I sat listening to Joanna's paranoid description of the future, that I began to think about Rob. If she was right about the father of our turkeybasted babies then how on earth was it going to be when my time came? How would Goran react to the discovery of a new man in my life? How would he deal with the threat of a second father for my unborn child? Even if I carried on allowing Rob to believe that the baby was his, supposing Goran decided to prove otherwise? We were no longer living in a world in which it was possible to deny who was the biological father of your child – DNA would find you out.

I left the hospital a little after two in the morning and got a taxi back to my flat. It wasn't until I climbed into bed – and encountered the warm naked flesh of another person – that I realised that Rob must have driven all the way back from Hampshire to be with me that evening.

'That was a very long picnic,' he said looking at me through one bleary eye.

'Joanna went into labour, I was with her, Rob, it was amazing . . .'

'What did she have?'

'A boy,' I said, 'an ugly, little runty boy. But somehow a very beautiful, ugly runty boy.'

'You know how people always say, Chrissie, that they don't mind whether it's a boy or a girl just as long as it's perfect?'

'Yes,' I replied as I put my arms around him and began to kiss him all over his bare, bald chest.

'Well I do mind . . .'

'Yes,' I said again as I pulled myself on top of him and began to make love to him.

'Chrissie, it's a terrible thing but I really want a boy. I want our child to be a boy.'

I felt my body tense at Rob's words. It had been a long day and for a while I couldn't work out what it was he had said that had so disturbed me. And then I remembered the way in which Goran had rebuked me at the picnic, and the exact tone of voice in which he had said the words '*our* child'.

Long after Rob had fallen, sated, back to sleep I lay awake thinking about Goran and Carole and Joanna and me. What had we done?

Chapter 11

The last months of my pregnancy were terribly stressful. I was huge – those big, blossoming bosoms that I (not to mention Rob) had so joyously embraced were now so bloated and blue-veined that they made me when I looked in the mirror experience what you might call the early evening sickness of pregnancy. I have never been a body fascist, although perhaps that is because I am one of those people who genuinely never have needed to worry about their weight, but I really wasn't comfortable being fat. My small frame – which had previously never weighed much more than eight stone – was now hitting the scales at something approaching eleven and a half stone.

Clothes, too, have always been a passion with me and the horror of being denied access to my pretty little slip dresses or my skintight leather trousers made me feel even more as if I had mutated into some huge Roseanne Barr character.

Rob was wonderful with me. If I found my own image repugnant, he never gave me any indication that he thought that I was anything other than the woman of his dreams. Some women, I know, experience a surging libido when they are pregnant only to discover that their partners, probably frightened by the baby within, are no longer able to physically make love to them. With Rob and me it was rather the reverse, my feeling so ugly and distorted that I could not bring myself to respond to the hungry kisses he would give me as, I suppose, some kind of preliminary foreplay for pregnant love. It didn't matter how many times he told me that I was beautiful, that I was 'like the most fabulous flower in full bloom', I couldn't really believe that I was desirable. Not that my lack of response, and my occasional irritated rejection, seemed to bother him. He was content, at least so he said, to just look, to just cuddle, to just sleep alongside me.

In so many ways he was more prepared for my pregnancy and its ultimate end product than I was. He took a far more practical role in organising things for the baby than I did. It was Rob who turned the spare room of my flat – which was a fashion victim's chamber of horrors, the place where I stored every absurd item of clothing that I had ever bought, but barely worn, into a nursery. Not some fluffy pink or baby blue heaven but a beautiful room painted in big squares of primary colours. As I have said before Rob was very good with his hands and those green fingers proved very adaptable. He created the most wonderful and imaginative space for the baby, filled with all sorts of magical things he had made and painted to fit with his colour scheme. And the best of it was that he didn't even tell me he was doing it. I just came home one day and, in the course of searching for an old jumper I had a sudden yearning to wear, discovered this wondrous room all ready and waiting for my baby to come home to.

He was supportive in other ways, too. Making me rest when my ankles swelled. Reassuring me, again and again, that I looked radiant when I resembled nothing so much as a jumbo sack of extra large baking potatoes. Feeding me, and Pushkin, when I was too tired to do anything but flop at the end of my working day. He had read somewhere that unborn babies can respond to certain sounds – calming music and the loving endearments of their parents. Every night that we were together he would put on a CD he had bought of specially soothing classical music. And last thing, before we went to sleep, and first thing the next morning he would kiss my belly and whisper 'good night' or 'good morning' to my baby.

We still weren't officially living together, partly because of Rob's commitments to Green Piece and partly because of my fear of how Goran and Carole might react to my having a full-time, long-term relationship. We talked a lot about the future and we had all sorts of fanciful plans for changing the way we lived. But we both accepted that it wasn't practical for us to be permanently together until we had sorted out the details of our working lives. It was, as I pointed out to Rob at the time, very fashionable for couples to keep separate homes. The papers were always offering insights into the lives of rich and famous people who loved each other but lived apart. But having said that there was this unwritten, unspoken agreement between us. That we would be together, forever.

We managed to spend at least two, sometimes, three weekday nights together and we often went down to Hampshire at the weekend. Paul and Anna seemed genuinely thrilled about the baby and if Anna had any lingering doubts about my suitability she didn't voice them. Their only concern, given their own conventional and conservative lifestyle, was that we should be married as soon as possible. It was Paul who first raised this point, in the middle of a Friday night supper we were sharing round their kitchen table.

'When are you going to name the day, then, Rob?' he asked.

'Yes when?' echoed Anna.

'I think,' said Rob glancing at me to check my reaction, 'that Chrissie would like to wait until after the baby is born. It's quite fashionable nowadays to have your child in attendance at your nuptials.'

'And your child's delicious cousins as page and brides-maid,' I added, trying to suppress a sudden feeling of panic at the thought of the whole of my baby's oddly extended family attending some bizarre marriage ceremony. All the children – all the half-siblings – in attendance when the presiding vicar would ask those dreaded words, 'Does anyone here have good cause,' giving Goran the perfect opportunity to stand up and denounce me in a crowded church.

I am not sure whether the food that night – pheasant in an over-rich cream sauce – or the talk of weddings brought on my first attack of heartburn. But I was so overcome by the awful sensation that was erupting up from my stomach through to my throat that I had to leave the table.

It was, I suppose, a measure of Anna and Paul's affection for me that, even without a wedding date or an engagement ring, they were so keen to endorse our relationship that they had even taken Pushkin, who travelled everywhere with me when possible, into their hearts and had gone to the trouble of replacing the little single bed in Rob's childhood bedroom with a double divan (for sentimental reasons we kept the Messerschmitt mobile.)

But the pressure put on me by Rob's family was as nothing, I was to discover a week or so later, when compared to the pressure I was about to experience from Goran. It wasn't until I turned up for an antenatal appointment the following Wednesday afternoon, to discover him already sitting in the hospital waiting room, that I began to question just how involved he intended to be in the birth of my baby.

'Chrissie,' he said, standing up and kissing me on both cheeks.

'Goran, what are you doing here?' I asked as if it were really possible that this was some kind of coincidence. That he was here by chance rather than by design. It only took me a couple of minutes to work out how he had come to discover the date, the time and the place of my appointment. The prolonged telephone campaign that Carole had been conducting since the first weeks of my pregnancy, ringing me up and interrogating me about everything from my latest weight gain to the predicted date of delivery, was obviously part of a covert plan to gather intelligence and feed it on to the spy master – or sperm king – Goran.

'I thought you might need some support,' he said with the kind of smile that, a few months before, would have offered me enormous comfort. But by now, having listened so often to Joanna's fearful tales of our imagined future, I, too, was beginning to become scared and intimidated by the man I had, at the outset of our story, imagined to be the physical and intellectual ideal.

'I'm perfectly OK, really I am,' I said with an artificially bright smile.

'This isn't something a woman should go through on her own,' he said putting an arm around me in a way that made me recoil from him.

'But I always knew I would have to go through this on my own,' I replied.

'I am not the kind of man to let you do that,' he said.

I am not sure why I didn't insist on him leaving. I think in the end I went along with him in order to prevent some difficult scene from erupting in such a public place. Instead of confronting him and telling him to go, I sat beside him and indulged in the kind of meaningless small talk that people exchange at dinner parties. How were the children? What did Carole want for her forthcoming birthday? Had he seen Joanna lately?

When the nurse called my name, Goran stood up and walked in beside me, shaking the hand of the duty doctor (I had never actually met the consultant whose name appeared on my notes), introducing himself as 'Chrissie's partner' and explaining his own medical background. His credentials might not have impressed the BMA when he arrived in this country but they certainly won over the doctor who proceeded to ignore me and talk over my head to Goran about the progress of my pregnancy. It was almost as if I didn't even exist, as the two of them discussed my state of health. In the past Joanna had often told me of the way in which men like to dominate and take over a woman's pregnancy. It was one of her obsessions, actually, that the world of obstetrics and gynaecology was a carefully maintained male preserve. Since they couldn't actually give birth themselves, she would say, they had long since decided to control the way in which women delivered. It wasn't the female, she used to say, that envied the male his penis, but the male who was deeply jealous of the womb. And sitting listening to these men talking about me as if I were some kind of reproductive machine made me think that perhaps she was right. She had told me once how, during her labour with Emma, the houseman had come up to her and told her to stop making such a fuss. 'You're not even in labour yet, you wait till you really start to feel real pain,' he had said. He dismissed her protestations that not only could she feel the pain she could also feel the baby coming by telling her she had a 'very low pain threshold'. Twenty minutes later Emma had been born.

For the first time during my pregnancy I felt vulnerable and powerless. Goran's obviously far more informed questions about possible complications in childbirth, full of complex medical jargon, prompted answers that filled me with fear.

By the time we had walked out of the hospital entrance and into the dingy backstreet where I had parked my car, that fear had turned to anger and for the first time I found the strength to tell Goran how I felt.

'Goran, I really don't want you coming to one of my hospital appointments ever again,' I said, as I opened my car door and attempted to fit my lumbering hulk into the driver's seat.

'Chrissie, I don't understand how you can object to my showing interest in your health and the health of our baby,' he said sweetly, although I detected a note of malice in his use of the word 'our'.

'Goran, you must see that you were only ever meant to be a silent partner in this. I understood that your direct involvement would end at the time that I washed out the last of those jam jars,' I said, unable to contain my temper.

'My experience of parenting is rather more extensive than yours, Chrissie. And one thing I have learned is that it NEVER ends. You might as well accept that you will never be able to wash me out of your life. In fact I will be part of your life for as long as the child you are now carrying is a part of your life. It wouldn't be fair, would it, to bring a child into the world without a father?'

This last remark, delivered as he turned, waved and walked away, really chilled me. I went home that day so disturbed that I felt physically ill. When I got in I played back my messages – one from Rob saying he would be staying down in Hampshire that night and that he hoped everything was alright at the clinic, one from Joanna asking me to call her and one from Carole.

'Chrissie, I just rang to say that Goran has booked you into the NCT classes in Booth Road. It's a four week course starting on Thursday the 8th at six. Hope you are well, darling, and that you are looking after yourself.'

What woman, I asked myself after I had replayed the message for the fifth time, would willingly allow her husband to have children with her two closest female friends without any apparent show of jealousy or resentment? I realise that it might seem a little strange that it was not until this moment that I began to question the role Carole was playing in our unfolding story. I think perhaps it was linked to the fact that, over the years, I had come to regard her as you would a sibling, I didn't analyse her behaviour in the way that you might someone you weren't convinced was part of your own particular chosen warm and loving family. But the sound of her voice intruding on my private space that day effected a shift in me and I found myself judging her, concluding that her involvement in the day-to-day life of a woman her husband had impregnated wasn't natural. But then, of course, none of it was natural.

What really, really bothered me about that message, though, was the fact that Rob might so easily have heard it. Holding on to a lie – as I had been doing these past months – was incredibly stressful and suddenly I needed to talk to someone about my misgivings. There was only one person who could really be my ally and I decided that it was time to confide in Joanna.

I rang her up straight away and asked if I could go round and see her. With Rob away for the night there was no time like the present. She sounded a little dazed and sleepy but she was evidently pleased to hear from me and said, as I knew she would, come now. On the way I picked up a Chinese takeaway and a bottle of champagne. Old habits die hard.

When I arrived, a little after eight-thirty, Emma let me in which was a bit of a surprise. Joanna had always been one of those very routine mothers. Well, she was a routine woman, really. Very organised, very tidy and very analytical about things. Emma had always been fed, bathed and in bed by seven. Tom's arrival, I quickly realised, had impacted on their lives in a devastating manner. The house, normally so pin-neat, was a terrible mess, there was no sign of Joanna but there were loud and disturbing signs of the new baby. Not just a trail of dirty disposable nappies and stained babygros, but the screeching presence of the boy himself.

Emma went and picked him up and sat down on the sofa with him, which only served to alarm me more and provoke a higher note of screaming from the baby.

'Where's Mummy, darling?' I enquired gently.

'She's having a bath,' the little girl replied.

I took the baby from Emma and carried him through to the kitchen which was even more of a mess. The table was like one of those conceptual art pieces they have in the Tate Modern – more nappies, Emma's colouring books and crayons, several decapitated Barbies, two dummies, half a dozen dirty coffee mugs, empty crisp packets, two half-eaten biscuits and a bowl of muesli that had been there so long it looked as if it might be pre-set concrete.

It was a full half an hour before Joanna emerged from her bath, her face curiously impassive as if she were on some kind of calming drug. Never known – or often called on – for my practicality I had, nonetheless, used the previous thirty minutes to great effect. I had managed to get Tom to sleep in his bouncing baby chair with the aid of a dummy and a bit of rocking motion, I had cleared that table, loaded and set off the dishwasher, cleaned the floor in the living room and put a pile of mixed coloured washing in the machine. I had even cooked Emma some fish-fingers, potatoes and peas and washed the kitchen floor.

Not that Joanna noticed. I realised that far from her being my confidant that evening, I was going to be hers. I sat her down, clamped Tom onto her left breast and put a glass of champagne in her right hand. Then I took Emma upstairs and bathed her, found some cleanish pyjamas, put her to bed and read her a story. She was so tired and so grateful for the attention that she was asleep before I had finished.

And so, when I finally got back downstairs, were Joanna and Tom. I carefully lifted the baby off his mother's breast, noting, as I did so, that he still didn't much resemble a human being, and laid him in his Moses basket in the corner of the room. Just as I was preparing to leave, reckoning that a good sleep might be of more use to Joanna than a Chinese takeaway and a chat, she woke up.

We sat at the kitchen table and ate the by now congealed Peking duck and plum sauce. I was, by that point, exhausted and after one glass of champagne I felt so intoxicated that I just blurted out that I was in love.

'That's nice,' Joanna said in a vague voice.

I got quite cross then and said that I needed help and advice and, to be fair, she did manage to focus on what I was saying. I told her everything – that Rob believed the baby was his, that I was too frightened of losing him to summon up the courage to tell him the truth and that I was beginning to share her misgivings about Goran.

Joanna got up when I had finished and came round and hugged me.

'Oh God, Chrissie,' she said. 'I knew that something had changed for you, I knew you were holding back from telling me something. And although I know it probably sounds terribly selfish, I am really pleased that you are now doubting Goran's motives. I had been feeling so alone, you know. So isolated and so exhausted that I began to worry if this thing about him wasn't all in my mind. If I wasn't having some recurrence of my old problems . . .'

She was trembling, I noticed, when she sat back down. She wasn't interested in talking about Rob, only about Goran and after a few minutes I began to wonder if, in fact, she *wasn't* suffering from a recurrence of her old problems. But I had no one else to talk to, no one else in whom I could confide my concerns.

'Joanna, what am I going to do about Rob? I don't think I could face losing him but deceiving him in this way is killing me.'

'There is only one thing that you can do. You have to tell him and tell him as soon as possible. If he really loves you then he will accept what you have done. If he doesn't then he probably isn't worth bothering about anyway,' she said coldly.

'But it isn't that simple, it isn't that easy. It isn't just the whole turkeybasting thing that I have to explain away, it's the deception that followed. My allowing him to think this baby was his, naturally conceived during an act of love.'

'Love?' said Joanna in the cynical tones she always adopted when talking about men. 'For goodness' sake, Chrissie, how long had you known him before this apparent conception took place – a week, a day, an hour? I know you so well, you want to believe it was love but it was probably just lust. You won't understand the meaning of the word love until you give birth to this child, so don't get distracted now by the idea that your bloody prince has come. You would be better off worrying about Goran than this man. Just tell him and have done with it, which is probably what he'll do with your relationship,' she said with a high, hard, brittle laugh.

'And what about you, Joanna? Have you managed to gather the courage to tell your daughter exactly who fathered her little brother?' I spat angrily back at her.

'Don't say things like that, Chrissie, please, please don't talk like that to me,' she said breaking out in a long strangulated sob that, in the minutes that followed, developed into the kind of cries that leave you, when you are a child, hiccuping and unable to speak as you fight for air. She was so distraught that I felt terribly guilty about having turned up that evening expecting to further add to her emotional burdens. It had been absurd to imagine that Joanna, in her current state, would be able to offer me proper counsel about Rob. Particularly when you took into account her mistrust and dislike of men. I realised that she simply wasn't able to take on anyone else's problems at a time when her own life was in such evident crisis.

I got up and went over to her and began to try to soothe her. As her cries slowed and she became a little calmer, they were replaced by the urgent screams of the baby in the next room. I went and fetched him and began to rock him until she was ready to attempt to comfort him herself.

'God, Joanna, it's not surprising you are so tired,' I said gently as the baby began to gulp from her breast. 'Coping with a new baby and Emma must be so stressful. I don't think this is anything to do with your old problems, it's just a little postnatal depression.'

'It isn't the baby or my hormones that's the problem, it's *him*,' she said.

She was in such a state that night that however hard I tried to steer the conversation away from the subject it always returned to Goran. She began to tell me more and more fanciful stories about his behaviour. How he had developed this habit of dropping into her cottage on his way home from work, apparently with Carole's approval. How he had begun to bully her about the way in which she was handling the baby, insisting that she should breast feed Tom for at least the first six months of his life.

'And the thing is, Chrissie, is that he is such a hungry baby and I don't think I am making enough milk. My nipples ache and at night I want to sleep so much that I started to give him formula and Goran just went mad when he found out. He was shouting and swearing at me, terrible obscenities some of them in a language I didn't understand. It was as if he were talking in tongues, like the devil. Chrissie, sometimes I think he *is* the devil.'

I tried to point out to her that English was not Goran's first language and that maybe he was just speaking in his native tongue, not 'in tongues'. But by now it was impossible to hold back her wildest fears and fantasies about the man whom we had chosen as the father of our children. At the time those mad ramblings didn't, despite my own experience with him that day at the hospital, deepen my misgivings. Instead they served to make me realise how deeply disturbed Joanna was – I had, after all, witnessed a previous period in her life in which she had displayed symptoms of paranoia.

During the difficult time after Harry left her – which had resulted in a month-long hospitalisation in one of those discreet up-market psychiatric clinics – she had been as obsessive and fixated about him as she was now about Goran. Even her terminology rang alarm bells with me. Hadn't I heard her, in the past, describe both her abusive father and Harry as the 'devil incarnate' in rather the way she was now referring to Goran?

I could see that he might be intrusive but the idea of his being dangerous was, at that point, totally absurd. I think then that I put his unexpected interest in our babies down to the fact that he was, after all, a doctor. It seemed, if I didn't stretch my imagination too far, to be a perfectly acceptable – responsible even – reaction for the father of a child to attempt to exert a little influence over the lifestyle and behaviour of his baby's mother. I tried to put this across to Joanna in order to calm her down and reason with her because by now she seemed almost possessed herself.

'I'm just so tired of it all, Chrissie, I just want it to all end,' she sobbed.

Tired as I was I couldn't just leave her like that so, as I had done with Emma, I helped her upstairs, undressed her and put her to bed. Then I carried the now sleeping

Tom upstairs in his Moses basket and placed it in its stand in her room.

As I left her that night she told me again to 'tell that man the truth' as soon as I could. I must not put off the moment until after my baby – due in six weeks' time – had been born. If I did that, she told me – her eyes wild with what seemed like real fear – it might be too late. She kept on and on about how she didn't want to get on the wrong side of Goran and that I should be very, very careful.

But I didn't listen to her because I was utterly convinced that she was mentally unbalanced. Maybe she was as unhinged now as she had been after her father had died, and when Harry had left her. Goran, I told myself, was no real threat to me. Not enough of a threat, that is, to give me the courage to tell Rob the terrible truth.

Chapter 12

❦

In the last weeks of my pregnancy, I began to have disturbing nightmares about the birth of my child. Some of them were totally absurd – in one I delivered a fluffy Persian kitten and in another I pushed out without drugs or an epidural, a fully formed, fully dressed five-year-old boy. But a few of them were the kind of nightmares you cannot dismiss from your mind at noon on a sunny day. One night I dreamed that Goran and Carole were present in the delivery room – Carole knitting like Madame Lefarge beside the guillotine and Goran gloating as he cut the bloody cord and snatched my baby away.

Variations on this particular nightmare played on my mind so much that I decided to change my plans. I still didn't really believe that Carole or Goran were involved in some sinister plot, but I reasoned that the best way to ensure that they didn't intrude on the birth of my baby was to remove myself from London. As soon as I took maternity leave I would go and stay with Paul and Anna in Hampshire. Since they didn't know the real due date of my baby – Rob had calculated it to forty weeks after we had got together on the Barbour – they would not think it was odd that I was prepared to be so far from University College Hospital so close to my delivery date. They wouldn't know that I now planned to have my baby in Christchurch Hospital, far, far away from the prying, proprietorial eyes of Goran and Carole.

I saw Joanna several times in the weeks before I left work. Her state of mind seemed to be slightly improved; she was still depressed and confused, but she was marginally less obsessive about Goran. I think now that maybe she realised that I was concerned about her sanity and that she made a conscious effort not to talk about him to me.

Instead she encouraged me to talk about Rob which I was only too happy to do. She seemed genuinely interested in our relationship, offering me, in place of her initial cynicism, the impression that she was really pleased for me.

It was inevitable, I suppose, that she would want to meet Rob.

Throughout our long friendship it had been customary, whenever one or other of us met a new man, for the others to want to cast their eyes over him. And so, since Rob had been pressurising me to introduce him to her since Tom had been born, I warily agreed to take him round to supper. I didn't much like the idea because while I was sure I could trust Joanna not to say anything to Goran or Carole about Rob, I was frightened that she might say something about them to him.

But it wasn't just my fear of an unstable Joanna telling all about the turkeybasting that made me nervous about her meeting my lover. I had reached that stage in pregnancy when you feel very physically insecure. Having bosoms, as I have said before, had been a lovely novelty at first but now they were just, well, another couple of things that weighed me down. I had always been thin and I only really knew how to dress for thin. The few things left that I could still wear looked so absurd that I felt like

Dawn French in Kate Moss's clothes. It got so bad, during the heatwave that summer, that I was forced to buy three vast baggy dresses (more like marquees than tents) and wear them 'one off, one on and one in the wash' as my mother used to say when I was a girl.

Rob had nicknamed me the 'Hunny Monster' because of my craving for Sugar Puffs and even though I knew he loved me, I had become a bit clingy and possessive. I had this wild fear that he might fall in love with my beautiful friend which, combined with my worries about Joanna's mental state at that time, made me extremely anxious about their meeting.

But it all went much better than I had expected. Joanna seemed to be making an effort to get her life back in order. The cottage was clean and tidy and she appeared to have got Emma back into her old routine. She even managed to cook us a pasta supper and although I didn't ever quite relax, I was pleased that Rob liked Joanna in a non-threatening (to me, that is) kind of way. The best thing about that night was seeing the way in which Rob was with the baby. He was so gentle, so interested and so good with Tom that I was aware that even Joanna approved of him (he was the first man I had ever introduced to her that I sensed she had liked).

There was only one really awkward moment during the evening. Joanna had decorated the downstairs loo in her little cottage so that the walls resembled a modern version of a Victorian scrap-book screen. Every inch was covered with carefully cut out photographs that blended into each other and had then been coated with varnish. The effect was very Joanna. It was clever, dramatic and very striking. So much so that I often found myself, when I visited her, nipping in for a quick wee and staying there for fifteen or twenty minutes looking at the landscape of memories locked on that wall. Our whole lives – that is the tangled lives of Carole, Joanna and myself – were exposed in that tiny room. Laughing pictures of us taken together over the years interspersed with portraits of Emma and Sasha as tiny babies, as growing infants, as little people.

Not all the pictures – as in a Victorian scrap-book screen – were happy representations of the major players in Joanna's life. There were several beautiful but somehow tragic pictures of Joanna on her wedding day. Another of me on mine, a rather more low-key affair than hers, and, of course, lots and lots of pictures of Goran. Snaps taken of him when Carole had first met him, his hair too long, his face distorted by a ridiculous moustache and an ever-present gold sleeper in his ear. He was, on those walls, the dominant male. He hovered over us all – sometimes his arms draped around the three of us for pictures taken, by remote, on special occasions such as our birthdays or Christmas. His was the only male face that appeared in close-up after close-up – holding Sasha, cradling Emma, cooking a meal for us, pulling a face for the camera, chasing the children along the beach on a shared summer holiday.

It occurred to me much, much later in our story, when I stood in that room trying to understand when and where we had gone so wrong, how imperceptibly we had all changed over the years. Not just physically – the glow slowly but irrevocably leaving our faces as we grew older – but in the way that our responsibilities and worries could be discerned behind our carefree poses.

But on the night that Rob met Joanna I hadn't realised the significance of that wall of smiles, let alone considered what my lover might think when, some time towards the end of our meal, he put down his napkin and asked our hostess where the loo was. As soon as he had entered that room and closed the door, Joanna leant across the table and grabbed my hand.

'He's OK, Chrissie, he's really OK,' she said which was the greatest accolade I had ever heard her give a boyfriend of mine.

'He, is, isn't he . . . ? I mean, I think he's a really decent person,' I said.

'Tell him,' she urged.

'And risk what we have got?' I whispered, anxious that he would suddenly return.

'Don't tell him and you'll lose everything you have got,' she said darkly before resuming the role of happy hostess as Rob came back to the table.

'The man with the moustache,' Rob asked ingenuously to Joanna as he sat down, 'is he the father of your children?'

I realised then that there were no pictures on display in my own minimalist flat and that Rob had never seen or heard much about Goran. What's more I had, I am not sure why, never offered Rob any information about Joanna's circumstances except to say that she was a single mother. He knew that Carole was married but I had spent less time telling him of our emotional entanglements with men than I had in relaying to him the strength of the bond that existed between us as women.

If Joanna was nonplussed by his question, she covered up her embarrassment very well, hesitating for only a few seconds before replying.

'No, no the man with the moustache is our friend Carole's husband. My ex-husband doesn't feature on those walls because I very carefully edited him out, with a pair of very sharp scissors,' she said with what passed for a glib little laugh.

'He looks like a good bloke, Carole's husband. I'd like to meet him,' Rob persisted.

'Oh you will, you will. In time,' Joanna said quickly.

'What's his name?' he said.

'Goran,' Joanna and I replied in unison.

'Where's he from?' Rob asked.

'Bosnia, he came from Bosnia but he's a British citizen now. He's played a very important part in our lives, hasn't he, Chrissie?' Joanna said, perhaps thinking that I might make my confession to Rob then and there.

'Yes, I suppose he has,' I said dismissively as the shrill cry of baby Tom, for once a welcome diversion, interrupted our conversation.

By the time that Joanna had fed and settled him again the subject of Goran had, thankfully, been forgotten and when we left her that night I felt full of optimism. I believed – mistakenly as it turned out – that Joanna had been suffering from a temporary postnatal depression and that she had put her outlandish thoughts about Goran out of her now much less disturbed mind.

I began to believe, in the days leading up to when I was due to leave work, that I had everything under control. That it was all going to be all right. If I hadn't quite been brave enough to tell Rob the truth I had certainly been courageous enough to confront Carole and Goran. I told them I had made my own antenatal class arrangements, that I was practising my breathing and that I had every confidence that I could achieve, without their help, a natural delivery. And I found a way of confounding Carole in her attempts to check up on my progress by doing something I should have thought of ages before. Unplugging the answerphone.

I had even managed to go, urged on by Rob, to visit my mother in the home in Bath where she now lived, something I had been putting off for far too long. Rob, who came from such a warm, close family and who had lost his own beloved mother so tragically young, couldn't understand my distance from the woman who had taken me in as a baby. He knew about her Alzheimer's – which had reached the stage where she could barely recognise or acknowledge anyone – and he had heard me occasionally refer to my unhappy childhood, but he still believed I ought to be a more dutiful and forgiving daughter. I thought that if he saw her, if he came with me, he might understand how very difficult it was for me.

She didn't acknowledge me when I arrived, but later she displayed a brief period of lucidity in which she referred to me by my childhood nickname, 'Nonnie' (don't ask) and talked sternly to me as if I was still a six-year-old child, rather than a heavily pregnant woman, something else she failed to notice. Her coldness to me, at the moment when she seemed to know who I was, had the desired effect on Rob. He realised, he said on the drive home, that love was not at the heart of all families. It was incredibly liberating for me to have this confirmed by someone other than Joanna or Carole whose own experiences of adoption obviously gave them a more empathetic view of my early life.

That night I talked far more openly to Rob about my relationship with my family – my father had left my mother when I was small, something she openly attributed to my 'difficult behaviour', and never bothered to make contact with us again. Until that point in our relationship,

I had held back about the damage done to me as a child, perhaps because I thought it would put him off me. But exposing my vulnerability to him – and allowing him to see the scars I still carried – brought us closer together and helped me to resolve the guilt I nonetheless felt about my current neglect of my mother.

The following week I left work after a rather over the top sendoff. Jean had organised a collection that had raised enough money to buy me a state of the art designer buggy and my boss threw me a lavish farewell party. Their apparent delight at my departure did, I admit, alarm me a little. I was only too aware of the kind of prejudice that women with babies suffer in male dominated workplaces. I suspected they all rather hoped that I would never come back, which probably accounted for the generous sendoff.

The next day Rob drove me and Pushkin down to Hampshire. I cannot describe the feeling of relief I experienced as I left my old life behind and journeyed towards a new future with my new family. It might sound fanciful, and indeed foolish, but I really believed I could pull it off. That I could relocate, have my baby and live happily ever after with Rob. But then don't they always say that ignorance is bliss?

Chapter 13

✧

The weeks that followed were, despite the awful physical side effects of late pregnancy, pretty much blissful. Anna now went into little-mother mode with me too, offering me lots of helpful hints about child-rearing and sitting with me for hours instructing me on how to achieve a natural delivery, even though, given the fact that her twins had been born prematurely, she had no experience of delivering one great big full-term baby. But my desire to bond further with her, and to hide within the security of her family, was such that I gladly, happily, listened to her every word with a transfixed smile on my big fat face (yes, my cheeks had blown up along with the rest of my body).

I slipped very comfortably into the mould of a *Country Living* and *Good Housekeeping* reader. I went for long walks, picking blackberries or flowers along the way and generally absorbing myself in my surroundings. I ran little errands to the village and got to know the local postmistress and the woman who ran the Spar grocery. There was a rhythm to life at Glebe House that really suited me in those last weeks of pregnancy, although I daresay that had something to do with my hormonal confusion. Normally the idea of being more than thirty minutes away from Harvey Nichols or a branch of Starbucks would have driven me crazy. As would the thought of spending every day following the same monotonous pattern – one of the joys of my job had always been that I never knew, from one week to the next, where I would be or what I would be doing.

Anna's life could not have been more different from my crowded chaotic, city existence. She rose at the same hour seven days a week, gave the children their meals at the same specified times, took them for their daily walk at exactly three, put them in their bath at five and finally slipped them into bed at six in order that she could have the meal for the adults on the table at precisely seven-thirty p.m. I learned a lot from her during my time under her roof; apart from the old wives' tales she passed down about babycare, she also instructed me on the fine art of making the kind of nursery food the Rider brood loved to eat – proper fish pie, Lancashire hotpot, steak and kidney pudding, apple crumble and home-made custard. And while I was not a natural (my previous philosophy had been 'why put something in the oven on five for two hours when you can pop it in the microwave on high for two minutes?'), I quite enjoyed the process of putting food on the table and watching everyone eat it.

That time was magical, too, because I got to know the twins really well. Camilla and George – not quite two – were delicious and confirmed all the old prejudices about gender stereotyping. George was bigger, more physical and less able to communicate than the quieter, sleeker and more contemplative Camilla. But like all twins, the combination of their skills – his brute force and her intelligence – made them a formidable but highly dangerous team who had long since learnt how to slip out of their cots, their car seats and even the front door of the house itself. George's obsession with all things mechanical – cars, tractors, trains and, like his Uncle Rob before him, planes – made me seriously wonder if the bond between men and machines wasn't innate. Particularly when it was contrasted with Camilla's early fascination with dressing up – she loved nothing more than going through my little jewellery box filled, as it was, with brightly coloured beads, sparkly fake gems and the kind of cheap bold statement accessories I loved, ludicrous though they now looked pinned or hung around my swollen body. I found myself saying absurd things to Rob or Paul or Anna about the children 'George is such a *boy*' I would say, glorying in any overt display of masculinity in the little man. 'Camilla is such a princess', I would mutter when I found her wearing one of my sequinned cardigans or discovered her smearing her mouth in my best Chanel Rouge Noir lipstick.

My growing affection for the twins and their fondness for me gave me more confidence in my abilities with children. I had often wondered if my devotion to Emma and Sasha was linked to the extreme bond that existed between their mothers and me, but the fact that I enjoyed the twins, whose mother I liked rather than loved, confirmed my secret belief that I might be good at this baby thing myself. I could even imagine living a life like this forever, turning into a sort of sub-Anna, devoting myself to cooking, caring for my children and housekeeping. I even found myself, one long quiet day, seriously reconsidering my post-maternity wardrobe. Perhaps, I thought, I should abandon all those Voyage fantasies and shop instead in Jaegar or Country Casuals. Tweed, back on the catwalk, after all, might not suit me in my present vast state, but when my little hips snapped back to normal, as I was certain they would, perhaps I *could* just manage a pleated skirt.

I suppose I began to get really jumpy about five days before my baby was due in early September. It was still very hot and I had begun to suffer from sudden quite dramatic contractions which Anna kept telling me were 'perfectly normal'. I don't know how I got through those last three weeks. Obviously I wanted the baby to be late but I had read somewhere about the dangers of a pregnancy going on too long. I was torn between my need to produce a baby close to Rob's imagined due date and my terror that too much of a delay might result in a terrible disaster. In the end I went into labour two and a half weeks later than predicted, in the middle of a wet and windy night. I shook Rob awake and told him that I thought the baby was coming.

'But it can't be,' he said, 'it's not due for two weeks.'

'It's coming, Rob, it's coming,' I moaned.

Other women never tell you the truth about childbirth. Even though I had seen the pain that Joanna had gone through just a few months ago, I wasn't really aware of how agonising it is to feel a seven and a half pound baby make its way down the birth canal. Fat as I was, I still hadn't achieved what they call 'child-bearing hips'. Beneath the blubber my hips were still like a boy's and while this was a wonderful bonus when it came to wearing a pair of skintight jeans, I realised – during the seemingly endless labour I endured – that size does matter for women as well.

Then again I think I have a lower pain threshold than Joanna or Carole, never mind the martyrish Anna. Despite Rob's gentle ministrations, I needed an epidural within minutes of my arrival in hospital. My friend Jean said when I finally got to tell her the full horror of my experience that I behaved during the delivery in rather the way I behave in restaurants and shops. Making a fuss if I don't get what I want and always insisting on having something a little different from the regular menu 'chicken on rye but hold the mayonnaise'. Anyway I certainly wanted everything that was going that day. And little wonder, really, because at some point it became obvious that this wasn't going to be a natural delivery. I remember thinking, after the midwife had called in the duty houseman and he had declared that it was clear from the start this baby would be a caesar and why the hell wasn't I x-rayed beforehand, that it was odd that Goran, in his role as partner and medical advisor at my hospital appointments, hadn't realised that my small bones and narrow hips would not be able to complete the function for which nature had intended them.

With hindsight – how many more times am I going to have to use that word before my story is finished? – I think that it was fitting and somehow symbolic that both turkeybasted babies were delivered by caesarean section. It was almost as if, trite though it might sound, what had been begot by a kitchen implement could only be harvested by a sharp knife.

I think Rob was more frightened than me. But then again I had been through this before and even though I now wished I hadn't glanced over the screen during Joanna's c-section, I knew that probably the easiest part of the business was getting the baby out quickly and safely.

Rob was very squeamish about blood and gore but such was his concern, that night, that he managed to put on a surgical gown and boots and witness the birth. I think the memory of seeing him standing there with blood spattered over his boots and a look of love and concern on his face will stay with me all my life. And, with Rob's support, I wasn't upset that I didn't in the end achieve anything like a natural delivery. Sam (it was beginning to look very much as if Goran didn't 'do' girls) was perfect and delicious and not even the pain of my stitches interfered with my bonding with him. Rob, as pale as if it were he who had undergone surgery, was awestruck by the sight of the baby.

'It's a boy, Chrissie, it's a boy,' he kept repeating.

The doctors were very concerned about the amount of blood I had lost and they insisted on keeping me in recovery for the rest of the night, banishing Rob until the morning. They gave me morphine for the pain and I can remember feeling this great surge of wellbeing overwhelm me as it took effect. I must have drifted in and out of sleep for the rest of that night coming to, now and again, in order to marvel at the slumbering body of my perfect baby.

The first thing I saw the next morning was Rob standing over me with a huge bunch of flowers that he had picked from the garden where, all those months ago, we had made love. They were far more beautiful and far more welcome than any glossy, shop-bought and arranged bouquet might have been.

I can't begin to describe how I felt when I watched Rob gently pick the baby out of the cot. Holding him very carefully in his arms, he sat down on the bed and looked from Sam to me with a big smile on his face. I cried again then and Rob told me that if I didn't stop my blubbering I would set a bad example to our son.

He would probably, he said, spend his formative years copying his mother's tearful display.

Rob sat by me for most of that day. In the afternoon, Anna, Paul and the twins came to see me, pronouncing my son to be 'a real Rider'. Camilla and George clambered onto my bed and threw their arms round me but showed little interest in their tiny sleeping cousin.

A curious change had come over me in the twenty four hours in which I had become a mother. While I was, of course, happy to see Anna, Paul and their children, I had a growing need to be alone with my baby and Rob. It had been suggested that, when I was discharged from hospital in a few days' time, I should return to Glebe House. But now I just wanted to take my baby to my own home, to that nursery we had prepared. Rob felt much the same, strangely enough. Neither of us wanted anyone else around – even in the hospital – apart from each other and baby Sam.

I couldn't, though, avoid the inevitable visit from Joanna who arrived the next day having left her own two children in Anna's care. There was something rather alarming and depressing about her appearance, as if she was losing control again. She looked frail and frightened and thin, I thought, as she sat by my bed and examined my baby. There was none of the warmth and intimacy I had hoped for – no embraces, no emotional exchanges about the horrors of childbirth. All Joanna could talk about was Goran. Her thought processes, though, were so confused that it was difficult to understand what she was saying. She seemed to think that Goran was going to fight her for custody of Tom which was a ridiculous idea. I tried, as I had done on previous occasions, to calm her and allay her fears about his motives, but it was impossible to reason with her. 'But Chrissie, you don't realise what he's like,' she said her fingers playing with a bunched up piece of toilet tissue in her hand, 'he hasn't begun with you yet. But he will, he will . . .'

'Joanna, please let's stop talking about him, can't you understand that it's the last thing I want to hear right now? I want to enjoy my baby – isn't he beautiful?'

'He's got the eyes,' she said quickly.

'Joanna, what are you talking about? He's got blue eyes.'

'For now he has, but you look, they are changing already. They'll be as black, as dark as Tom's, as Sasha's, as Nino's, as Goran's,' she said still fiddling with the tissue in her hand.

'Blue eyes are a recessive gene, Joanna, maybe he will, maybe he won't have dark eyes eventually.'

'The devil's eyes,' she said.

'What are you trying to say, Joanna? That our babies are the spawn of Satan? This isn't a remake of *Rosemary's Baby* for godsake! Do you realise just how unbalanced you sound? Stop it, please, and either talk sense or just go away and leave me alone.'

'I'm sorry, Chrissie, I'm sorry, I so wanted to just come here and be happy for you, with you. Of course he's beautiful, he has beautiful parents,' she said.

'There you go again. You can't stop yourself can you? You must promise me something, Joanna, you must not say anything about this to Rob or Anna or Paul. Please, please for my sake don't go on about the dark eyes of the devil or anything in front of them. They see my son as a Rider, don't please disabuse them of that fact. I have now what I have always, always wanted – a real family. My family with Rob and, by association, his brother's family.

I am happy, Joanna, really happy with them. Don't let any of this destroy that . . .'

'Oh Chrissie, of course I won't say anything that would upset things for you. But I think you should face the fact that one day – and one day quite soon – Rob and his family will find out. Goran will see to that. You may think I am exaggerating but you don't know what I am going through with him,' she went on, unable to stop herself from repeating and repeating her message.

'You're overwrought, Joanna, you can't see things clearly right now. You have two young children and your work and really it's quite understandable that you might have got things a bit out of proportion,' I said, fighting to control my temper.

'Look, I know what everyone thinks about me, I know you think that I am suffering from some kind of depression brought on by the baby. That my mind is playing its old tricks with me, but it isn't, Chrissie, it isn't. This thing isn't in my mind, it's reality. It's caused by coming home and finding him sitting at my kitchen table as if it were his home. He is conducting a sustained campaign against me. Checking on everything I do with the baby, questioning the way I am feeding him, reminding me, at every opportunity, of his rights as Tom's father. If I sound mad, Chrissie, it's because he wants me to. He wants control, he has always wanted control. I just didn't see it before.'

'Why on earth would he want control of Tom? He and Carole have their own children, their own home and a limited income. What makes you think that he wants to take over your baby? He's just trying to help you. He understands how difficult it is to be a single mother to two young children. You should be grateful he cares, not trying to make it seem like some sinister plot.'

'He wants to take Tom away from me . . .'

'Don't be absurd, Joanna, no one can take Tom away from you. There isn't a court in the land that would take a baby away from its mother. I think you are being irrational because you are tired and stressed. You'll feel very different about all this in a few weeks,' I said, feeling rather resentful that I should be – yet again – trying to comfort Joanna at a time of my life when she should be supporting me.

What made her ramblings about Goran even more incomprehensible to me was the fact that, earlier that day – during one of Rob's rare absences from the hospital – I had plucked up the courage to ring Carole to tell her my news. I had my story all worked out – how I had been staying with a friend from work in the country and had gone into labour unexpectedly, how this friend and her family had offered to have me to stay for a few weeks, how I would call her as soon as I got back to London. I reasoned that this tale would, if nothing else, buy me a little time. Time that I could spend alone with Rob and my baby. But when I put the call through from the portable phone brought to my bedside by a nurse, Goran had answered. He couldn't have been more reasonable, more charming, more his old self. He was thrilled by my news, agreed that my staying with my friend sounded like a good idea and said that he and Carole looked forward to seeing me and the baby whenever I was ready to see them. The man I had spoken to that day and the man Joanna was obsessing about seemed like two entirely different people. He had put no pressure on me, he had given no indication of any proprietorial need to intervene in my life or the life of my child. I didn't tell Joanna about my conversation with him because I knew it would only prompt another tirade from her. And by now I was weary of her company and eager for her to leave.

'Tell Rob, Chrissie, tell him before it's too late,' she said imploringly before she went. I promised her that I would, of course, tell him as long as she promised me she wouldn't. She smiled and came over and gave me a hug. It was the only sign of affection she had given me that afternoon and, despite my irritation, I embraced her back. But the sense of relief I felt when she walked out of the ward that day was overwhelming. I determined, as I settled down to feed Sam – noting as I did that his eyes were still just about blue – that I wouldn't allow myself to fret over Joanna and her odd behaviour. Nor would I keep my promise to her. I had no intention of telling Rob about Sam's conception until I was ready. And, deep down inside, I wondered if I ever would be.

Chapter 14

❦

Looking back on those first precious weeks of Sam's life, under the gentle protection of Rob, still makes me want to weep. Rob had a rare gift for nurturing all forms of life – plants, people, Persian cats and most particularly, babies. He only had to hold Sam in his big, gardener's hands to stop him from crying. He only had to croon a few words of some old lullaby to make Sam slip into a deep sleep.

While I panicked at the slightest sign of discontent in my son, Rob would know instinctively what to do. He had, he confessed during the first few days of Sam's life, been reading up on babies. He knew about everything from the primitive reflex reaction in small infants that causes them to cling on to their mother's hands, to the best way in which to get up wind after a feed (laying the baby on its tummy and gently massaging its back). He knew about the burning effect of urine on the delicate skin of a newborn baby and how to counter that effect by applying zinc and castor oil and making sure they didn't lie too long in a dirty nappy.

He had even taken on board some new theories on the development of intelligence in the early days of a baby's life and had stuck a series of visually stimulating images around the inside of his Moses basket. It had been my idea, though, to pin Rob's own childhood mobile – the Messerschmitts that had hung over his bed in Hampshire – on the ceiling above the cot in which Sam slept, or at any rate was put down in, each night.

Rob's devotion to Sam and me aroused conflicting emotions; it made me happy and sad. Happy because I knew he loved us and sad because I so hated the fact that I had, however unwittingly, deceived him into believing that this really was 'our' child.

The baby seemed most comfortable, in those first few nights, sleeping between Rob and me. He seemed to fret more when he was separated from us. Rob had read some book by Desmond Morris – who wrote *The Human Ape* – which maintained that a secure infant needs to be able to smell the scent of its parents when it sleeps. And maybe it was some primal need in Sam that made him scream everytime I carefully lifted his sleeping body from our bed and placed it back in his own cot.

New babies are like little tyrants. It's impossible for anyone who hasn't been a parent to realise how despotic, how dominating such a small, defenceless scrap can be. It isn't possible, I discovered very quickly, to train a baby to feed every four hours (as my mother once claimed she had with me) and to sleep through the night. I wasn't in control of Sam. Sam was in control of me.

I felt, and I think that Rob shared the same feelings, that it was as if the rest of the world had ceased to exist. Before Sam had been born, I couldn't function in the morning unless I had looked at a newspaper or listened to the *Today* programme on Radio 4. I liked to think that I was an informed, intelligent person. But now even the most urgent and disturbing issues of the day – terrorism, conflict in the Middle East, bio-chemical warfare

– were of no interest to me. The only news stories that could hold my attention were those that concerned babies or small children. I was no longer interested or involved in the adult world.

But it wasn't just the wider world that had lost its appeal, I no longer really cared about the people who had previously been so important to me. I became quite reclusive, keeping the phone either unplugged or on answerphone all the time. The messages that I did play back were usually from Joanna and, selfish though I subsequently realised my behaviour was, I never bothered to acknowledge them because I was too tired to endure another tortured and doubtless delusional conversation about Goran's attempts to persecute her. It seemed to me then that there was no room in my life for anyone or anything else but Rob and my son. I understand now why so many people passionately believe that the best start you can give a child in life is two caring parents. Sharing all those silly but nonetheless disturbing worries with Rob was, I later came to realise, a wonderful luxury.

I can remember once waking up in the soft glow of the nightlight to see Rob standing by the window singing softly to Sam.

'Hello boys,' I said as I got out of bed and joined them.

'Hello Mummy,' Rob said as he gently passed the baby over to me to be fed.

'Goodbye Daddy,' I replied as I lay back down on the bed to feed Sam.

The image of Rob, watching my son gorge himself on my breasts, is imprinted on my memory as surely as it might have been had it been captured and placed on a photographic negative. Except that this vision was positive, revealing as it did, the powerful emotions that Rob felt, as he observed me feeding the infant he was, with the utmost certainty, convinced was his own child.

The only regret I had, in those first couple of weeks, was that I hadn't met Rob before I had become involved in our odd, convoluted plan. Why, I sometimes wondered, had nature been so cruel? Why hadn't I been allowed to come across Rob before – rather than after – I had embarked on this mad scheme?

I had come to realise, long before Sam had been born, that Rob was the man I had been preordained to meet. He was – if this doesn't sound too terribly corny – my other half, my soul mate. If only I could have reached him, recognised him, before I had given up hope of ever finding Mr Right and, instead, settled for an artificial substitute. If only I had met Mr Rider first.

Oh and how he spoilt me in those precious early days. He hardly let me do anything but lie amid a pile of plumped up cushions whilst he cooked, cleaned and dealt with all the dirty work, changing nappies, washing babygros and bathing both me and the baby.

Perhaps the most remarkable thing about those weeks was the way in which Rob and I managed to be so close and united without having sex. We cuddled and caressed each other but Rob showed no urgency to resume sexual contact.

Some evenings when Sam was briefly sleeping, I would give Rob a back massage or he would sit and gently brush my hair. But he never attempted, as I had heard was common amongst men whose partners had recently given birth, to reclaim his territory by having sex with me. We thought, you see, that we had all the time in the world. I remember once hearing someone talk about how people should have a 'babymoon' when their child was born and that is what we had – Rob, Sam and me. We had three weeks of beautiful, blissful ignorance together during which I believed, as I had done all along, that everything would come out right.

Rob went back to work at the end of those three weeks and our lives seemed to slip into a new routine. I was feeling more confident with Sam by then but still, by five in the evening, I was longing to see him.

My most poignant memory of that time came on his third day back at work when he returned home with a little square giftwrapped present. He knelt down in front of me and handed it to me with a big grin on his face.

'Open it, Chrissie,' he said.

Beneath the ribbon and paper I found a little leather box within which was a beautiful ring engraved on the outside with the words 'LOVE.TRUST.HONOUR' and on the inside with the message 'Chrissie, Rob and Sam – together forever'.

'I love it, Rob, I love it,' I said aware that I was in danger of crying. 'I mean I love you, Rob, I love you.'

'I should have asked you to marry me when you first told me you were expecting Sam. But I wasn't sure that you would say yes. You will marry me won't you, Chrissie?' Rob said.

I remember thinking, as he slipped the ring on the second finger of my left hand, that maybe I could have it all. Like some foolish princess in a fairy tale I think I had come to believe in magic. I had started to persuade myself into believing that, after all, Rob was Sam's father. I had come to think that it might be possible that I had made a mistake with my dates, even entertaining the fantasy that Sam was not the end product of a cold and clinical insemination but had, in fact, been conceived naturally exactly as Rob had thought in the garden of his childhood home.

'Is the answer yes, Chrissie?' he said a little nervously.

'YES, YES, YES, YES,' I shouted.

I went to sleep that night, locked in Rob's arms, feeling happier and more positive about the future than I had ever done before in my life. I slept so deeply that Rob had to nudge me awake when Sam woke for his feed at three. Half an hour later, I fell back to sleep and into a wonderful dream in which I was a beautiful bride and Rob a handsome groom. I can vaguely recall Rob gently kissing me when he left the flat at about seven-thirty that morning, but I was so sleepy, and so eager to get back into my dream that I am not sure whether I managed to say goodbye.

I spent the whole of that day preparing a celebration meal for us that evening. After all, it wasn't every day that you got engaged. I wheeled Sam down to Marylebone High Street and shopped in all my old haunts. I bought flowers, even though I knew Rob didn't really approve of cut blooms, I selected all sorts of delicious foods and I picked a special bottle of champagne. Everything seemed to take so much longer with Sam who, just as I was about to buy a present for Rob, began to scream in that urgent, persistent way that makes it impossible for you to think. I paid for the gift – a tiny solid silver pair of miniature garden secateurs – and then ran all the way home, the sudden speed shocking Sam into silence.

Looking back, I think I was like some old-fashioned fifties housewife that day. It was as if I was starring in an old Doris Day movie. Every now and again I would sneak a glance at the ring on my finger in the mirror and smile wildly at my ridiculously happy face. While Sam napped in the afternoon I had a long bath, washed my hair, changed into clean clothes and carefully made up my face in readiness for the return of my man. My hormonal confusion was such that I even cleaned up the flat, hoovering away as if it were second nature to me, before laying the table with candles and putting the champagne in the fridge.

I began to get agitated at about six forty-five. It was so unlike Rob to be late, and he had promised, when he went back to work the previous Monday that he would be home by six-thirty every day. Half an hour later, I was getting really worried and Sam had begun the crying that would in the weeks to come turn into terrible colic. I tried Rob's mobile but it was switched off. I rang Green Piece but there was no reply. By eight, I was frantic because in all the time I had known him, not that long I know, he had always rung me when something had delayed him.

At eight forty-five, the front door bell rang. He's forgotten his keys, I thought with relief, as I held the screeching Sam in my arms and ran to answer the door.

But it wasn't Rob. It was Goran with this solicitous smile on his face that, with the inevitable hindsight that I now lend to the scene, I think of as particularly sinister. He took Sam from my arms, walked into the room and sat down at the table that had been so carefully laid for two. It was the first time that Goran had encountered Sam and I felt curiously repulsed by the sight of my son nestled in the arms of his biological father. It seemed terribly, terribly wrong particularly when I contrasted it with the way in which Rob, when he had first held Sam, had looked so natural, so right.

'Chrissie, I am so, so sorry. I have bad news,' Goran said gently, looking at me with compassion over the head of my still screaming baby. My mind went into overdrive then. Something terrible had happened to Rob – some awful injury, some hideous accident, some life-threatening terror.

'What's happened?' I said, my voice taking on the same screeching, wailing tone as my son.

'Your friend,' Goran said softly, 'your friend came to see me today, at the garage.'

'My friend?' I said blankly, unsure what Goran was trying to say but aware, still, that some catastrophe had occurred.

'Robert Rider,' he said as he made a vain attempt to calm Sam.

'Why would he come to see you? How would he know where to find you?' I said because, confused though I was, I was certain Rob had no idea where Goran lived, let alone worked. 'What's happened to him?'

'Why didn't you tell us, Chrissie, about Robert? Why didn't you tell us you had fallen in love. Do you think we didn't want you to be happy?'

'Tell me what's happened to him, please, tell me?' I said taking Sam from Goran and clasping him to my chest to comfort him, to comfort myself.

'He came to see me because Joanna had called him and told him to. He was confused and nervous and at first I couldn't understand what he was saying. If only you had told me that you had met this man, everything would be alright,' Goran said.

'What did you say to him, what did you tell him?' I said as my brain began to grasp that something more terrible than an accident had felled Rob – the truth about Sam.

'How could I know that this man thought he was the father of your child? When he asked me who I was and what my relationship was to you and Sam I eventually said – because he was very insistent that he should "know the truth" – that I was your child's biological father,' Goran said, bringing his hands up to his head in a gesture of despair or regret.

I sat down then and began to almost involuntarily rock Sam backwards and forwards in an effort to silence him.

'What did he say?' I asked after a few moments.

'He was distraught, he was broken by what I said. At first I thought he might become violent towards me, he was so upset, so angry, so disturbed. But then he just cried, Chrissie. I tried to comfort him, he is a good man, but he could not be comforted. In the end he allowed me to call someone for him – a brother or brother-in-law I think – and while we waited he talked to me about your betrayal, your deception. Why did you lie, Chrissie, why did you risk losing such a man because of a lie?'

'I didn't lie, I just didn't tell the truth. Oh Goran, you have to understand that his believing that Sam was his wasn't a deception on my part, it was a misunderstanding on his. I got worked up to tell him everything – about you and our plan – but when I said I was pregnant he didn't let me say any more, he was just overcome with happiness because he just assumed it was his.'

I broke down then, and began to sob. Goran came and gently took the now sleeping Sam from me and laid him down in his Moses basket. Then he came and sat next to me and tried to stop my tears.

'Where is Rob? Where is he now?' I said.

'It's too late now, he's gone, Chrissie,' Goran said softly. 'He went off with this man, the brother. He said he couldn't face seeing you or the baby again, he couldn't be accountable for what he might do if he did confront you, he just wanted me to tell you that it was over. I tried to persuade him that he should give you another chance, that it wasn't as if you and I had a sexual relationship but he said truth was everything in a relationship and that he could never forgive the lies. I talked to him of true love and how it was about giving and forgiving but he just shook his head.'

I had always known that Rob's philosophy on life was a simple one, that a lie – and a lie as big as this – would be like a death blow to our relationship. I suppose if I thought about it at all I vaguely imagined that in time our love would have grown so deep that it might withstand such a deception. But I knew that at this stage, in this situation, the truth would have been untenable for him. Goran, who had been watching me with soulful eyes embraced me in the way you might a child who had suffered a terrible shock.

'I'm so sorry, Chrissie. I promised him that I would pack up his things and get them to him. You have to face the truth, Chrissie, as he has had to do. He won't be coming back.'

I nodded my head because I could no longer speak. I accepted what he said because my guilt was such that I didn't think to question anything. I just found myself going along with what he said and what he told me to do. While Goran filled a case and two black bin liners with Rob's possessions and then carried them down to his car, I served up the supper I had cooked for my lost love. Goran ate it all.

Meanwhile Sam had woken up again and I began to try to calm him again. It was curious, really, but Goran never seemed very interested in my son. That night he seemed absolutely oblivious to his screams. Much later I came to believe that a major part of Goran's motivation was territorial and no doubt fired by an excess of testosterone (what Joanna, ages ago, had defined as male 'testostitorial behaviour'). I think he felt about our babies in rather the way that some men feel about their ex-lovers – I don't want her but I don't want anyone else to have her either. He couldn't bear the idea of another man raising his child.

But I am rushing ahead of myself again and on that night I was so devastated and confused that I didn't think to question Goran further about Rob's reaction. Besides, I was so ashamed about the way I had treated him and so upset by the thought of how hurt he must feel that it never entered my head that it was actually unlike Rob to just walk away. But like everything else in this story I just didn't see it until it was too late. I just took what Goran said at face value. It didn't even occur to me, at this point, to resent the way in which Goran had told Rob or to blame Joanna for having put the two of them in touch. I didn't even feel – as I would some time later – disappointed that Rob didn't love me enough to allow me one, albeit vast, mistake. There was only one person, I thought that night, who could truly be held responsible for the breakdown of my relationship with Rob. Me.

Chapter 15

❧

The following few weeks were probably the hardest of my life. Not only was I struggling to come to terms with the loss of Rob but I was also finding it increasingly hard to cope with Sam's colic. He would cry from about four in the afternoon until late at night – a desperate, persistent, high decibel noise accompanied by an odd contorting of his body that frightened me and made me tense with worry about the pain he must be feeling. Some evenings I would sit alongside him and silently weep with him, wringing my hands and fiddling with the ring that Rob had given me – which I was never to take off – as I replayed the events of the previous months and weeks.

It was as if my world, my dream of happiness and a family, had suddenly been shattered and in its place was this awful reality – a difficult, unhappy baby, a terrible feeling of failure and of solitude and, to make things worse, an increasingly worrying financial situation.

Although we had never really talked about it in those wonderful early weeks, I had been thinking about giving up work, or perhaps returning on a part-time basis. It would have been difficult – we couldn't have lived, at least in the same way, on Rob's income – but it would have been possible to scrape by.

Until Sam had been born I had no idea what people

meant by a 'maternal instinct', perhaps because I had never really known, or at any rate had no memory of, being mothered myself. I had always suspected that I might, contrary to everyone's expectations of me, be a good enough mother but I wasn't a natural nurturer. I loved Sasha and Emma – and my involvement in their early childhood had probably triggered or at least set the alarm on my biological clock – but the feelings they had aroused in me were as nothing when compared to the emotional pull I felt towards my own baby. I think now that the instinct was particularly strong in me because of my own family history. Because Sam was, you see, the first real blood relation I had ever had. I did attempt to trace my birth mother when I was twenty-one but I was informed that she did not want contact with me and I never bothered again, even when they changed the law.

The discovery that all my childhood fantasies of being the much-loved baby of some mysterious woman who had been forced, against her will, to give me up were just that – fantasies – had devastated me. I think that the knowledge that my mother had, in fact, not only rejected me at birth but was also rejecting me as a young adult had a profound subconscious effect on the way I viewed my own child.

I know a lot of women pour scorn on the idea that there is some instant bond between mother and child but it was like that for me. Within minutes, actually seconds, of his birth I had known inside that I wanted to devote my life to him, I wanted to be what all those childcare books call 'the primary carer'. I didn't want to give him up to a child minder or a nanny.

And even in those bleak days, when I felt so helpless and unhappy and it almost seemed as if Sam was voicing – well, crying and screaming – my grief for me, I still couldn't bear the thought of being parted from him. But the clock was ticking away, and this time it wasn't biological, it was the doomsday clock counting out the time before I must return to my job. Not that I let myself think about it, I didn't really let myself think about anything. I just shut myself off from the world and went to pieces, occasionally pulling myself together enough to get dressed in order to take Sam out to the baby clinic or to the shops.

The only sense of real satisfaction I got, during that period, occurred during my outings with Sam. I found myself beaming with pride and pleasure whenever some little old lady in Sainsbury's commented on Sam's beauty. And I positively crowed when the health visitors who ran the clinic recorded his increasing weight and marvelled at how well, despite the evening colic, he was doing. 'Gold Top' one of them said to me one day when Sam tipped the scales at twice his birth weight.

Unlike Joanna I had no problem with my milk. Rather the reverse, actually, my breasts working like a twenty-four-hour dairy producing ever larger quantities of milk. Just as, I swear, I had felt my hormones scream before I conceived Sam, I could feel my mammary glands throbbing and churning as they produced a steady stream of mother's milk. But if my body was functioning my brain wasn't – or perhaps my mental state was connected to this particular body function because looking back I think the best way to describe me then was as bovine.

At some point, the time sequence of that phase of my life is so hazy now that I am not sure exactly *when*, I received a letter from Rob. I knew from the moment I opened it that there was no point in my replying or in attempting to see him to explain my actions. It wasn't cruel or even condemning but it was cold and somehow resolute. He had, he wrote, decided to start his life anew. He was moving out of London to be closer to Paul when they expanded their business interests. I don't know now why I didn't pay more attention to the signing off line – it seems so obvious all this time later – but I just pushed the paper into my deep kitchen drawer, in which unopened bank statements, credit bills and income tax demands nestled darkly together. 'I hope with all my heart that you *will* be happy together' he had written and it wasn't until much later that I understood the sinister significance of these words which did not, as I then assumed, refer to Sam and me.

Sometime later I received another, more damning, letter from Anna. It was such an emotive, raging letter that reading it cut even deeper into my heart. Anna accused me of the 'grossest form of deception'. She told me that I hadn't just let down Rob, I had let down the whole family. Her own personal distress at discovering that the woman she had taken in and regarded as a kind of surrogate sister had turned out to be a callous cheat was not, she said, something she would easily get over. That I had the nerve to not only seduce her brother-in-law but also her children had shaken her faith in human nature. Had I, she asked, at any point felt any real affection for any of them? It was exactly the sort of letter that I would have expected from good, decent Anna and much as I longed to write my side of the story, offer up some defence, I knew that it was useless. In a big postscript written in capital letters, Anna had written across the bottom of the last page 'PLEASE DO NOT THINK OF REPLYING TO THIS LETTER, I NEVER WANT TO HEAR FROM YOU AGAIN.'

My self-esteem, by now, was at an all-time low. I honestly believe that if I hadn't had Sam to cope with I would have done something desperate at that time. He was my only reason for living and the only way, I reasoned, that I could vindicate myself. If I could prove – to myself as much as anyone else – that my commitment to Sam was such that I would put his life before my own then maybe I could, in some small way, redeem myself.

It's very curious how society has positioned the single mother as some kind of selfish, pernicious influence. We are constantly being told by the voice of Middle England that single mothers are lazy, amoral creatures who undermine the future of the family. That women who have babies outside conventional relationships regard their children as state-funded meal tickets. In the minds of many people, single mothers are responsible for the breakdown of society – they are held culpable for everything from juvenile crime to rises in taxation.

In truth, of course, it is single mothers who are actually struggling to hold the family together in a world in which men and women seem less and less able to live happily together.

No one ever thinks how hard the life of a single mother can be. No one ever tells you about the loneliness, the depression and the pressure of responsibility which falls on a parent without a partner. No one ever talks about how difficult it can be to cope with a small baby – there are so many worries, so many uncertainties and illogical fears – when there isn't another adult to lean on. Believe me, being a lone parent certainly isn't an easy option.

The weeks after Rob had left, when Sam developed colic, were the most physically exhausting of my life. Some days I didn't even have the energy to get dressed, let alone brush my hair or look in the mirror or cook myself a meal. Some nights when the baby had been crying for hours on end I became so frightened and so panicked that I thought morning would never, ever come. I had no support network, I couldn't turn to my mother who, even before the onset of Alzheimer's, had never been very maternal towards me. I had no siblings to lean on, no cousins, no loving aunt.

The only people I had ever really been able to depend on had been Carole and Joanna whose own family experiences were so similar to my own that we had been – at least until now – like an alternative family unit. But what had seemed like the ultimate plan to extend our friendship to a real kinship had, in the event, only served to push us apart. I no longer wanted to confide my mistakes, my worries in either of them. My relationship with Carole had gradually but persistently deteriorated during my pregnancy. I had come to find her interference in my antenatal care and her endless desire to offer me advice about motherhood patronising and intrusive. My alienation from her was further compounded by the feeling of failure – not to mention the humiliation – that Rob's departure from my life had prompted after Sam was born. I felt that she was looking down on me, that she saw me as somehow wanting not just as a mother but as a woman. And as a result, doubtless as much to do with my own pride as her rather bossy matriarchal behaviour, I no longer regarded her as a suitable or sympathetic confidant.

Meanwhile I had turned Joanna, in my head, into a kind of scapegoat for all my current troubles. I think the need to deflect some of the blame for your own mistakes is one of the strongest instincts that modern men and women have developed. We have come to believe in the so called 'blame culture'. We are living in an age in which no one is prepared to take responsibility for their own actions – it's always someone else's fault. What do you do if you are so bad at your job that you are passed over for promotion? You sue your employers for sexual discrimination. What do you do if you are so drunk that you fall over in the street? You sue the council for not repairing the paving stones. What do you do if you fail your GCSEs? Why, you sue your school. And although I couldn't exactly sue Joanna, in my head and my heart I held her responsible for my losing Rob. This was, of course, unfair because if I had taken Joanna's advice and told Rob the truth I might just have managed to save my relationship. But I had trusted her with the truth, I had relied on her as my confidant and she had betrayed that confidence by contacting Rob and telling him to ask Goran for the truth.

To her credit she did turn up on my doorstep – I had refused to take her calls – a couple of days after Rob had gone. But I wouldn't – couldn't – accept her pathetic explanation as to why she had failed me so badly. She attempted to mitigate her actions by reiterating her tedious claims that Goran had subjected her to a sustained campaign of intimidation and interrogation that had affected her ability to think properly. In contacting Rob, she said, she had not meant to destroy our relationship, she had only meant to help, she hadn't thought of how he might feel to discover that Sam wasn't his child from Goran. She wept as she told me this but I felt no compassion for her. I knew how emotionally frail she was and I was well aware of her history of depression but I was so angry, so hurt and so preoccupied by my own problems that I wasn't prepared to even consider how she might feel. Later I would come to wonder if my cold rejection of her –

and my subsequent refusal to talk to her – might not have played a part in her own downfall.

My sense of isolation, then, in the weeks after Rob's departure was compounded by my estrangement from Carole and Joanna. Without the support and companionship of the two women who had once meant so much to me – and with whom I had so foolishly but willingly entered into this strange blood alliance – I felt lost and yet more confused and I became increasingly reclusive shutting myself off from everything and everyone. It seemed to me that the only thing I could depend on was Pushkin, my faithful and devoted cat. Such was my troubled state of mind at that time that I began to talk to Pushkin as if he were really able to listen and respond to me. Long before I had got myself into this – during my disastrous relationship with John – someone had given me a mug bearing the legend 'Behind Every Successful Woman is a Cat'. And soppy and sentimental though it might sound, I came to think of that as one of the great truths of life. Well my life at that time, anyway.

I lived not so much from day to day as from hour to hour with no real routine or view of what was going on in the wider world. I had to go on because of Sam but there were moments during those weeks when I felt so tired and so lost that I just wanted to lie down and never get up again. The flat was filthy – heavens, many days *I* was filthy – although Sam was always clean and cared for, even if he didn't stop crying. It was as if I, that is the old Chrissie, had ceased to be.

Tired as I was, and there is probably no time of a woman's life when she is more tired than during the infancy of her first child, I could not sleep. My mind was constantly sifting through the events of the past year. At night, during the precious hours when Sam had stopped crying and was finally sleeping, I would lie in my bed remembering, and trying to make sense of, the sequence of events that had led up to our big idea on that sunny day that seemed, now, a lifetime away. How shallow I had been, how foolish and unthinking I was to have imagined that I could have it all and not pay some kind of price. The image that stayed in my mind most was of Joanna, on the day that she fell and went into labour, screaming in pain and talking about 'her punishment'. I could even recall her exact words 'It's a punishment, Chrissie, I know it is. I've done a terrible thing'. Was the loss of Rob – and my beloved friends – *my* punishment?

Chapter 16

❧

It was, ironically enough, Carole who eventually took charge of my life and made me face up to the future, turning up one afternoon to find me wandering round in a milk and muck-stained nightdress, muttering to myself as I attempted to sway Sam to sleep. She was, she told me later, profoundly shocked by my appearance. I had lost all the blubber I had put on during pregnancy and a little bit more so that I now looked, Carole said, like some starving survivor of a Nazi concentration camp.

Such was my desperation, when I opened the door to Carole, that I forgot my fears and my misgivings about her behaviour and embraced her, breaking down in her arms and spilling over her not just my tears but all the pent-up worries of the previous weeks. Pushkin suddenly seemed a poor substitute for a real live walking and talking human friend.

Quite simply she was a godsend that day. She listened to me and comforted me and held me tight against her in a way that made me feel safe. When she felt I was sufficiently recovered she turned her attention to Sam. And, really, despite all that subsequently happened, she *was* genuinely wonderful with children. She took Sam from me and instantly he relaxed. They do say that a new mother can pass her tension on to her child and it was almost as if you could see the relief on Sam's face as he felt himself held by firm, sure hands.

She could only stay for two hours on that first visit because she had to pick up her own boys – Sasha from school and Nino from his childminder – later that afternoon. It didn't occur to me then to ask her why she wasn't at work, well, it didn't occur to me to question anything at that time in my life and I was just grateful for some adult human contact. And she was like a tornado in my life in the time she had that day. She ran me a bath, ordered me to wash my hair and relax while she went out, taking the sleeping Sam in his buggy with her, to do some shopping. When she returned, Sam still soundly asleep, she filled my fridge with fresh wholesome food and then began to clean up the accumulated mess in the flat.

I became very emotional again when it was time for her to go, beseeching her to stay with me a little longer.

'Chrissie, I have to get back, but if you want I'll come again tomorrow.'

I did want and she did come back the next day, this time bearing yet more gifts – fresh baby clothes for Sam that Nino had long since grown out of, a wind-up illuminated baby mobile that she claimed could lull even the most fretful infant to sleep and, most thoughtful of all, a beautiful top from Vivienne Westwood that she had found in a sale and thought might cheer me up. It was time, she said, for me to start thinking of myself again.

In the next few weeks I slowly came to depend on Carole again, feeling the old bond return. It may be that my life would have improved without the resumption of my relationship with Carole, but at that time I attributed every upturn in my circumstances to her influence. Sam might have naturally grown out of his colic and he would,

I suppose, have begun to be more contented without Carole's intervention. But I didn't think that the fact that Sam smiled at me for the first time on the day that Carole had come back into our lives was a coincidence. It was only later that I was able to realise that at about six weeks of age all babies begin to properly smile and that the pain or colic gradually fades as their digestive system becomes more efficient. But because I had totally lost confidence in my own abilities to make either myself or my child happy, I made up my mind that it was all down to Carole.

But I didn't just fall back into my comfortable old relationship with my friend, I also fell back into my old relationship with her husband.

I saw him as I had done on that sunny day when he inspired our mad idea. The man who I had begun to doubt during my pregnancy – and whom Joanna had so constantly attempted to turn me against – had become, again, the kind, dependable person I had always assumed him to be.

My relationship with him improved to such an extent that all the fears that Joanna had tried to awaken in me gradually faded. He was a good, decent family man, I decided. If he had been a little dictatorial in his approach to me when I was carrying Sam it was only because he cared about us, it was only for our own good.

Most Sundays, Goran would come and pick Sam and me up and take us over to Acton to have lunch with them and I no longer felt awkward with him. Indeed, ironically enough, he was the only person I could even mention Rob's name to because he had been a part of that terrible night. I remember, in particular, one conversation we had one day on the journey from my flat to his house.

'How is your heart, Chrissie?' he asked, and I can vividly recall his deep, black soulful eyes looking at me as we sat waiting at the traffic lights.

'Not so good,' I said, looking away from those eyes, trying to blank those eyes from my consciousness because, of course, they were my son's eyes and Joanna's son's eyes and Carole's boy's eyes.

'I think you loved him a lot, Chrissie. But I think he cannot have loved you enough,' Goran said.

'I don't think I behaved very loveably, do you?' I replied.

'True love between a man and a woman is unconditional, Chrissie. It might have wounded his pride to discover that Sam was not his child, but if he had loved you enough he would have understood. It is not, is it, as if I were anything other than a friend to you? We were never lovers, it was not an infidelity.'

'It became an infidelity when I allowed him to believe Sam was his, I think. But there is a part of me, Goran, that feels betrayed as well. As if everything I thought I had with Rob was not as it really seemed.'

'Then, Chrissie, maybe your heart is beginning to mend,' he replied, squeezing my hand in a gesture of support.

I didn't think that my heart would ever mend, but I was aware that my feelings towards Rob had changed in the past weeks. I was angry with him now, I felt cheated and not a little foolish, as if the whole period with him had been like some mad teenage crush. Sometimes when I was lying feeding Sam in the middle of the night I would retrace the course of my relationship with Rob and examine all the little details which, at the time, had felt so special, so preordained but which now I began to doubt and question. How could I have known, so soon, that he was the man I had always wanted, particularly when I remembered how ill I was on the night we got together? How could I have fallen so totally, so utterly for someone who was too cowardly to come and tell me how he felt face-to-face? I even began to question his motives for embarking on our relationship – maybe with all that odd obsession with sowing seeds his real intention had only ever been to have a baby. And once he discovered that it was not his seed that had been sown, on that Barbour, he had lost interest in both the mother and the child.

Having Goran and Carole back in my life had restored a bit of my old confidence, I did not feel so isolated. In fact it was rather like going home, being back in your old familiar surroundings. So although I was by no means happy, by no means over Rob, I began to feel more positive about my role as a mother to my child.

I didn't think too much how things might develop as Sam got older – typically I preferred to ignore the issue of my child's paternity and who my son, when he could speak, would call his father – because I needed to be part of a normal family. Well, what I imagined then was a normal family.

We never talked about Joanna and her problems. I didn't want to talk to or see her and Carole, who still maintained contact with her, respected my feelings. I missed her, of course, but I still couldn't forgive her for letting me down and causing such heartache in my life. In rather the way that Joanna and I had come together and shut out Carole during our pregnancies, I now moved closer to Carole and shut Joanna out of my life.

In any case Carole, and of course Goran, offered me much greater physical and emotional support than Joanna ever could have done. Joanna, much as I had loved her, had always been more dependent than dependable. She couldn't possibly have provided me with the kind of practical help that Goran and Carole offered me during the early months of Sam's life. Help which made them crucial, at that time of my life, for my survival.

Goran was there for all those stupid things I could never quite cope with – to change the wheel on my car, for example, or to come, as he did once, late at night to mend a fuse that had blown the lights in the flat. And of course, to calm me if I became overly concerned about Sam's health – it was wonderful to have that safety net of Goran's medical knowledge to call on.

Meanwhile Carole helped me to get my head back together, to sort out Sam's feeding and sleeping patterns and to return my home to something of its old order. She had always been more domestic than me and since she was now an experienced mother she could pass on to me little tips and truths that are, I suppose, what have traditionally been called 'old wives' tales', such as when to begin weaning, what to do when your child develops croup (which in addition to everything else became another worry in Sam's infancy), and what to do when they are teething. While other new mothers pored over Miriam Stoppard or Penelope Leach, I turned to Carole and Goran. They were, quite simply, the only people that I felt I could totally trust.

As time passed, I began to worry less about my son and more about myself. I had only four weeks left before my statutory maternity leave was due to end and although it was possible to extend that time I would no longer be paid a salary.

There was absolutely no question of my being able to give up work. I had never been good with money, had always lived life on overdrafts and on the edge of my credit limit. I had a mortgage to pay, a child to feed and debts to pay off. But I had made no arrangements about childcare, probably because I wasn't ready to face the idea of leaving Sam with a stranger. I couldn't stand the thought of leaving my baby with a child minder or a nanny or, worse, in one of those institutionalised day nurseries with a deceptively sweet name such as 'Buttercups' or 'Jumping Beans' which belied the fact they were, at least it seemed to me, nothing more than baby borstals.

The only person I felt I could trust with Sam, the only people I was happy to leave him with for more than a minute were, of course, Carole and, to a lesser extent, Goran.

I still don't know if my new dependence on them was part of any big master plan. Were they, even then, scheming against me or had we just slipped back into something more like our old pre-turkeybaster relationship? It was Carole herself who prompted me to come up with another solution to my childcare problems. She had got into the habit of dropping in to see me, if only for a few minutes, every couple of days. And on one of these visits she began to talk about how fond she was of Sam and how much she liked being involved with another baby – Nino was now a sturdy toddler.

Then she told me, almost as if it had just occurred to her, that what she would ideally like to do was to give up work and be a full-time mother. Goran worked so hard, she said wistfully, but as a mechanic he still earned less than half her salary and there was little likelihood of her ever being able to escape from work. She told me – and if anything should have sounded alarm bells in my head it was this – that she worried about the balance of the relationship between a man and a woman when he earned less than she. Men, she said, have a primal need and a right to be the masters of their own homes, the main breadwinner. Had Joanna been there she would, I feel certain, have thrown up her hands in horror and reminded Carole of where giving into a man's primal needs left a woman – with lower wages, inferior status and, very often, a black eye and a couple of broken ribs. But since I, too, at this point could understand Carole's yearning to be at home with her children, I didn't even think to quote my favourite feminist definition ('I myself have never been able to find out precisely what feminism is: I only know that people call me a feminist whenever I express sentiments that differentiate me from a doormat or a prostitute', Rebecca West, 1913). I just let her carry on talking about her domestic dreams and her new fantasy of taking a Montessori course and starting her own little school, somewhat different from starting her own women's cable channel with links to the worldwide web.

At the time it didn't seem like a calculated conversation but of course it must have been. She knew how vulnerable I was – what with my new baby, my broken heart and the worries about my imminent return to work – and she must have known I would clutch at her dream and come up with a solution for both of us. And of course I did, a couple of days later.

'How serious are you, Carole, about changing your life?' I asked as she sat on my sofa playing with Sam.

'More serious than I have been about anything else I have ever said to you,' she said, giving me one of her intense, loving gazes.

'I don't know how to put this, but if you really mean it maybe we could, well, help each other,' I began, actually nervous lest she reject my proposal.

'What do you mean, Chrissie?' she said, laying Sam down and offering me her total, rapt attention.

'The thing is, I do understand how you feel. I think that if my circumstances were different – if I had a proper partner that is – I would want to be a full-time mother. But obviously I can't do that, I am a single mother.'

'What are you trying to say, darling?' she said gently.

'I suppose I'm trying to say that maybe at least one of us could be a proper mother to their children. I thought that maybe if you gave up work that – you must tell me if you hate this idea, Carole – I could pay you to look after Sam as well. I mean, I know whatever I could give you wouldn't make up for what you would be giving up financially but nannies cost over £200 a week and a full-time nursery just a little less so it would be enough to at least put food on the family table,' I said, my tone becoming increasingly nervous because I was fearful of offending or patronising her.

'But Chrissie, that's just the most brilliant, brilliant, brilliant idea,' she exclaimed as if this possibility had never occurred to her. 'Do you really, really mean it?'

'God, Carole, you would be doing me the bigger favour. I can't even think about the idea of leaving Sam with some stranger or in some awful childcare establishment. I think I can face the future, at work that is, if I knew you were looking after my baby,' I said.

'It's just perfect – I could do a correspondence course

in the evenings and build up to the possibility of starting my own Montessori school. God knows the house, when we get rid of all the tenants, is big enough to house a nursery school. Oh, Chrissie, Chrissie I'm so excited, I can't wait to tell Goran. He will be so happy. I can't tell you how much he has wanted for me to be just, as he says "wife and mother",' she said kissing Sam, and then me and then Sam and then me until the baby, thinking it some mad game, began to laugh. The sound of a baby's laugh is the most infectious thing in the world and within moments all three of us were convulsed with laughter. It was the first time I had felt happy since Rob had left.

What was so clever about all this, I realised much, much later, was the way in which she managed to engineer all our discussions when we were alone and not when Goran was present. It was like the old days, just two friends supporting each other. And I know it's stupid that I should so blindly, happily even, have rushed to further enmesh myself in their family life but it just seemed like the obvious solution. And I realise that it was idiotic of me not to look at the whole thing more objectively. But then objectivity, when you are a new mother, is something that somehow vanishes along with the natural cynicism which, in the old days, would have made me question Carole and Goran's real motives. My hormones, rather as they had done before I conceived Sam, were doing my thinking.

Chapter 17

⟡

Just as I had an unrealistic view of the problems that might arise from the way in which I had conceived my child, I had an equally blinkered and rosy idea of what it is to be a working mother. I never really imagined that having a baby would alter my life. I think I thought that working and looking after Sam would be a slightly more proactive version of looking after Pushkin my cat. I mean, I thought babies, like cats, spent most of their lives feeding and sleeping.

I didn't, for one second, resent Sam's presence in my life. I knew that he had fulfilled a terrible need in me and I loved him more than I could imagine loving anyone or anything, even Pushkin and certainly, by that time, Rob. But I was so very, very tired.

Going back to work, even with Carole's backup, didn't make my life any easier. For a start I felt very awkward going into the office. My life had been so totally changed by Sam's birth that I almost felt as if I were a different person. The only thing I can really compare it to was the year – when I was seventeen – that I returned to school after the summer when I first fell in love. I probably didn't look that different to my classmates, apart from a radical haircut, but I felt that I was now a fully functional woman and not a schoolgirl. I no longer belonged in their world.

Anyway, it was a little like that at the office – me feeling somehow apart from the others because of course no one else at work had changed, and nor had the job. The atmosphere was still fiercely competitive and there was still that strong culture of 'presenteeism' – the person who arrived first and stayed the latest on any given day was somehow afforded a kind of moral superiority.

What I hadn't realised – although of course in the past I had griped enough myself about women who couldn't forget they were mothers at work – was that there would be no allowances for me now that I had Sam. I was still expected to arrive in the office at eight-thirty – much, much earlier when we were shooting a commercial – looking like something that had walked out of the pages of *Vogue*, (rather than *Mother and Baby* magazine). I was still expected to work late on quotes and to be prepared to go away, at a moment's notice, when an ad was being shot on location. Some days being apart from Sam felt like a piercing physical pain. Breast-feeding had come easily to me and had intensified my bond with my baby. I loved the smell of my baby, as he suckled me, as much as he loved the smell of my milk. And the way in which his eyes would lock with mine in a state of mutual adoration was one of the greatest pleasures of motherhood for me.

Weaning him on to a bottle, in preparation for my return, had been one of the hardest things I had ever had to do. He had never liked teats, he hadn't even been able to take water or juice from a bottle and in the end the only way I had managed to get him to take milk from anything other than my breast was to literally starve him into it. Carole made me go out of the flat for a whole day while she attempted to feed him. It was no good my trying to give him formula because if he could smell my milk he would scream and push away the bottle demanding the real thing, not this poor substitute for mother's milk being dropped into his mouth through a rubber teat. Right from the start Sam was a very stubborn little boy and it took Carole some six hours, most of which time he spent crying, to persuade him to take a couple of ounces of formula from the bottle. I had to give up feeding him that very day because to put him back on the breast would undo all she had achieved.

The physical effects of suddenly ceasing to breast-feed your baby are well known. I became engorged and although the doctor gave me some pills that were meant to stop me from producing milk they weren't very effective. I still felt a tingle everytime Sam cried and I still dripped milk every four hours or so for weeks after I had returned to work. Not, you understand, that anyone else noticed.

Trying not to talk about Sam or fret about being parted from him was very difficult and further served to set me apart from my colleagues. Even Jean, who had been so supportive during my pregnancy, seemed to find any mention of my son during my working day tedious. I knew that her resentment of me was probably prompted by the fact that her most recent attempt at IVF had failed, but I had expected her, on my return to work, to be my one office ally.

But what I failed to recognise was that Jean and all my other workmates only had to worry about doing their jobs and pursuing their very singular lives, while my own schedule was rather more punishing. In order to drop Sam off at Carole's by eight, I had to be up by six-thirty, occasionally having barely gone to bed.

It took me at least forty minutes to get from my flat to Carole and Goran's house in East Acton. Because of the geographical distance between our two homes, I would drive Sam to their house, leave my car for Carole to use during the day, and travel on into work by tube. When I did pick up Sam, who was usually bathed and sleeping soundly, I was so overcome by guilt and withdrawal symptoms that instead of putting him to bed when I finally got home I would wake him up so that I could be with him for a few hours.

This is, I have discovered, a common mistake made by many working mothers. I was terrified, in those early days, that he would forget I was his mother and rather than give him the kind of set routine that babies like I tried to make him adapt to my schedule. So that, as he grew older, he became so used to sharing late night suppers with me and to sleeping beside me and Pushkin in my bed that he became what people call a 'difficult sleeper'. Refusing, no matter how tired and fractious he was, to go to sleep at night unless I was lying next to him, holding his hand as he dropped off.

I think I felt, during my early days back at work, as if I was a failure in every area of my life. I didn't see enough of my child to be the kind of mother I wanted to be and my concerns for my son were affecting my performance at work. I needed my job, well my salary, so much that I was terrified that anyone at work might think that I had lost my old drive and enthusiasm, which, of course, I had.

So I wasn't just spending my evenings trying to make it up to Sam for my absence, I was also attempting, during the working day, to compensate for the fact that I could no longer give my job everything I had got.

Carole and Goran were very supportive. Willingly agreeing, sometimes at just a few hours' notice, to keep Sam overnight when I had to go off on location. Keeping up a smiling face, and focusing on the job, were particularly difficult when I was trying not to think about Sam. And made all the worse by the continued references, from my colleagues, to Rob. For some reason I was unable to tell anyone at work, even Jean, that Rob was no longer a part of my life. Perhaps I thought that I would seem an even more vulnerable and dependent member of the workforce if I was perceived as a single mother.

Anyway I somehow managed to perpetuate another lie in my life by letting everyone believe that I lived with Rob. Which made it even more difficult for me to get out of going away on location because the standard response of my immediate boss, whom I sensed, believed I was no longer really earning my way at work, would be to say, 'For goodness' sake, Chrissie, your baby will be fine. He's got a father, hasn't he? Rob will look after him.'

The most depressing experience of those first weeks back at work was the shoot I organised for my ex-boyfriend John. I hadn't worked on anything that he had brought into the company since our split and I still felt awkward and nervous when I encountered him.

He was the kind of man, I could now see, who regarded every woman he met as a challenge. And as one of the few women who had ever ended a relationship with him, rather than, as was more common with John, the other way round, I presented an even more tantalising test of his charms.

I found out later that he had specifically asked for me to be involved in the production of the commercial he had brought into the company. It would mean a three day shoot in Jerez, in southern Spain and although the thought of being away for such a long period gave me a very heavy heart, I knew I was in no position to refuse to go.

I know it probably sounds churlish to say that flying off in the middle of a cold wet winter to stay in a five star hotel in temperatures close to 25°C was a miserable prospect for me, but it really was. I knew that John would take every opportunity he could to humiliate me in front of my colleagues. And that it was inevitable that he would attempt to get me alone and try to re-establish some sort of sexual relationship.

But I tried to put a brave face on it and to be as much a part of the social scene on shoots as I had been prior to Sam's conception and birth. I went through the motions, on the first evening, of putting on one of my flirty little skirts and going out to dinner with the client and the rest of the crew.

It was difficult, though, to appear engaged and happy when my heart was back home with my baby. Beneath the glossy exterior that I had carefully put on that night, I was a completely different person from the one that everyone remembered from my past. I no longer even liked alcohol very much, I had given up smoking and I certainly didn't find the vulgar banter of my colleagues – let alone the alarming woman-to-man ratio – very stimulating. By eleven, I could stand it no longer and I made my excuses and left everyone else drinking in the bar.

I suppose I should have guessed that John – vain bastard that he was – would misinterpret my reasons for leaving so early. But I was tired and distracted and eager to call home to Carole to check that Sam was alright. When the knock came on my hotel door, it never occurred to me it would be him, holding a bottle of champagne.

'Chrissie, Chrissie, you don't know how much I want

you,' he said as he pushed his way into the room and slammed the door shut after him.

'John, please let's just keep it as a precious memory,' I said aware that it would take all my ingenuity – and maybe physical strength – to prevent him from becoming my lover again.

'Chrissie,' he said again, lunging at me and pushing the cold bottle hard against my thighs in what was clearly intended to be an obscene and suggestive gesture. He was drunk, his breath stank of booze and cigarettes and I wondered how on earth I could ever have found him attractive. But such was his strutting male arrogance, that night, that he assumed that I still did. He pushed me back on to the bed and began kissing me, forcing his tongue into my mouth and simultaneously slipping his hand up my skirt. I had never found myself in that situation before and I had no idea how difficult it was to push an amorous, six foot, seventeen stone man off you. I wanted to scream and shout but he was kissing me so hard and so insistently that I could scarcely breathe. What's more with that weight wedged on to my slight, eight stone frame, I was unable to fight back with anything but my fists which made little or no impact on his ardour.

'John, I'm not ready for this,' I managed to say when he surfaced for air at some point.

But he seemed to think that my resistance was some kind of game.

'You know you are, Chrissie, you were always ready for it,' he said, pushing me back down and kissing me again in rather the way that you might attempt artificial resuscitation. Only in this case it was as if his life depended on it, not mine. At some point I knew that he would have to take his mouth from mine, if only to take in some air again, and that I would be able to scream at him to stop. But when he did and I shouted 'No, No, No' at him, he then clamped a hand over my mouth and began telling me how much he wanted me, how much he needed me, how I was 'the best fuck he had ever had'.

With his other hand – isn't it extraordinary how dextrous a drunk man can be when he is aroused? – he managed to pull down my tights and my knickers and then to undo his flies and release his erect penis which sprang out in rather the way that Sam's favourite jack-in-the-box leaps out of its container when you press a little button.

I really think he would have carried on and raped me – although of course I am sure he wouldn't have thought of it as rape – had the phone on the bedside table not begun ringing. The shock of it made him move and in an instant I escaped from under him and grabbed the receiver shouting and screaming for someone to come and help me.

Within seconds, he had pulled the phone from my hand and cut off the call. But he didn't come near me again. He gave me a look of pure hatred then picked up the bottle of champagne and made his way to the door.

On the threshold, he turned and looked at me again.

'Bitch,' he said as he opened the door and walked out.

I ran over and locked the door and then went back and put the phone back on the hook. It rang again immediately. It was Carole. I told her what had happened and, hundreds of miles away though she was, she did her best to calm me down.

It is difficult for me to explain how profoundly that incident affected me. I didn't just feel physically violated and horribly humiliated, I felt something else. I had never really been aware, before, of the greater physical power that men had in this world. I had never thought to question the fact that men and women were equal, but I did that night. How often in the past, when I was with Carole and Joanna, had I referred to men as the 'weaker' sex? When all the time, I now knew, in the most fundamental sense, the very opposite was true. All Joanna's feminist theories about the redundancy of the male and a brave new female future suddenly seemed like silly childish fantasies. The feeling of vulnerability and weakness that I had felt when I was trying to escape from John had made me realise that the balance of power would never really be with women. Even those who had tried to play God with a Tiptree jam jar and a turkey baster.

Chapter 18

I suppose that if I am to get the chronology of our story correct I ought to explain here what was happening to Joanna. In order to understand what subsequently happened, it's important that our stories should appear side by side.

But it's also important to know that although I will now relate Joanna's story I did not, at this point, have any knowledge of what was going on in her life. We had, as I have said, stopped communicating with each other. She sometimes left the odd message on my answerphone imploring me to ring her and repeating how sorry she was that she had betrayed my confidence. But I wasn't ready to forgive her and even if I had been, I don't think I would have had the emotional energy necessary to take Joanna back into my life. I daresay that sounds rather callous bearing in mind how vulnerable she was, but sometimes in life you simply have to put your own welfare first.

It is difficult to work out exactly how and when Goran began to undermine Joanna but he must have known about her old problems long before she conceived his child. And it was, of course, my own knowledge of those problems that made me dismiss Joanna's increasingly hysterical ramblings about Goran as being in her head.

Joanna had never made any secret – at least in the old

days of our friendship – of anything in her past life. None of us had, really. Most women, heavens most people, experience some kind of mental, physical or emotional drama during their youth and our common link, our unhappy childhoods within adopted families, probably made us even more vulnerable. With Carole it had been an under-age pregnancy – and subsequent abortion – with me it had been a brief period of reckless drug-taking which had culminated in a conviction for possession. And with Joanna it had been a long history of depression that had involved psychiatric help and, on at least one occasion, resulted in a month-long stay in The Priory.

In truth, Joanna wasn't just your regular man hater. Her 'all men are bastards' philosophy had not been prompted by a series of ill-fated affairs or by Harry's brutal defection. It had much deeper roots than that: an alcoholic adoptive father who had beaten her mother and mentally abused Joanna and her younger sister.

It's ironic, I suppose, that what had led Joanna into this whole mess was her belief that Goran was the perfect man. She saw qualities in Carole's husband that she had never seen in any other male she had known and as a result, she idealised him. He was, she had said shortly before we came up with our ill-conceived (in its most literal sense) plan, the first man she had ever really imagined she might trust. I even think, now, that Joanna was a little in love with Goran at the beginning of our story. I certainly believe that her misconception (there I go again) of his true nature played a big part in her subsequent involvement in our crazy scheme. I merely followed her blindly in the unthinking, unpremeditated way in which I had always conducted my life.

With hindsight (if only you could buy bifocal glasses

that could give you a forward and backward view on life), I suppose that Goran was only too well aware that Joanna's tirades about the redundancy of the male and her insistence that we might face a future in which men were graded on their potency and used as sperm kings were not the normal ramblings of a thirty-something woman who had been let down by a lover (or two or three or four). And maybe, right from the start, he had played the part of the perfect man in order to fool her, to trap her and to eventually break her.

Over the long years of our friendship, Carole and myself had come to understand how fragile Joanna was and how much her childhood traumas – particularly the death of her sixteen-year-old sister – had damaged her. We had witnessed at first hand two of her most difficult periods – when her adoptive father had died and when Harry had been unfaithful during her pregnancy with Emma.

But Emma's birth seemed to mark a very positive change in her. There were still odd times when she could become depressed and despondent, but she was stronger, more resilient and it seemed clear that motherhood was, for her, the greatest anti-depressant in the world. Until, that is, she had Tom.

At about the time that Goran had carefully removed Rob from my life – although of course I didn't at that point realise that it had been a calculated move on his part – he had also begun to destabilise Joanna. He did it in all sorts of subtle but persistent ways so that she became more and more nervous and paranoid.

Poor Joanna had no one to turn to at that point. Goran had seen to that. He had cleverly manoeuvred the situation so that she had lost my friendship and although she kept trying to reach me I continued to reject her. I doubt, though, that even if we were still friends, I would have taken much notice of what she said. She knew that her attempts to influence me against Goran before the birth of Sam had misfired and she knew that anything she might add to that, in the months that followed, would doubtless have been dismissed, by me, as dangerous delusions and a prime example of her well known paranoia. Because let's face it, Joanna did often over-react.

Anyway in this case her over-reaction, before Tom was born really, was, as it ultimately turned out, spot on. But Goran began his campaign against her with such subtle stealth that even she knew that complaining about him would make her seem disturbed and obsessive. Particularly since what she saw as a sinister invasion of her life might seem, to anyone else, as merely the concerned interest of a responsible father. Was it so strange that Goran was actively interested in the health and wellbeing of his son since Tom was, after all, a rather sickly asthmatic child, and Goran was, or rather had been, a medical man? And at first this interest was, even Joanna admits, irritating rather than alarming – regular visits conducted like spot checks and numerous phone calls that might, of course, have been prompted by natural parental concern. Except of course that there was nothing natural about this parental relationship and Goran was not really interested in the babies themselves, only in controlling our lives.

Joanna was, she will freely accept, already depressed. To a lesser degree, because of course she already had Emma, the reality of having Tom, rather as my own reality with Sam had so surprised me, did not fit with her fantasy. It was that much more difficult for her to work from home, meeting the kind of deadlines she was used to, with a baby around.

Financially, too, things were more difficult because while Emma's father paid maintenance, there had never been any question of Goran supporting his turkeybasted babies.

It's important to realise, too, that Joanna was much more malleable than I had ever been. She was a much more ready victim than me. And, my goodness, how Goran capitalised on this.

He had long since begun an in-depth study of the intricacies of British family law and slowly began to use his knowledge to drip-feed fear into Joanna. Informing her of certain precedents in which a father – even a sperm donor father – had been awarded custody of a child. Sending her, through the post, newspaper cuttings he had gleaned from places as far off as California and Sweden, in which the rights of a father had been exerted over those of an unsuitable or unstable mother.

And then he began to step up those visits, dropping in on at least a daily basis to ensure that all was well with Tom. It became so that Joanna felt she had to be prepared, at all times, for his sudden arrival. Which, of course, only served to make her more tense, depressed and disturbed. At some point she discovered that Goran had made contact with the neighbours who lived in her street. He had, needless to say, used his legendary charm to get them on his side. Telling them, it later transpired, little snippets of her psychiatric history and imploring them, with a concerned expression on his noble face, to contact him if they heard or saw anything *untoward*. This part of his plan was a masterstroke because in the four years in which Joanna had lived in her home she had remained a very remote figure. Hers was the only cottage without an orange 'Neighbourhood Watch' sticker in the window and as a result, Goran affected a neat reversal of the usual aims of such schemes; he turned her neighbours' attention away from the enemy without to the enemy within. The odd woman next door.

It was, Joanna told me she felt at the time, a little like being under surveillance by some mysterious secret service agency. I mean if you think about it we are all a little vulnerable to the idea that we are being watched and listened to – everytime we walk into a shop our movements are traced on CCTV cameras and who hasn't, at some time or another, wondered if someone wasn't listening into and monitoring their telephone calls? Anyway suffice it to say that Goran used Joanna's neighbours as intelligence operatives, receiving back reports of every occasion on which Joanna raised her voice or the baby cried for more than five minutes or Emma was observed, on a school day, playing alone in the garden.

It was this last, increasingly common, occurrence which gave Goran the ammunition to take his campaign that little bit further. Joanna had been having problems with Emma, she didn't like school, she was feeling insecure since the arrival of her brother and, more than likely, she was aware of her mother's mental fragility. Some days it was much easier for Joanna to keep Emma at home than go through the exhausting emotional and physical process of getting her to school. Particularly on those days on which, during the previous night, Joanna had been up with Tom. Emma was only six but her presence in the little cottage made it easier for Joanna to get on with her work. The little girl could divert Tom, rock him to sleep and alert her mother when he needed something. Emma's absences from school became a sort of pattern – she might attend on a Monday and a Tuesday but towards the end of the week, and that soon became every week, she would miss one or two days.

It's not clear who first made contact with social services – Goran or the prying members of the nosy Neighbourhood Watch – but somehow or other Joanna's problems came to the attention of the authorities and her previous history of mental instability was discovered. Her regular health visitor, who had been unaware that Joanna was anything other than a responsible, middle class single mother, was asked to prepare a preliminary report.

It was only a matter of time before the school was alerted to the family's difficulties and Emma came under their frightening social spotlight.

Everything from her slightly anti-social behaviour to the bruises on her legs, caused by her new Rollerblades, was noted and analysed.

Within a few weeks a social worker was appointed to handle Joanna's case which, naturally enough, took her paranoia almost to the point of madness. And it was one of the regular weekly visits of the cold and critical Ms Edwards that brought Goran's clever campaign to a head.

The social worker arrived to find Emma trying to calm her brother during a frightening asthma attack whilst Joanna was upstairs asleep, so dead to the world that she didn't even hear the door bell ring. It was Ms Edwards who finally managed to rouse her from her slumber, noting as she did so, the half empty bottle of sleeping tablets on her bedside table.

A case conference was called and within forty-eight hours, Goran had applied for, and won, a temporary care order for both Tom and Emma.

When they took the children from Joanna, she became so hysterical that a doctor had to be called to sedate her. Two days later she lost custody of Tom and Emma and was forcibly hospitalised for an 'indefinite period'. I feel certain that had I been in contact with Joanna at this time I would have been able to help. But Goran's clever system of 'divide and rule' had been so cunningly implemented that I was blissfully ignorant of Joanna's problems believing, quite wrongly as it turned out, her to be the cause of my own life crisis.

Chapter 19

❧

Meanwhile, the mistakes I had made in my own life were coming back to haunt me. I have hinted, on and off throughout this account of our story, that I was not very good with money. I have always been extravagant and impulsive. Joanna used to say, years ago, that I earned in centigrade and spent in Fahrenheit and to some extent it was true. I did use shopping as therapy, I did compensate myself for an emotional upset with a new outfit or reward myself for a period of sustained hard work by an outrageous purchase. But then in those days, I only had myself to think of and, yes, I was spoilt and self-indulgent. I was the kind of woman who could find herself in the wrong place – most often a shoe shop – at the wrong time, a week before my salary cheque went into my bank account, losing my head and buying something because, well, I just *had* to have it. I suppose, in a way, it was the same with the baby. Having Sam was just an extension of my usual greedy and acquisitive behaviour. I just *had* to have him and I didn't care what it cost me, emotionally, physically – and particularly – financially.

New parents are not just expected to be overwhelmed by the need to nurture and protect their young, they are also expected to start behaving like responsible grown-ups. They become a prime target for the kind of commercial marketing that has always been a turn off to me – safe cars, private health-care, savings schemes, pensions, peps, ISAs (whatever the hell they are). But there must have been something missing in me because however much I loved my son, I was still incapable of opening a bank statement or replying to the entreaties of the Inland Revenue or, worst of all, sorting out my credit card repayments. Just as I didn't let myself think about the moral implications of Sam's conception, so I didn't concern myself too much about giving my child financial security and stability.

And while in the past I had always just about managed to get by without ending up in Ford Open Prison (well, I never actually committed fraud), the advent of Sam and countless new financial responsibilities, not least the money I paid each week in cash to Carole, pushed me into dangerous debt.

Not, you understand, that I acknowledged my mounting problems. I just carried on putting those horrid looking envelopes in my big kitchen drawer.

I did make cutbacks. I had totally stopped the 'me' spending. I didn't buy any clothes – truthfully, I didn't care how I looked – and I gave up things like facials, Nicky Clarke haircuts and Clinique cosmetics and cleansers. But these deprivations served no real purpose except to make me look and feel dreadful – and the debts from my past just kept accumulating interest.

I know that I sound completely stupid when I say that it was three months before I realised I had got into arrears on my mortgage. I might never have known – as I said I never dared open any of those official-looking envelopes – had it not been for the registered letter delivered one

Wednesday morning informing me that the mortgage company were foreclosing on my debt and were in the process of repossessing my flat.

I felt that day that everything was closing in on me. Work was ghastly – I was more and more of an outsider and was certain that the only reason I held on to my job was the fact that one of my clients, God bless him, remained absurdly loyal to me and would doubtless take the work he brought in to the company away if they sacked me. Not, you understand, that John hadn't put a bit of pressure on my boss to 'let me go' after the misunderstanding in the hotel in Jerez. I think that he was privately worried that I might bring some criminal complaint against him – he knew, after all, that all phone calls in and out of the hotel were logged and that whoever had heard me screaming for help that night, backed up by the phone records, would probably be a reliable witness in any court. For once, though, much as my boss valued the business John brought in, he stood up for me and rather than letting me go, instead turned John away. I found out later that this was not a touching act of altruism but a sensible reaction to a number of other, similar, accusations of sexual harassment made by several female members of staff.

I probably wouldn't have found my job such a strain if I had a life outside work to balance it against. But I had no time for anything apart from my job and Sam. I spent all my weekends cleaning the flat, shopping and trying to be – for forty-eight hours a week – the perfect mother to my son.

I didn't resent Sam. Well if I did occasionally question why on earth I had got into this whole business one smile, one deep throaty baby chuckle would instantly stop me, but I was aware of how much I had lost. My freedom, my lover, my old carefree life and now – very probably – my home.

But although I wept when I read that letter and although I began to fret about how I would be able to raise the deficit of £3500 within seven days, I didn't actually do anything. I just shoved it back in its envelope and put it in my handbag (a step up from the kitchen drawer) and studiously ignored it for a full three days.

It was inevitable, really, that ultimately I would turn to Carole for help. Because she was, at that point, the most important person in my life apart from Sam.

I never really gave a thought to what problems Carole herself had to cope with during this period. Of the three friends she had always seemed to be the most sensible, stable and strong. And since I imagined that she had chosen the role of matriarch I allowed her to be exactly that.

I had begun to call her my Mother Superior, not just because of the way in which she gave me guidance, advice and help with Sam, but also because of the way she now looked. Oh, I don't mean she wore a nun's habit, but her mode of dress and the way she carried herself had changed so fundamentally that even I, in the midst of my own crisis, noticed the difference.

I said before that Carole had the most spectacular body – when we had first met she was almost a pastiche of womanhood like that character Jessica Rabbit in that old movie *Who Killed Roger Rabbit*? And just as Joanna tried her very hardest to play down her beauty, Carole had always gone all the way to meet her own allure. Worn short skirts and high heels to properly display her extraordinary legs. Putting on plunging necklines that revealed the depth and breadth of her breasts. No-one would ever have called Carole understated.

I suppose the change must have been gradual and I don't doubt that her pregnancies and the subsequent alterations of her body shape played their part in her physical transformation. But it has to be said that the shift in style that Carole had adopted was, well, strange.

I can remember, so clearly, the day on which I fully absorbed the change that had taken place in her appearance. I was dropping off Sam as usual and on this particular morning she was fully dressed (I arrived so early sometimes that often she would still be wearing her dressing gown). She was wearing something so hideous – a long floral frock made of some kind of highly inflammable synthetic material – that before I could stop myself I had made a comment.

'My goodness, Carole, you didn't get that from Escada or MaxMara, did you?' I said realising immediately, from the blush that spread across her face, that I had embarrassed my friend.

'I've put on so much weight, Chrissie, none of my old clothes fit me anymore. And besides what do I need with MaxMara and Escada now? I don't have the money and anyway this is so much more practical,' she said clearly anxious to deflect my scrutiny.

Which, of course, only served to make me even more curious as to why on earth – and where on earth – she had acquired her beige and navy, flower-sprigged overall-style garment.

'You don't look as if you have put on weight. At least you wouldn't if you wore something that was more like your old style of dress,' I said trying to make out, through the impenetrable high-sheen material, if there really was any discernible weight gain.

'My appearance really isn't my main priority in my life now, Chrissie, my children are. Anyway, Goran likes me in dresses. Actually he bought it for me,' she said dismissively.

'But he always had such good taste,' I replied before I could stop myself which only prompted another embarrassed blush from Carole.

'He's much more traditional than you realise,' she said in a rather mysterious tone.

After I had left her, I began to think about Carole and clothes and I realised that during the previous few months – probably since Sam had been born – I had never seen her looking like *her*. Not a glimpse of Lycraed leg or Wonderbra-bolstered bosom. We hadn't, it's true, gone out anywhere together so I suppose there hadn't really been any reason to dress up, but Carole had always been the kind of person to dress to excess even when she was just hanging out at home.

Lately, though, everytime I had seen her she had been wearing something long and concealing rather than short and revealing.

I didn't, though, give much thought to the deeper shift these surface changes might indicate. But then of course my own problems, at that time, seemed far more pressing. So much so that, a day or so later, I found myself breaking down and unburdening myself on the already overburdened Carole. I have tried, recently, to justify the way in which I leaned on my friend without much considering the harsh realities of her own life at that time. The only excuse I can come up with, as I have done throughout this story, is excessive hormonal confusion which, combined with the exhaustion of coping with a new baby and the pressures of competing in the workplace rendered me incapable of concentrating on anything but my own feelings and emotions.

Anyway, on a rainy, grey morning, having spent half the night coping with Sam's teething, I arrived at Carole's house and found myself collapsing in a tearful state into her outstretched arms when she opened the door.

I told her about my mortgage arrears. I told her about my credit card bills. I told her about my overdraft and my unpaid bank loan. I told her everything and she tried her best to make me feel better – stroked my head, said soothing things and promised me she'd help me sort myself out.

I felt like you do as a child about your mother, although I can't remember ever feeling that way about mine. I felt as if she *would* sort everything out for me, fight my fight and solve all my problems. She made me feel confident enough, when I had repaired my make-up, to make my way to work although I did feel a bit as if I had come to the end of the line (East Acton, as it happened).

Carole repaid my belief in her, too, because when I came out of the office at the end of that day, weary and despondent, she was sitting in the car waiting to drive me home, my sweet, smiling son strapped alongside her. Goran, she told me, was so concerned about me that he had come home early to look after the boys so that she could come and be with me.

While I put Sam to bed, Carole cooked us a quick pasta supper – without wine for once – and we sat down together to talk.

'Have you any idea what your exact outgoings are,

Chrissie?' she said pushing in front of me some paper and a pen.

'Well I know how much my mortgage is and how much I pay you but nothing much apart from that,' I said.

'Write down your monthly income at the top there, and then put down everything you can think of – from nappies to tampons – that you have to pay out each week,' Carole said, as if she were explaining basic economics to an alien.

Of course I had no idea how much I spent on food (I have never been the kind of woman who could remember the price of a pint of milk or a loaf of bread), let alone any conscious knowledge of how much my phone, electric, or gas bills were each quarter. But Carole was ruthless with me that night making me do something that I never thought possible – opening all the brown envelopes that had, for months now, been tucked away in my kitchen drawer.

I don't think Carole ate much that night; she said that the gap between my incomings and my outgoings had so frightened her it took away her appetite. She sat there, surrounded by bills and final demands, with a forlorn expression on her face.

'Christ, Chrissie, how do you sleep at night?' she asked when she had worked out, as far as she could, the extent of my debts.

'Oh, you know me, when I don't like something, when I am frightened of something I just ignore it. Compartmentalise it, pretend it doesn't exist,' I replied with a weak smile.

Vague though I was about finance I had always known that I couldn't really afford my flat. I had fallen in love with it and bought it, madly exaggerating my income in order to get the mortgage I needed. The down-payment had been lent, and more or less paid back, by my bastard ex-lover and would-be rapist John. But its central London location, (albeit on the seedy outskirts of Soho) and its increasingly fashionable look and New York Loft lay-out had made it, surprisingly for someone as impulsive and impractical as me, a sound investment.

'There's only one thing for it, darling, you are going to have to sell this place. It's your only asset, and you have so much equity that you could clear all your debts and buy something much bigger a bit further out of London.'

'But I love my home. I couldn't possibly even think of moving anywhere else,' I said, trying my hardest to stop myself from crying.

'For goodness' sake, Chrissie, you have responsibilities now, you've got Sam. You've got to accept that your life has changed forever. Being close to Harvey Nichols and Carlucci's isn't important any more. Being close to a good school and somewhere Sam can run free and safe should be your priority now.'

'Hyde Park is only ten minutes away,' I said a little plaintively.

'Grow up, Chrissie, and look around you. Is this flat really what you might call child-friendly? What are you going to do when Sam is mobile – are you really happy with the idea of him falling down a flight of sharp-edged stone stairs onto unyielding limestone floors?'

'I'll put in lots of child-gates, I'll make it safe, I promise you. Carole, you know how important the look of things is to me, you know how I always loved this flat, I can't face the idea of compromising, of giving it up for some hideous semi-detached in suburbia. No, what I'll do is extend my mortgage. I mean that's a much better idea because this is such a sound investment, the price of these apartments is rising much faster than the interest rate.'

'Chrissie, you can't cope with the repayments you have now and since the mortgage company are about to repossess, you aren't going to be eligible for the kind of extension you need. The only way you can get at the capital that is held up in this flat is to sell it. It will be a fresh start for you, think about it,' she went on.

I can only marvel at the way in which, very slowly and very subtly, Carole talked me round to the idea of selling my home that evening. And, really, it wasn't possible to fault her arguments.

I couldn't argue with anything she said – I knew I couldn't afford the repayments on my current mortgage, I knew with all my other debts I would never get an extended mortgage and I had, in any case, begun to worry about the prospect, within the next couple of months, of Sam struggling to walk round my flat. I had already constructed disastrous mental pictures of his precious, tender little body being bruised and battered by the hard surfaces of my *Architectural Digest* home.

The only sensible way out of all my problems, and not just my pressing financial crisis, was to sell my flat as quickly as I possibly could. That way I could forestall the mortgage company and emerge with enough money to buy myself a more suitable home in a more suitable area.

It has to be said that I had always been very resistant to the idea of living in a 'suitable area'. Well, I loved being in the centre of the city and I hated the whole concept of suburban family life.

But I knew that much of what Carole was telling me was true and within no time at all she had not only convinced me to sell up she had also somehow managed to make the idea of a terraced Victorian cottage – in the hinterlands of London – seem almost attractive.

Worse, she had even raised the spectre of my looking for somewhere near her because, as she cleverly pointed out to me, I might then also improve the quality of my life by having more time at the beginning and the end of every day with Sam.

I had never previously been able to appreciate the allure of Carole's neighbourhood. They had chosen East Acton because it was cheap, had great public transport facilities and was close to Goran's workshop. It had always struck me as a mean and run-down area which, despite constant predictions of gentrification, would always remain thwarted by its proximity to so many notorious tower block estates and its worryingly high crime rate.

But the following evening, when I picked up Sam after work, she gave me a clutch of house details and I began to understand its appeal. For two-thirds of the price of my own minimalist flat I could buy a proper house with a garden. Perhaps I *could* adjust to East Acton.

The next morning following Goran's advice I called two competitive estate agents for valuations and the flat was officially on the market within three days.

Chapter 20

‹❧›

I sometimes wonder – useless though I know the whole business of 'what if' is – what might have happened had my flat taken longer to sell. If the time between putting the place on the market and selling it had been longer, things might still have ended, if not happily, then quite differently. But it was difficult to turn down, just a week later, what my agent described in awed tones as a 'cash' buyer (which I mistakenly imagined meant my getting all the money in £20 note bundles packed in a suitcase). Particularly since they were offering a few thousand more than the asking price.

I was only too aware that things were going too fast – one of the conditions of the sale was completion within four weeks and there was no way that I was likely to find the house of my dreams, or even my compromise cottage, in that time. And if I did it was unlikely that I would be able to move straight in. It seemed inevitable that I would have to rent for a few months whilst we looked for a new home.

What I am trying to explain, what I am leading up to, is why I made what would prove to be such a fatal move. The last place on earth I ever thought I would find myself living when I put my flat on the market was Carole and Goran's big, dark, ugly house.

Carole had, as I mentioned before, inherited the place from her maternal adoptive grandmother. The old lady had lived on the ground floor and had converted the rest of the house into flats. And although Carole and Goran had subsequently managed to extend their living space when the tenants on the second floor had moved out, the rest of their huge home was still divided into four more flats – two small bedsits in the attic, one two bedroom flat on the third floor and a similar sized space in the basement. Their dream was to eventually have possession of the whole house but they still had three sitting tenants – one in the attic and one on the third floor – and insufficient money with which to buy them out.

It was Goran who suggested that I could save some money on rental by lodging temporarily in their basement flat which they planned, in a few months, to renovate for their own use. Overwhelmed by the horror of organising my move, which was far more complicated than I had imagined, this idea seemed sensible to me. Particularly since it was unfurnished which meant that I wouldn't have to put my things in store, I could move straight into the flat and take some time looking for a suitable house.

Even now I can see the sense of going along with such an eminently practicable arrangement – Carole was, after all, looking after Sam and being able to just take him upstairs and then make my way to work each morning would make my life so much easier. What's more it would offer me an inexpensive way of seeing if I could, indeed, adjust to life in East Acton. And meanwhile what was left of my capital would be gaining interest in the building society. I realise now that moving – even on a temporary basis – into Goran and Carole's house was a terrible mistake. But as I have said before, and will say again before the end of this story, I *trusted* Carole and Goran. They were, after all, family.

I had, I must again reinforce, no knowledge of what was happening in Joanna's life and I had no real reason to doubt the sincerity of the two people who had, as I believed, supported me through such a difficult time.

It wasn't until just after I had sold my flat, but before I had moved into the basement of number 12 Milton Gardens, that I discovered that Joanna had become 'clinically depressed' again. Although, needless to say, the story I heard from Carole was rather different from the one I have previously related.

It may well be that Carole was unaware of her husband's involvement in Joanna's downfall – hell, it's possible, I suppose, that at that stage she was blissfully ignorant of everything.

I am not sure, though, that she would have told me when she did had it not been for the fact that, one evening when I picked up Sam, I was greeted at the door by Joanna's daughter Emma. I was, naturally enough, alarmed by the sight of Emma's anxious little face and it was then that Carole told me what had happened. Having settled the children in front of a video, a rare treat in Carole's strictly controlled household, she took me into the kitchen.

'It's Joanna,' she said her face contorted with concern.

'What about Joanna?'

'She's alright, Chrissie, she's OK. It's just that she took an overdose and – oh God – I didn't tell you because I knew you had so much on your plate already. It was her health visitor who found her, Emma let her in – it's a real mess but at least the children haven't been taken into care. They're staying with us until Joanna's discharged.'

'I must see her, Carole, I feel so terrible. I've been shutting her out of my life and not thinking, at all, about how she might be coping. All I can ever think about is my own awful life. Where is she?'

'They've put her in The Abbey. But you can't see her. They have got her on some sort of intensive treatment and she's not allowed any visitors for the first four weeks.'

'Four weeks? How long is she going to be in there?'

'They don't seem to know. And even when she is discharged there may be a problem with her getting the children back.'

'Christ, Carole, that will finish Joanna. What can we do?'

'Nothing, Chrissie, except be there for her when the time comes. Meanwhile I'm doing my best to keep the children happy.'

'But how will you cope, Carole? I mean haven't you got enough on your hands what with Nino, Sasha and Sam? With Emma and Tom that's five kids under the age of seven.'

'For goodness' sake, Chrissie, that's nothing. Goran's mother raised eight children without a washing machine or a fridge,' she said.

'That's probably normal in Eastern Europe but it's bloody unusual in East Acton,' I said briefly dispelling the frown from Carole's face by provoking a small smile.

'You know I love all the children, I love being at home and Goran's the kind of man who believes the more kids there are around the better,' she said apparently unaware of the significance of this statement.

'I suppose I will soon be living in the basement and I can help you a bit in the evenings and at the weekends,' I said, the thought of being able to give her a hand giving me an added incentive to move in. I can remember thinking that maybe, after all, it had been the *right* thing to do. Fate even.

'It will be lovely having you here,' she said with another little smile when I left that evening.

Again and again, as I tell our story, I am struck by my own stupidity and my absolute inability to question anything. My only excuse for not checking out Carole's account of Joanna's problems was that I was so taken up with my planned move that I simply didn't have time to think too deeply about what had gone on.

I had never really believed that old tale about moving being one of the top three traumas alongside divorce and bereavement, but I did now. There were the removal men to organise, the packing up and the throwing out (I was astonished at how much rubbish I had accumulated in five years), the change of address cards, the long list of utility companies that had to be informed, the new telephone line and so on and so forth. I took a week off work which I rather resented because I would have preferred to have spent all the holiday time I had just lazing around being with Sam. Instead I was irritable, exhausted and – about three days before our moving date – I became overwhelmed by this sort of presentiment of doom that I couldn't explain but which I supposed had something to do with the huge life change I was about to make.

This feeling, this hovering, depressive cloud, didn't go away but rather, during the following day, gathered force so that by the evening, when the door bell unexpectedly rang, I was so taut and tense that I jumped with the kind of fear you experience sometimes when you wake after a nightmare you cannot quite remember. I wasn't expecting anyone and it was late and I found myself cautiously looking through the peephole that I had put in just after Sam had been born. When you look through those things they distort the person, it's like a fish-eye lens, and for a moment I didn't recognise the man who was standing on my doorstep. It took me a while – and another, harsher ring on the bell – to realise that it was Rob. And although I had often fantasised about just such an event I was so apprehensive that I almost didn't open the door.

'Oh, please come in,' I said, as you would to a neighbour come to borrow a cup of sugar, when I finally managed to pull it open.

'Er, thank you,' he said nervously as he came in, carefully avoiding making eye contact with me and instead glancing round at the mess that surrounded us – packing cases, piles of baby clothes, the entire contents of my kitchen cupboards.

'Would you like a cup of coffee or something,' I asked him as if we were co-stars in one of those banal soap-style commercials, rather like the one we were shooting when we first met.

'Yes, that would be nice,' he said as he followed me into the kitchen and watched me make a cafetiere of freshly ground French roasted beans (well, at least it wasn't a cup of Gold Blend).

Then we went and sat amid the chaos of my open-plan living room, him on one white sofa and me on the other. I wanted to tell him how I felt, I wanted to deliver the speech I had been planning for God knows how long, since way back in my pregnancy, about how he would always be the perfect father for my child even if the conception of Sam hadn't been 'the first seed he had planted with all his heart'. But along with my guilt for what I had done to him I also now felt angry at the way he had treated me. So rather than talk about the really important issues I began instead to babble about the progress the baby was making.

'He's very stubborn but really very advanced. The health visitor said his responses were at least six months ahead of his age. Heavens, I sound like one of those pushy mothers who puts their child in full-time education as soon as they can walk,' I wittered.

'No you don't, you just sound like you love him,' Rob said gently.

'I had no idea how complex loving a baby was. I mean it brings out the best and the worst of your instincts. Like my boasting at the clinic about what he's doing and comparing him to the other babies and thinking very smugly that he's the best looking, the cleverest, the most physically forward of them all. I'm really rather ashamed of the way in which I want him to be the best because it isn't just about him, it's about me. He's got to be the best because he's my son, you know what I mean? But at the same time having a child is the only thing that's made me in anyway selfless. In the last few months he's the only thing that has kept me going, his life is much, much more important than mine,' I said, incapable of not at least alluding to the pain I had been through since Rob walked out.

'Does he look like you?' Rob asked.

I went silent then because, of course, Sam – like Sasha, Nino and Tom – shared Goran's distinctive black eyes, with their prominent yellow flecks.

'It's difficult to tell at his age,' I managed to say after a while.

Curiously it was Sam – whom I believed to have prompted the rift between us – who brought us back together. Rob's obvious interest in him and his tentative request to see the sleeping baby provoked the first connection – and the first direct eye contact between us.

He walked into Sam's room and looked down into his cot with an expression of such tender regret on his face that I found myself fighting back tears. I left the room and waited a few moments outside, desperately trying to control myself, before returning. He was standing with his back to me, looking down at Sam, and when he heard me come in he suddenly extended one of his hands out behind him, as you might for a small child to catch and grip, and I seized the moment. Placing my hand into his and squeezing it in an attempt to show him the depth of my feeling. And it was then, as he felt the ring that he had given me on the second finger of my hand (LOVE.TRUST.HONOUR), that he seized me, spun me round and held me.

He led me out of the room, gently closing the door behind him so that he didn't disturb the sleeping Sam. Then he pulled me to him and tried to kiss me, but something, a feeling that if I let him back into my life he would go again, made me move my head away so that his mouth collided with the side of my head.

'What happened to us, Chrissie?' he asked in anguished tones.

I started to cry then. All the grief I had felt in the previous months seemed to come out of me in great gulping sobs. Rob held me and stroked my hair and tried to calm me.

'Shhhhhh, Chrissie, you'll wake the baby,' he said in the soothing tones I remembered from our first days with Sam.

I did stop, eventually, apart from the odd very

unglamorous hiccup. I had looked a mess when he had arrived and now, feeling increasingly insecure and uncertain, I got up and went to the bathroom. My face was as red and blotchy, swollen even, as it was possible to get but I made an attempt to pull my features together, patting some concealer beneath my eyes, putting a little gloss on my lips and brushing my now quite long hair.

He was sitting on one of the white sofas when I came out and I felt a surge of relief that he hadn't gone. I sat down next to him and smiled in an encouraging but absolutely unprovocative manner.

'It broke my heart, Chrissie, when I found out you had been unfaithful,' he said, looking directly in my eyes and holding the contact between us.

'I was never unfaithful to you, Rob, what do you mean?' I said.

'Your relationship with that man, that's what I mean,' he said angrily.

'What man? I never had a relationship with another man from the moment I met you. And I hadn't had a relationship for months before then.'

'What do you mean you weren't having a relationship? You were carrying this man's child when you met me. When I look back on those first days, those first weeks we had together I just feel so betrayed. That you could continue with that man, that you could deceive me into thinking your child could be mine,' he went on, more enraged than I had ever seen him.

'Let's get something clear here, Rob – I had a relationship with a jam jar and a kitchen implement, not a man. Just because your male pride is upset by the discovery that Sam was conceived before I met you doesn't make what I did infidelity. It was bad timing, it was an idiotic idea but my son is the end product of that and I cannot go back on it. I cannot even really regret it. What I do regret is that you aren't man enough to accept that,' I shouted back at him.

'Are you denying what Goran told me? Are you trying to say that you didn't have a proper physical relationship with him?'

'Of course I didn't, you must have misunderstood what he was saying. There was never anything physical between him and me or Joanna.'

'Joanna?' he said, his face, with every passing moment, becoming more confused.

'Didn't Goran tell you about Joanna?'

'Goran never mentioned Joanna. He told me that Sam was his baby, that you and he had been having an affair for years. That you loved him, that you were going to be together and that you wanted to end things with me but couldn't face me,' he said, the words tumbling out of his mouth as his brain began to take in the fact that there had been a misunderstanding. A big misunderstanding.

'But why would he have told you that?' I said, my own mind racing now with the possibilities. It didn't, for one second, occur to me to question the truth of what Rob was saying. I knew Rob was incapable of a lie – even a white lie – it was a quality that I found both infuriating and endearing in him.

'Tell me what happened, Chrissie, tell me the truth,' Rob said.

'I wanted a baby so much, Rob. It was like a physical ache. I had been stuck in this relationship – this was ages before we met – with a married man. I told you about John, the one at work? Anyway I broke up with him and I became more and more convinced that I would never find the right man. You know how women are always going on about their biological clocks – well it was like that for me. I suddenly understood what it meant – I had a finite time within which to have a baby and I was never going to find the man of my dreams. It's easy now to say I should have waited because you were just a few months away. But how was I to know that I would find you?' I paused for a moment and Rob put his hand in mine and gave me a smile, the first since he had arrived, that revealed more than his teeth and gums – it exposed his love for me.

'Go on, Chrissie,' he said gently.

'Well, I told you a bit about my friendship with Carole and Joanna. We were so close, closer than close. Coming, as all three of us did, from such disturbed and similar backgrounds in which we all saw ourselves as displaced, as adoptive changelings – if you can understand that. We weren't just friends we were each other's family. I've told you about Joanna's problems with men, the abusive relationship with her stepfather, with her husband. And I suppose, in a way, I had absorbed a lot of her pessimism about male/female relationships. I began to believe that the only way I was ever going to be able to have a child was on my own as a single mother. Oh, God, I'm not sure I'm saying this right, I'm not sure this can make any sense to you,' I said looking at Rob.

'You are making more sense now than you ever have before. There was always, in my head, a question mark about your past, your relationships and your attitude to men. Go on, Chrissie, I want to know everything.'

'Over the years, obviously, there were men in all our lives. But none of them could ever really understand the importance of the relationship between Carole, Joanna and me. Until Goran, that is. Goran, like us I suppose, was an outsider. He didn't know anyone in Britain apart from us and we became his family here. He understood us, he encouraged us, he became a part of us. We weren't just a threesome, we were a foursome. I am trying to explain how this madness started. Carole was very pregnant with her second child, Joanna was divorced from Harry and aching to give Emma a sibling and I, well I was just a mess. And then one day we just started talking about what we wanted, I was just so, so broody. I think it was Joanna who voiced the idea first and it might sound mad now but it wasn't then. It seemed sensible, it seemed like the perfect answer. And Carole, because of the strength of her feelings for us – at least that's what I thought at the time – she went along with it. Because you see, Rob, it was never going to be a sexual thing. Goran, who seemed then to be the perfect man, was going to be a donor. More than a donor, I suppose, he was going to be a kind of godfather to us. And that's what I thought he was, until now. Why did he do that, why did he tell you such lies?' I said, fearful of confronting the full implications of the way in which Goran had misled Rob and, in the process I now realised, deliberately removed him from my life.

'Maybe he just became more possessive about you, maybe he wanted you, I don't know, Chrissie. Maybe it was like a biological reaction – he just couldn't face the idea of another man rearing his child,' he said running his hands through my hair with such tenderness that I found the tears running down my cheeks again.

Only this time I wasn't crying for what I had lost, but for what I had found again and when I looked into Rob's eyes, I noticed that he, too, was crying. And then we were embracing, our kisses tinged with the salty flavour of our tears.

We went upstairs then and made love. Our lovemaking had always been tender, it had always been different from the kind of quick, and occasionally brutal, couplings I had experienced in the past. But that night it had an added intensity. Rob had changed my thinking on sex when I had met him because he was the only man I had encountered who seemed to take as much pleasure in foreplay as I did. He never hurried, he wanted to cuddle, he wanted to caress, he wanted to kiss every inch of my skin. Slowly, oh so slowly, we moved towards the actual consummation of our refound love. With Rob I felt safe as well as sexy. He was the man who had proved to me that fucking wasn't about male invasion and possession, it was about giving and taking, it was about establishing an intimacy and mutual trust that is only possible when a man and a woman love each other. It was a merging, it was a coming home and it went on for most of that night. Just before dawn the baby woke up and Rob got up to calm him, bringing him back to the bed and placing him between us as he had done in those precious early days of Sam's life.

Chapter 21

❧

'When will I see you again?' I said the next morning as I watched Rob sharing a Petit Filou with Sam.

'Well, actually, Chrissie, I'm going away for a week. It's a business thing with Paul, to do with the vineyard. Some big French producer is interested in linking up with us so we are having some meetings in Burgundy,' he said a little sheepishly.

'So it was just a one-night stand was it?' I said, trying to keep the panic from my voice.

'It will take a little time, Chrissie, for me to learn to trust you again.'

'That's not how it seemed last night,' I said sharply.

'We can't just take up where we left off,' he said scooping a spoonful of yoghurt into Sam's gaping mouth.

'Why not?' I said angrily.

'Well for a start I don't think I can move into Goran and Carole's basement with you, do you?' he said.

'So you aren't my knight in shining armour come to rescue me at the last moment. You won't be sweeping me off to live happily ever after with you,' I said in the tones, I suppose, of a rather spoilt and unhappy child.

'You know that's impossible. It isn't as if I still have the flat in London. We have a live-in manager there now. When we broke up I went back to live in Glebe House and I think it will take a little time to bring Anna and Paul round to our being together again,' he said.

'Well then, if it's alright with you I've got rather a lot of work to do. I move out of here tomorrow. I think you'd better go,' I said angrily.

Rob tried, just a little, to placate me but it was clear that his feelings that morning did not match those he had expressed the night before. He kissed me gently, and maybe somewhat regretfully, on the top of my head as he left.

'I'll call you, Chrissie,' he said offering, I thought, Sam a more enthusiastic farewell than the one he gave me.

'I won't hold my breath, Rob,' I said as I closed the door on him.

I had known, of course, that by then it was far too late for me to back out of my move. But I had still somehow hoped that Rob coming back in my life would offer me an alternative to life in Carole and Goran's basement. I suppose I should have realised that we couldn't just come back together as if nothing had happened but nonetheless I was disappointed by the way in which he had breezed in the night before and breezed out that morning.

Wary though I obviously now was about Goran's motives there was nothing else for me to do but move into – for as short a period as possible – their basement flat as planned.

I didn't, though, let myself think too deeply about Goran's deception, probably because I couldn't cope with the consequences of accepting that, all along, Joanna had been right. I was, of course, shocked by the story that Rob had told me the night before but I was too frightened to allow myself to take this new knowledge to its logical conclusion. I wasn't ready to confront the thought that Goran – and by implication, Carole – meant me harm. Nor did I put two and two together and question Joanna's fate; I just pushed the whole messy business to the back of my troubled, troubled mind.

I did shed a tear or two, the following day, when I left my lovely flat. And I did have a growing feeling of disquiet about living under the same roof as the man who had turned Rob against me. But I balanced that against my loyalty and love for Carole and the fact that it was only temporary. I would just have to bide my time.

When the removal men had put all my possessions in the back of the van and had driven off to my new home (if I could call it that), I spent half an hour, wandering nostalgically round my echoing empty flat. Then I loaded Sam into his car seat and put a very neurotic Pushkin in his cat-carrier and drove off to East Acton.

It broke my heart to see the contents of my beautiful minimalist flat filling the horrid four rooms of Goran and Carole's basement. Somehow they were rendered almost as ugly as their surroundings, pushed up against replacement windows, chipboard partitions and artexed walls.

I couldn't escape a family meal with Goran, Carole and the children that evening. But I did observe him rather differently, noting, as I hadn't on previous visits, the fact that he now sat at the head of the table in a big, upholstered carver whilst the rest of us nestled uncomfortably on cheap knotted-pine chairs. And that, during the entire meal, Carole waited on him like some harassed housemaid, shushing the children whenever one of them tried to speak when their father was already holding forth.

It was the first time, too, that I had really appreciated the uncanny physical resemblance between all the male children seated round the table. Each of them had the same distinctive black, flecked eyes – their father's eyes – and each of them had similar dark glossy hair and creamy skintone. What prompted the comparison was the presence of Emma whose pallid complexion and white-blonde hair made her stand out like an albino cuckoo in a nest of starlings.

It was Emma's anxious face – and Goran's harsh treatment of her during that meal – that made me resolve to do something about Joanna. I would, regardless of what Carole had told me, make contact the next day. The full horror of what had happened to Joanna – who had never been parted from Emma or Tom before – suddenly struck me. How terrible it must have been for her to have had her children taken from her and placed in the care of the man she regarded as her enemy. And who, I was now beginning to think, was my enemy too. I suddenly felt terribly ashamed for the way in which I had rejected and blamed Joanna after Rob had left.

I was able to avoid any meaningful discussion with Carole, seriously concerned that I might break down and tell her about Rob's brief re-entry into my life, because Sam was tired and fractious and I wanted to get him to bed so that I could spend some time sorting out my things. I thanked them profusely, I even kissed Goran on the cheek as I left, and made my way down the back stairs to my new MFI MDF front door.

When I did finally get Sam bathed – in water heated by a rusting old Ascot – and settled in his cot, placed next to my bed in the dingy back room with its sinister barred windows, I was almost ready to drop off myself. At ten,

I abandoned my impossible task – making my ghastly rented flat look like a real home – and collapsed on one of my white sofas where I drank a whole bottle of white wine and, for the first time since Sam's birth, smoked a whole packet of Marlboro Lights.

I woke up feeling frightened and disorientated, aware that some sudden noise had disturbed me. When I checked Sam was sleeping soundly, but above me – somewhere in the house – I could hear crying. It must have gone on for at least an hour, the shouting, the screaming and the echoing noise of doors banging and furniture crashing. I carried Sam into bed with me and cuddled his sweet-smelling body against mine, my concern about what might go on in this house turning from a vague disquiet to a real fear. If only Rob were with me.

Things always seem less pressing, less disturbing by day than they do by night and the following morning I was able to put my fear, in part anyway, down to my exhausted and emotional mental state. I even wondered if I hadn't dreamed or imagined those sounds.

It was a Friday, the last day of my week's leave, and I had so much to get in order before going back to work on Monday that it wasn't until midafternoon that I remembered my resolution of the previous evening. I had to see Joanna.

I went upstairs and knocked on Carole's door – I hadn't seen her since the previous evening and I suddenly felt terrified lest she might appear with a black eye or a broken arm. But there was nothing to see, no indication of what might – or might not – have gone on the night before. She was pale but then she wasn't wearing make-up (she seldom did nowadays) and she was wearing one of her new regulation long overall style frocks.

I didn't tell her that I was going to see Joanna, I just asked if she could look after Sam for a couple of hours whilst I did a few chores and, as ever now, she was sweetly, almost submissively, compliant.

It took me an hour to find The Abbey in Richmond and a further forty minutes to get my way round the bureaucracy. Eventually I managed to talk to someone in a white coat who explained to me that Joanna was in the middle of a very intensive treatment and that patients in her state were only allowed visitors who were close family. Something about the attitude of this patronising woman put up my hackles and I found myself explaining that I was the closest family Joanna had got apart from her two children. Which, in more ways than one now, was true. I would not leave, I said with such firm resolve that I even impressed myself, until I had seen her.

The woman began thumbing through files in an agitated fashion, from time to time glancing up at me as if she was appraising just how serious a threat I posed. After a few minutes she got up, went through a door into an adjacent office and made, from what I could see through the window, a series of urgent phone calls. Finally she told me that it would be possible for me to see Joanna but that I might have to wait a while.

They put me in a large, sumptuously decorated drawing room that was littered with antiques and had the kind of soft lighting you might expect in a discreet five star hotel. I was, by now, feeling a bit paranoid and disturbed myself. I had this quite distinct feeling that I was being watched. That behind one of the oval gilt framed mirrors eyes were trained on me.

After about half an hour, a woman who looked like a

regular nurse came into the room and asked me, a sweet smile on her face, if I would follow her. On the way down endless carpeted corridors past numbered rooms, again very much like a rather smart hotel, she explained that Joanna might seem disorientated because she was being treated with very strong anti-depressants. She added, as we reached the door and she unlocked it with a key from a chain that was attached to her uniform, more in the fashion of a prison warder than an angel of mercy, that I should ring the bell by the bed if I needed her.

Joanna was sitting in a chair by the window looking out onto the grounds below. She didn't seem to notice that I had come into the room, her eyes remained focused on the sweep of grass, flowers and trees outside her room.

'Joanna,' I said gently but she didn't look up.

'Joanna,' I repeated more forcefully but there was no reaction.

Eventually I went over, knelt down beside her and took her terribly thin hand in mine. She started as if she were shocked and looked at me with an expression of alarm on her beautiful – but worryingly vacant – face. She was wearing what was, I suppose, a nightdress, beneath a dressing-gown, stained with food, that made her look slovenly (and Joanna was normally almost anally fastidious about personal hygiene).

'Oh, Joanna, I am so, so sorry that I didn't help you'll more. I'm so, so sorry that I didn't realise how difficult things were for you,' I said in the way you might address someone in a coma – I had no idea whether she was taking in anything I was saying.

It must have taken her five minutes or so to try to make sense of the stranger – as I think she thought I was on my arrival – kneeling beside her. It was as if she were trying very, very hard to make her memory break through the fog of drugs and mental confusion, and all the while she was doing this, I talked.

'When I left today Emma was making some biscuits with Carole. She's really such a great help with the babies, a little mother. It's all going to be alright, Joanna, you'll see. We'll get you back feeling fine again and we'll all be together like we used to be, like a family . . .'

'Chrissie,' she said so softly I wasn't sure at first that she was saying my name.

'Joanna, you can hear me?' I said.

'Chrissie, Chrissie, Chrissie!' she repeated again and again with mounting urgency as if, I think now, I were the cavalry that she knew would one day come to rescue her but who had taken so long that she had almost given up hope.

It's difficult to recall our exact conversation. At first it was just nonsense. The closest thing I can compare it to was watching a foreign film that had been badly dubbed into English so that the words that the actors say don't quite match the movements of their mouths. Only in this case it was the reverse. It was as if her mind was out of sync with her mouth – as if her brain wasn't translating her thoughts in quite the manner she intended. But gradually she became more coherent.

'Chrissie,' she said as her head seemed to clear and she began to sound something like her old self. 'I'm sorry that I ruined things for you and Rob. I'm so sorry.'

'Joanna, it's me that should be sorry. I don't need to forgive you for anything. All I need is to get you out of here as soon as we can.'

'You don't know how I miss the baby and Em. You don't know what it's like to have lost them,' she said.

'But you haven't lost them, Joanna,' I said putting my arms round her to comfort her.

'Goran has taken them from me. He did this to me, Chrissie.'

'What do you mean?' I said warily.

'It was all part of the big plan. I tried to tell you, I tried to, Chrissie, but you thought I was imagining it all,' she said.

'Look, darling, I'm beginning to come round to your way of thinking. I found out about something that Goran said to Rob and it's made me question everything. So tell me exactly what happened.'

She looked at me carefully, fully focusing her eyes on mine as if to measure whether or not I was serious or just humouring her. Then she began, her voice growing in strength as she progressed, to tell me her version of the events leading up to her overdose.

'It was like I told you, he seemed to just slowly but surely undermine me. Little things at first, Chrissie, but intrusive and – oh you know how easy it is to upset me. I think it was the constant questioning of the way I was handling the baby that got to me. And I was so tired anyway, so very tired. When you had Sam, when you shut me out of your life I began to lean more and more on Emma. I know that sounds absurd but she was always such a mature little girl, she was always there for me. And some days, when Tom was being difficult it was so much easier to keep her home from school because she could help me and she was company for me. I almost saw her as a kind of protection against Goran. Anyway it got so that she was going to school less and less and I was more and more dependent on her as another pair of hands. Small hands, I know, too small and I feel terrible about that.'

Terrible about the way I pushed so much responsibility on to such a small child. But there was no one else and I was desperate,' she said prompting another burst of guilt ridden apology from me.

'Joanna, Joanna, I really let you down, didn't I?'

'No you didn't, I understand why you didn't want to accept what I was saying. With my history, it was easy to just dismiss this thing with Goran as a paranoid delusion. But it wasn't, Chrissie, it wasn't. I am sure it was Goran who contacted social services and I even think that it was him that switched my bottle of paracetamol tablets for sleeping pills. So on the day that the social worker arrived and found me unconscious and Emma looking after Tom, I hadn't knowingly taken those pills, I thought I had taken a couple of Nurofen or whatever they were. I was completely out of it and it isn't difficult to imagine how it looked to this woman. And of course when I did manage to emerge from the influence of the pills, I became completely demented when I found out that they were giving temporary custody of the children to Carole and Goran. It was the worse thing that had ever happened to me, it broke me, Chrissie, I just crumpled up, gave in and here I am,' she said by now quite lucid and fluent.

I stayed with her for about two hours. The effort of overcoming the stultifying effects of the drugs she had been prescribed had clearly exhausted her. But tired though she was it was obvious that our conversation had been cathartic for her and it occurred to me that what she had needed during the time she had been at The Abbey was not sedatives and psychotherapy but the counsel of a friend that loved her. The woman I was leaving was dramatically different from the woman I had encountered when I arrived.

'We'll get through this together, Joanna,' I said gently before I left.

'You do believe me don't you, Chrissie?' she said.

'Yes. I believe you. Absolutely I believe you.'

'Thank goodness for that,' she said holding my hand in both of hers.

'If we stick together, Joanna, we can stand up to whatever Goran tries to do to us,' I said.

'I hope so, Chrissie. God, I hope so,' she said plaintively as we parted.

Chapter 22

❧

Later that same afternoon, when I finally got back to my hateful new home, my growing misgivings about Goran took on a sinister new twist.

When I went to pick up Sam, I found Carole and the children out – at the park I assumed although it was rather late for that – so I went downstairs to my flat.

As I opened the door I was instantly aware that I wasn't alone. I moved through the sitting room, which remained as I had left it the night before; empty wine bottle, glass and the ashtray full of lipstick-coated Marlboro Light stubs, towards the bedroom where, through the half-open door, I could make out the form of a man.

The really worrying thing about the whole incident was Goran's apparent lack of concern at my finding him there. All the old pretence, all the old sweet, soothing caring act that, I realised now, he had previously put on for me, had gone. In its place there was a coldness and a censoriousness that was frightening to behold and was intended, I thought, to reinforce this message he was giving me that he was now in control of my life.

I am sure that the fear on my face as I confronted him going through my diary gave him the mental equivalent of the physical thrill a rapist gets when he corners his victim. Very slowly he closed the diary, placed it back on the bedside table, and looked ominously at me.

Then he walked out of the room and stood looking at the mess on the floor of the sitting room.

'Chrissie, you don't seem to understand the house rules here. I do not permit smoking or the drinking of alcohol in my house,' he said angrily.

'Fuck off, Goran,' I spat back at him.

He went mad then. He began shouting at me in rather the way he must have done to Joanna, half in English and half in his own native tongue. His words – in any language, mine or his – were vile. He called me a whore and a slut and kept repeating a phrase *marsh u pichku materinu* that I was to hear repeated so often in the subsequent weeks that I eventually discovered it meant (in rough translation) 'a pox on your mother's genitals'. He told me I was a bad influence on his family, that I was disgusting and decadent and that it was time that I learned how to behave. This last sentence was delivered in such a menacing manner that I screamed at him to get out of my flat. Before he left he turned round and in a chillingly detached way reminded me that it was *his* flat.

Of course I realise now that I should, at that point, simply have got myself together and left. I should have stopped to grab a few essentials, Sam and Pushkin, and then I should just have driven off. But for all sorts of reasons – not least cowardice and my weakened mental state – I didn't.

Besides, despite my external display of bravado during my confrontation with Goran, I had lost my nerve. Carole and Joanna, back in the days before we had all been caught in Goran's nasty, sticky web, had always regarded me as the most rebellious and outgoing one of the three of us. I was the one whom everyone assumed didn't give a damn about authority figures or convention. But so many things had tested me in the last few months, Rob's defection (I still hadn't heard from him) being the final straw, that I was beginning to feel, and behave, like a timid, terrified child. My old swaggering confidence had almost gone and finding Goran in my room confirmed the feeling I had since the incident with John in the hotel in Spain, that I was just a weak and powerless little woman.

I didn't even dare confront Carole, although I had half a mind to as I suspected that she was very nearly as unhappy as Joanna and myself. But I wasn't foolish enough to risk telling her how I felt about Goran. He was, after all, her husband and their relationship, at least in the past, had always seemed pretty much perfect.

Anyway, I couldn't afford to antagonise her because I was due back in the office that Monday. And although, in a way, I felt a little more liberated now that I had money in the bank and a clean financial slate, I was still acutely aware that I needed to hold on to my job.

But I did make certain plans and resolutions that weekend. I visited Joanna several more times and slowly managed to fit together the pieces of her story. My presence seemed to reassure and help her, a fact that even the staff confirmed. On the Sunday afternoon I had a brief telephone conversation with her consultant who agreed that if Joanna continued to make progress she might be released in the next week, although only social services could make any decisions about her regaining custody of the children.

I had a growing conviction that if Joanna and I could stick together we could regain our old strength. Some master plan was forming in my head whereby Joanna and I would live together, perhaps putting our assets together to buy a house big enough for us all. Meanwhile I would play a waiting game, giving Goran and Carole the impression that all was well, whilst privately plotting like mad to make my escape.

In the following week I made two important discoveries. The first happened by chance as I walked from East Acton station to the house on the Monday evening.

I was making my way down an alley that I had discovered was a shortcut home when I became aware of some menacing looking youths, sitting on a park bench about a hundred yards away, shouting obscenities. As I pulled level I realised that they were not, as I had supposed, jeering at me but at a woman who was hurrying past them pushing a double buggy.

There was, I can remember thinking, something vaguely familiar about the back view of the woman but it took me a while to realise, actually when I caught sight of Emma's brilliant blonde head bobbing along beside her, that it was Carole. She had a scarf tied in a rather eccentric manner round her head. Headscarves, even in the age of the pashmina, had never really been Carole's thing and I was rather alarmed by this further indication of her dramatically changed image.

It was only when I caught up with her that the significance of the way she was dressed finally hit me. Carole's scarf was draped round her neck and over her head so that it totally obscured her brow and entirely covered her hair. In the Moslem way.

It was then, I suppose, that I got my first inkling of the hold that Goran had over Carole and what I –

not to mention Joanna and our babies – might be up against.

'I didn't recognise you, Carole,' I said a little breathlessly as I fell in step beside her.

'Why ever not?' she said.

'The scarf, it's not, well, it's not very YOU is it?'

'It's very me, now, Chrissie,' she said meaningfully.

'I can't think of any occasion in the past when I have seen you wear something like that. I remember that phase you had when you used to wear a little pillbox hat with a veil, you always looked so terribly glamorous. You had a thing about the forties, do you remember?'

'My scarf isn't a fashion statement, Chrissie. I've grown up. Maybe it's time you did,' she said coldly.

'But surely you can still look good, take pride in yourself when you are grown up,' I said.

'I wear this scarf like this because it makes Goran happy. It's a tradition in his country,' she said.

'But he doesn't live in his country. Shouldn't he be adapting to our traditions?' I said, determined to get her to open up about her odd physical transformation.

'I like his traditions. I like the idea that the only man who can see me is my husband. I feel protected, I feel safe,' she said.

'Oppressed more like. For God's sake, Carole, whatever happened to the independent post-feminist woman I used to know?'

'The teaching of Islam does not oppress women, Chrissie. Quite the opposite. It's about respect, it's about honour, it's about being cared for. This obsession you have about equality is ridiculous. Equality can never work, it destroys the balance between men and women. Men and women are different, they compliment each other but the woman is only really happy if she defers to the man,' she said.

'Oh come on, Carole, you can't really believe that. Making women cover their hair, their faces, their bodies in public isn't about respect and honour. It's just another example of the age old paternalism that has kept women down for centuries. Christ almighty, you were always complaining about the chauvinism inherent in our society, what on earth has made you embrace a culture in which women are just the possessions of the men they marry?'

'You are showing your ignorance, Chrissie. Like so many British people you make assumptions about something you cannot possibly understand,' she said angrily.

'I don't think it's something that I want to understand, thank you,' I said.

'One day you will, Chrissie, I can tell you that for nothing,' she said as we reached the front door of the house.

I was rather alarmed by this exchange because Carole was so cold and inflexible and because there seemed to be some kind of threat in her last statement. It struck me that she was behaving more like some meek and brainwashed member of a weird religious cult than the outgoing, outrageous and outspoken woman I had previously known and loved. I unstrapped Sam from the buggy and took him downstairs to my flat without saying a proper goodbye. Behind my front door I clutched my baby to me and began to cry, forlorn tears falling onto his dark, downy hair. What would become of us?

The second discovery of the week took place at almost the same time on the very next day. When I got home on the Tuesday, I noticed a white van parked about fifty yards from number 12. As I walked past it, the driver's door flew open and a man jumped out and caught me in a clumsy embrace. Such was my state, at that time, that my first reaction was to scream. But then some sense in me, comforted by the familiar smell of compost and potting plants, realised that it was Rob emerging from his Green Piece van.

'Chrissie,' he said tenderly, 'I love you.'

'You didn't call me,' I said.

'I told you I was away. But I thought about you all the time – first thing in the morning, last thing at night and a great deal of the space in between.'

'And what did you conclude?' I said growing bolder and more confident with every word he said.

'That I can't live without you. That I want you and me and Sam to be a proper family,' he said.

It was as if the sun had suddenly burst through a brooding, dark cloudy sky and reversed the course of a day, well my life really. The knowledge that he loved me and wanted to be with me had such a powerful effect that it somehow banished all my worries and doubts. I felt certain – poor deluded fool that I was – that everything was going to be alright.

I was still sufficiently jumpy and nervous, though, not to dare to fall into his arms in the street outside the house. I knew it was risky taking him into my flat – hell if Goran didn't allow drinking and smoking he was hardly going to condone fornicating – so we arranged that I would go in and pick up Sam and signal to him when I had established whether Goran was around.

Five minutes later, with the coast clear, Rob came creeping in from the bushes.

Curiously the sight of Rob in those rooms suddenly made them seem like home. We smiled at each other,

Rob, Sam and me and, after a moment or two he took the baby from me.

'Bloody hell, you're heavy, old chap,' he said, pretending to drop Sam in a way that delighted the baby and produced a loud chuckle.

Despite all that had happened, Rob was so sweet with Sam. He didn't, as a lesser man might have, resent Sam or noticeably change in his approach to him. It was as if he still regarded him – in everything but the biological sense – as his son. And oddly, although of course he was still only a little blobby baby, my son seemed to have the same feelings about Rob. His face, with those black eyes that would be a life-long reminder of his true paternity, would light up when he was with Rob. It was as if, fanciful though it sounds, there was a real empathy, a real bond between Sam and Rob. A bond that was never ever there with Sam and Goran – I think my son was as instinctively wary of his true father as I now was.

'Would you like to bath him while I get something to eat?' I said.

'How do you feel about that?' Rob said to Sam as he carried him off to the bathroom.

In the little galley kitchen, as I prepared a quick pasta meal, I could hear laughter, splashing and then the sound of Rob singing.

'Don't be too noisy, boys,' I shouted. 'You might disturb the neighbours.'

I got Sam out of the bath and put on his nappy and his sleepsuit and then Rob gave him a bottle and we both put him down to sleep in his little cot.

'I talked to Paul about you, he is rather more forgiving than Anna. But they'll come round, I know they will. Anyway it's about time I escaped from the family home. We could get somewhere in London, or in Hampshire or any bloody where, just as long as we are together,' Rob said when we were finally alone, the curtains carefully drawn across the window lest Goran or Carole might see us.

'The important thing is to just get the hell away from my landlord. And to get Joanna out of The Abbey and her children back,' I said, giving him a brief résumé of my conversation with Joanna.

When we had eaten, we went and sat on one of my sofas and slowly, as was always the way with Rob, we began to make love. It doesn't matter how hard you try to make it otherwise, the reported speech of lovers always sounds horribly clichéd. But even if what we said to each other that night was nothing more than the much repeated reassurances and endearments used by millions of other couples, they sounded beautiful and fresh and new to me.

I felt like a nervous young virgin. Partly because I was feeling so emotional – and still a little weak and frightened from the experiences of the past months – and partly because I was terrified that Goran might have come home and would, at any moment, walk in on us. It even occurred to me, as I tried to prevent Rob from expressing his lust and love too loudly, clamping my hand over his mouth at one point, that Goran might have been planting hidden cameras on the day I had disturbed him in my flat. And that even now, on some screen in the big ugly house above us, he was watching us making love.

But Rob's reappearance in my life really did have a miraculous effect on my outlook and mood. I mean I knew – Rob and I both knew – that we couldn't be together whilst I was living in the basement of number 12, but finding him again gave me the heart to think about a future. A future away from this horrid flat beneath the roof of that horrid man.

Until I could make my escape, we would have to keep our relationship secret and be very careful not to arouse any suspicion. Goran had pushed us apart once and we wouldn't give him the opportunity to come between us again. At the time we thought that the sneaking around, the hiding of Rob's presence in my life from Goran and Carole was a bit of a joke. I suppose it even gave an edge to our love. It was like two teenagers fooling overstrict parents. But of course, I eventually discovered, we were only fooling ourselves.

Still, I look back on that time with the same soft-focus sentimentality with which I look back on the blissful days after Sam's birth. We spent all the time we had alone together making love and talking, talking, talking. For us that phrase 'the truth will set you free' was absolutely right. In the past my secret, my lies had always been a kind of mental barrier in my ability to communicate with Rob. But now he knew – and accepted – the truth of the whole turkeybasting business it was as if I had been liberated, I felt now I could tell him anything and everything. My hopes, my fears, my dreams for the future. We had so many plans. We would start a business together so that I could give up my ghastly job and we could be together twenty four hours every day. We would go and live in France. We would buy a farm in Northern Spain. We would live in an old Romany caravan and have seven children. Oh, the plans we had . . .

Chapter 23

Every day that I spent in Carole and Goran's house gave me new insights into the way they lived their lives. On the Friday of the week in which Rob came properly back into my life they asked me to join them for dinner to celebrate some new contract Goran and his partner had just secured. I didn't dare refuse.

It was, in every way you can imagine, a totally different social function to the ones we used to have back in the days before we had come up with our big plan. Not least because this time it was the males, not the females, who were the dominant influence and no alcohol was consumed.

I had met Vedo, who had grown up in the same small town as Goran, briefly before but I had never encountered his wife Jasmina. The moment I saw her I realised that she must have played a considerable part in Carole's transformation – there was something worryingly similar about the two women despite the fact that they were physically so different.

They were dressed almost identically, in ugly synthetic clothes designed, I now realised, to cover their bodies from the prying eyes of any man other than their husbands. But it wasn't just their outfits that matched, their mannerisms were similar and they worked together, preparing and serving the meal, in a way that suggested that they were a team.

I became aware that evening, too, that Carole's conversion to the Moslem way involved more than just the adoption of the 'veil'. When Goran said prayers over the food Carole joined in the responses – and not in English. And her attitude towards Vedo was as strained and respectful as Jasmina's approach to Goran. Both women sat with downcast eyes in the presence of the two men.

'Chrissie, what do you think of the traditional customs and food of my country?' Goran said quite genially to me when we were eating.

'The food is wonderful but it's all very different from our old evenings together,' I replied in cautious tones.

'Family changes you, it makes you want to retrace and recreate your own childhood. Women, Chrissie, need rules, routine for their security. Carole, as you can see, has never been more secure,' he said glancing over at his wife.

'Secure? You mean like a prisoner held behind bars for his own good and the good of society in general,' I said before I could think better of it.

'Carole is not my prisoner, Chrissie, and I resent your suggestion that she might be,' he said.

'I didn't mean to offend you, or Carole. It's just that I wasn't really aware, until I came to live here, just how much her life had changed,' I said fearful that I had made a huge mistake in questioning their lifestyle.

'Carole and I thought it would be good for you to see how we live now. We enjoy a simple home-based existence,' he said as Carole and Jasmina, in response to a nod from Goran, began to silently clear away the plates.

Perhaps I would have been more surprised by this odd display of female subservience in a contemporary London setting, if I hadn't already observed the power that Goran could exert over his wife. I had noticed, in the previous weeks, that he was able to control her behaviour almost by remote-control. He had a series of signals that would work on his wife like a zapper on a multi-channel TV. So that a slight move of his hand, and a glance from his cold, dark eyes, would have her rushing off to obey his command.

Immediately after we had eaten, after another prompt from Goran, Carole and Jasmina rose and indicated to me to leave too. It was a little like that old English custom of the women withdrawing whilst the men smoked cigars and drank port. Only, of course, no one that night had a drop to drink.

While the men carried on eating and talking round the table, we cleared up in the kitchen and drank peppermint tea. Every now and then Goran would shout something – in the manner of a commanding general – and Carole would jump up and go back into the dining room to fetch or carry whatever it was he wanted. Try as I might, I couldn't help but question this custom and Carole's apparent compliance with Goran's traditions.

'Do you remember how Goran used to cook for us – Joanna, you and me – in the old days?' I said when Carole sat down again like some harassed waitress in a crowded restaurant.

'Things were very different then. It is a woman's joy and a woman's destiny to serve her husband,' she said looking anxiously across at Jasmina for approval.

'It must have been difficult for him, back then, waiting on us while we all banged on about how men were such selfish, useless bastards. It must have been as alien to his culture as this is to mine,' I said.

'Chrissie, we had no culture then, nor manners nor any sense of propriety,' Carole said catching Jasmina's eye and saying something to her that I couldn't understand in what was clearly now a common language. One, that is, that I could never understand.

'You ought to know, Carole, that I have been in contact with Joanna,' I said, aware that I needed to talk about our mutual friend's progress but wary of saying too much.

'You've written to her?' Carole replied, her eyes suddenly alarmed.

'No, I've been to see her. She's doing well. I felt so guilty about not having done something to help her earlier. I had no idea she was in such a terrible state,' I said.

'Don't tell Goran,' Carole urged.

'Don't tell Goran what?' I replied.

'Don't say anything about Joanna, having seen her,' she said almost jumping out of her skin when, from behind her, Goran suddenly spoke.

'What about Joanna?'

'I have been to see her, Goran. She's doing well. I think it's time that we made it possible for her to see her children,' I said.

His face became even more grim at this news but he didn't venture any further comment until after Jasmina and Vedo had left.

'What makes you think you have a right to interfere with Joanna's treatment?' he asked me sharply as soon as the door had closed on his friends.

'Goran, you know full well what gives me the right. Joanna is very important to me. Have you forgotten the bond of family that exists between us?'

'Chrissie, I will never forget the bond of family that exists between us all,' said Goran with a chilling little laugh before adding, 'but that doesn't mean you have any right to go creeping around in secret behind our backs. Joanna is a very sick woman.'

'No she isn't. I admit she's emotionally fragile but she's much, much better. I think she's almost ready to go home, to have the children back,' I said.

'She is not a fit mother. I am not sure she will ever get her children back,' he said ominously.

Carole, I noticed, had become more and more anxious as our conversation had progressed and was now wringing her hands in the lap of her horrid long, floral frock. Her fear of her husband was almost palpable.

'Goran, you might imagine you have a superior know-ledge of Joanna's mental state because of your medical background, but actually the people treating her are in agreement with me, not you. They have agreed that she can be discharged into my care tomorrow. Social services will make the decision about the children,' I said.

'Joanna will never be welcome under my roof. Nor do I believe she is ready to resume her responsibilities as a mother,' he said.

'Well, she'll be welcome under my roof. For the time being she can stay in the basement with me,' I said, so firmly that I reminded myself of the bold Chrissie of old.

I think that knowing that I had Rob must have made me feel stronger and more able to stand up to Goran. At any rate, although he looked at me with undisguised hatred, he didn't argue any further with me, just turned his back and went upstairs.

I spent the following day preparing the little flat for

Joanna's arrival, clearing out the tiny bedroom at the back so that it looked something other than an ugly prison cell. I knew that she had huge misgivings about living at number 12 and I wanted her to feel as relaxed and at home as was possible in such miserable and unattractive surroundings. In the afternoon I drove, with Sam strapped into his baby seat, to my old stomping ground in Marylebone High Street. Being back in the heart of London lifted my spirits and I indulged, as best I could with a lively baby in tow, in a delicious shopping spree. Buying lots of my favourite foods from the specialist shops I used to frequent and then moving on to the Conran shop where I bought some beautiful linen for Joanna's bed and some for mine, three exquisite white orchids in white containers and three new sets of fairy lights (I am an all-year-round fairy light fanatic). On my way home I stopped at Penhaligons and spent a fortune on a whole range of beautiful bath oils, scented candles and lotions. When I got home and arranged all my purchases around the flat I decided that, at least after dark, it would be a glamorous, glowing, sweet-smelling refuge for us.

Later that afternoon I went to pick up Joanna who was waiting for me in the rather grand drawing room in which I had sat on the day of my first visit. She had washed her hair, put on a bit of lipstick and regained some of her old beauty. She had cut back on the anti-depressants she was taking and she was so excited by the thought of seeing Tom and Emma that I had to hold her hands to stop them from shaking.

In the car I told her a little of what had been going on at home. It was an edited version of events because I wasn't yet sure she could cope with the more sinister aspects of Goran's behaviour. She was frightened enough of him already and it had been quite a struggle to persuade her to stay with me whilst social services assessed her. Her compliance, I suspect, had much to do with the close proximity of her children.

When she had dumped her things in the bedroom she would sleep in, we went upstairs to see the children. Joanna could hardly contain herself as she waited for the door to open. Carole greeted her with what looked to me like a real, warm smile followed by a long, tight hug. If Joanna bore her any ill-will she didn't show it.

The cry that Emma let out when she saw her mother for the first time will stay with me forever. My conscience had been badly troubled, in the last weeks, by Emma. Her brother was too young to be affected by his separation but Emma and Joanna had always had such a deep bond that the events of the last month or so must have had a profound effect on her.

Joanna held her as if she would never let her go but she didn't cry. I felt very intrusive watching the reunion but I noted, as I observed mother and child, that Joanna was very controlled, hard even. I sensed – and later she told me that I was right – that she was now absolutely determined to win the battle for her children. I even thought, quite astutely as it happens, that she would do anything that was necessary to regain control of her life, her babies.

Tom was a little nervous of her, clinging to Carole when she tried to hold him out to Joanna and I think that cut like a knife through her poor, broken heart.

She stayed upstairs until she had settled her children into bed, making her exit before Goran, who had discreetly gone out for the afternoon, returned.

I cooked a shepherd's pie that evening and it was almost like old times, except that Carole was missing and in her place, smuggled in through the kitchen window with a contraband bottle of wine, was Rob.

I had, by now, more than forgiven Joanna for her mistake in telling Goran about Rob. Something in her manner that afternoon told me that, no matter what Goran might do, I could trust her never to repeat that mistake. It was only the second time that Rob and Joanna had met and the circumstances were so different from that first meal we had shared – when I was burdened by a seven pound baby in my belly and a terrible secret in my head – that it was, in effect, the first time the three of us had relaxed together. Emboldened by the wine, we were able to talk very frankly about our feelings. Listening to our different accounts of the way in which Goran had taken over our lives and undermined us was fascinating. Joanna retelling the story of the sleeping tablets, Rob describing Goran's chilling charm on the night he told him he was Sam's father, me recalling the occasion on which I had disturbed him going through my diary. By the end of the evening we were a unit of three dedicated to extricating Goran from our lives.

In truth, of course, we were totally deluded. Holding a conference of war within the very heart of enemy territory. But then however much we feared Goran and however much he dominated our conversation that night, I don't think any of us had any idea how far he would go.

What disturbed me, an hour or two after Rob had disappeared into the night through the kitchen window, wasn't the sickening sounds from above, but Joanna urgently shaking me awake.

'Chrissie, Chrissie, something terrible is happening upstairs,' she said as I emerged from a deep sleep feeling confused and frightened.

'It's happened before,' I said when I had made sense of my surroundings and the noise from overhead.

'It's awful I can't bear to listen – he's been shouting and screaming for half an hour and the worst of it is that the only response has been these low moaning sobs. God, Chrissie, I could even hear him hitting her. We have to do something.'

'I don't think it would be safe to intervene,' I said nervously.

'But what about the children? Supposing he turns on them? I can't just sit here and do nothing,' Joanna said.

She wanted to go and knock on the door, she talked about ringing the police but by the time we had gathered the courage to make any move the sounds suddenly stopped. Tense and too wide awake to sleep, we made some peppermint tea and took it back to my bed, Joanna climbing in beside me.

'How on earth did we get into this situation?' I said.

'You know how we got into this situation. The real question is why didn't we ever suspect that this was going on, how could we have been so clueless about Goran?' Joanna replied.

'I think something changed between Carole and him when we came up with our plan. I think that he has only recently begun to assert himself, I don't think we could ever have known that he had this side to him. I've been running the past through my head so much recently looking for the signs and I honestly can't think of a single occasion – before we became pregnant – when Goran was anything other than the perfect man we believed him to be,' I said.

'But it must have been there, underneath, mustn't it? He must have resented us even though he put on this caring, compliant act. We just took him at face value, we just believed in him. We didn't question anything,' Joanna said.

'When I look back now, having seen this new Goran, this controlling, macho man, I can see how naive we were. For a man from his religious and cultural background, for a man so sure of his innate superiority to women, we must have seemed like monsters. How patronised he must have felt when he overheard our drunken talk about male redundancy while he cooked us supper and did the washing-up. God, how he must secretly have loathed us for having everything that he had always assumed was naturally his by right – the money, the control. And meanwhile there he was – highly skilled, highly intelligent and educated, reduced to servicing cars in a back alley in some awful London suburb.'

'It's a bit ironic isn't it, when you think about it. The two of us – independent women who had always been so convinced that "sisters could do it for themselves" – finding ourselves caught out like this. It's almost funny, really. We were so certain in our belief that we could just procreate like amoebas. We didn't need a man. God, Chrissie, do you remember how I used to say no woman needed a man? How I used to bang on about how we were living in a world in which men were superfluous, in which scientific advances would shortly enable us to create new life without the aid of man. We could have a baby without having a relationship. And what has happened? We have ended up hopelessly trapped and controlled by our sperm king,' Joanna said in despairing tones.

Again and again, we kept returning to the fact that we had never seen it coming. Never, for one second, suspected that Goran was difficult and domineering and desperate to exercise some form of control over his wife's two closest female friends. We had thought he was the only man who could truly tolerate our relationship and it had turned out that he was the only man who could come between us. We should have realised just how much Goran had lost in moving from his own country to ours, and just how much he hated exchanging the status he had enjoyed as a skilled surgeon in Bosnia for that of a cheap motor mechanic in Britain. It had taken years for him to find a way to gain control of the situation, but he had finally achieved his goal. Goran had the dominant role now. Not just with Carole, in the room above, but with of all of us.

When I did finally fall asleep, long after the birds had begun singing, I had this dream in which Goran turned out to be Satan. It was like *Rosemary's Baby* in a contemporary setting. Carole, Joanna and me breeding babies in some awful satanic cult – the symbol of which wasn't an inverted cross, but a solid gold turkeybaster.

Chapter 24

I remember once, years and years ago, a friend of mine telling me how she had heard her neighbours – a very middle class, Middle England kind of couple – having a very violent argument and how, despite seeing the woman the following day looking bruised and battered, she had said nothing. At the time I was convinced that if I ever found myself in a similar situation I would wade in and confront the man. But I realised, the following morning, that it wasn't that easy. I understood why so many people turn a blind eye and ear to domestic violence.

This, though, wasn't some vaguely known neighbour, it was Carole, and I couldn't pretend it hadn't happened. It was now almost impossible to match the woman who lived above us with the one Joanna and I used to meet up with for our weekly suppers. And not just because of the way in which she now looked and dressed. Her old spirit, her old irreverence had gone. Carole had always been outrageous – she had always had this ability to say exactly what she meant, however rude or obscene other people might find it. And she had always had such a wicked sense of humour, delivering jokes in her rich Geordie accent and punctuating the punch lines with her loud, earthy laugh. Where had that Carole gone? How had she changed from a confident woman who strutted around on six-inch spike stilettos into this meek, submissive woman who covered her hair and cowered in the presence of her husband? And, more to the point, why hadn't I noticed the terrible transformation as it was taking place?

At about ten, I forced myself to go upstairs and knock on their door. A Goran quite different from the one of the other evening answered. He was like the old Goran – that charming, sensitive man who, all that time ago, had prompted our mad plan. Carole, he said in a considerate, conspiratorial whisper, was sleeping. On Sundays, he said, they took it in turns to get up with the children, it was his turn today. From what I could see everything inside was in order, Emma was drawing at the kitchen table while the boys were playing with toys on the floor. My resolve to confront the situation disappeared and I left, vaguely uneasy about my weakness. Had I been more forceful, had I been more determined, perhaps I could have prevented the horrors that followed.

And now I reach that part of our story that haunts me the most. The twist in our tale that still has the power to make me feel physically sick.

It's still difficult for me to describe the sequence of events because every time I try to concentrate on what happened, I mentally flinch at the prospect of visualising those terrible last hours. Psychologists say, don't they, that in order to overcome a trauma you need to re-live it again and again. But I don't think I will ever overcome what happened and I don't think I will ever be able to re-live it without breaking down.

But I do remember every detail of the last time I saw Rob, the last precious, precious time that the two of us spent together. And I re-live that day again and again and again in the hope that it will eventually become as clear and real as a video that I can instantly replay – rewinding and pausing at the best bits – in my head.

It had been hard trying to conduct a relationship in the circumstances we found ourselves in – him working and living in Hampshire, me temporarily living in Goran and Carole's flat. I was now so spooked by Goran that I found it impossible to relax beneath his roof and so, even on the rare occasions when I was able to smuggle him in, I couldn't enjoy being with Rob. In any case, even if it had been possible for us to openly live together at number 12, it would have been virtually impossible for us to be alone. Because of course as well as baby Sam there was now also Joanna.

It was Joanna, actually, who suggested that Rob and I should escape somewhere together for a day. I felt very guilty about it at the time, taking a sneaky day off work and not spending it with my baby, but the memories of that day have sustained me and, I suppose, ultimately made me feel less guilty about what happened to Rob. At least I can comfort myself with the knowledge that we had that last perfect day together. I think I have said before that the subterfuge made the meetings we did manage all the more exciting. That last morning I left the flat and dropped Sam off with Carole at exactly the same time as I would have done were I going to work. I even wore my smartest work clothes. Rob's white van, with its Green Piece logo, was parked, by prior arrangement, two streets away, just near East Acton station.

I climbed into the van and he pulled me to him and kissed me.

'I love you, Chrissie,' he said as I broke nervously away from his embrace – I could never feel entirely comfortable with Rob in public when we were so close to my new home.

'I love you more,' I said as he started the engine and we drove off.

It was a glorious day, we had been having a minor heat wave, and we had decided to drive to a place Rob knew in the New Forest – a wood bordered by a stream that he had called, when he was a child, The Stepping Stones.

The only shadow on the day was the increasing doubts I now had about Goran's behaviour. On the journey there I told Rob about the sounds of violence and distress that Joanna and myself had heard.

'When I was on my own I half thought that I might be imagining it, but when Joanna heard it too, I realised I wasn't. The thing is, Rob, that we don't know what to do about it. With this whole thing with social services still hanging over Joanna's head we have got to be very careful. Goran is such an arch manipulator, God knows what he wouldn't do if he thought we had contacted the authorities, so we daren't show our hand too soon. But at the same time there's Carole, and more importantly the children, to think about.'

'Couldn't you report it anonymously somewhere? There must be some kind of number you can ring, like *Crimestoppers*,' Rob said thoughtfully.

'I think with domestic violence it has to be the person involved. Until Carole's ready to do something about it there's nothing we can do. But again I don't know how to reach her, to talk to her about it. She's so detached from me and Joanna at the moment.'

'What we really ought to be doing is planning to get you out of there. We've got to sort things out so that you and I can be together – with Joanna and her children if needs be – then we can just shut the door on Goran,' Rob said, almost losing control of the van as he looked away from the road and straight into my eyes.

The idea of closing the door on Goran was so attractive but somehow so impossible that I didn't offer a reply. I just began to muse, as I watched the lush green landscape rush past the window, on the possibility of a world without Goran.

It took about two hours to get to the New Forest and the excitement I felt at the thought of finally being alone with Rob for a whole day made even the interior of his van, filled as it was with bags of compost, spades, trays of plants and dozens of terracotta pots, seem the most romantic place on earth.

When we got to the little wooded glade, and Rob had parked beneath a big tree, I felt that rush of anticipation you have when you are a small child on a day trip to the seaside.

I think Rob must have felt much the same because when he began to unload things from the back of the van, it was obvious that he had given our day together a great deal of thought. He had packed a hamper full of food and had brought a proper tartan picnic rug which he spread out in a very secluded sun-dappled spot.

It was the most perfect picnic. There was champagne and smoked salmon, quails eggs and cold chicken, raspberries and a French cheese that you could almost see ripening and melting in the heat. Not that we were really hungry for anything but each other.

I suppose all couples have their favourite places and positions for love making. What turned Rob on most – as I already knew from that first day on the Barbour in the garden – was sex beneath the sky. I don't mean that he got some vicarious thrill from making love in public places. It was just that Rob really was happiest when he was at one with nature (and me).

So before we had got to the food, after just one glass (he had even packed real fluted glasses) of champagne, we got to each other. And maybe, when I think about it, he did get some extra sexual charge from feeling the bare earth beneath our bare bodies. At any rate, what with all that food so beautifully arranged on the rug, there was no room for us and when I lay down on a blanket of moss, grass and leaves, carefully avoiding a nearby clump of stinging nettles, Rob seemed to go almost mad with desire. And really, despite my fear of creepy crawlies and the fact that the ground was a little damp, it was the most powerful sex I had ever had. Not what Carole used to call – way back in the days before she had met and married Goran – 'a full throttle thrust fuck'. It was still, as ever with Rob, tender and intimate.

It's a curious fact, and another comforting thought, that before I had met Rob I had never made love in the open air. In truth I am not sure I had ever really made *love* at all before I met Rob. At any rate, I had never, ever been so absolutely conscious of being *in* love. Cynic that I am, I am not even sure that I ever believed that such a thing as real, true, romantic love existed. But that day I knew it did.

Looking back I am amazed that no one disturbed us during that long afternoon. But maybe we were just oblivious to everything and everyone else in the world. We made love three times and we didn't bother to get dressed between our bouts of lovemaking, although I did drape my pale blue pashmina round my shoulders, because whenever the sun disappeared behind a cloud it became quite cool.

If anyone had stumbled across our little picnic place, I am sure we would have been as startling a sight as that famous painting *Déjeuner sur l'herbe*. Lolling nonchalantly, as we were, in the nude round a rug filled with food. There's something a little decadent about sitting naked in the sun while you drink champagne, fill your face with food, and, well, fuck.

But there was much more to our day than sex. Our relationship had followed such an odd stop-start pattern that we were still at that talking stage when you both take extraordinary delight in hearing stories from one another's childhood. Stories that, to anyone else, would be stupefyingly boring but which, from the mouth of your one true love, are more fascinating than anything you have ever heard before.

Not, of course, that all the tales from my own past were as traditionally happy as Rob's. But even I, lying so secure in his arms on that blissful day, was able to conjure up a few happy memories from my dysfunctional early life.

'I remember once my Aunt Julie giving me this fantastic dress for my birthday – I must have been six or seven. My parents didn't really approve of Aunt Julie but I think now she was really the only positive female role model I had. She had been married twice which was very much frowned upon particularly since her second husband had been black. And she had this wild taste in clothes. I don't think I ever saw her without high heels and lipstick. She was always dressed up – a bit like Carole used to be actually – and she just seemed so glamorous to me because my mother was such a cold, puritan person. Anyway, she gave me this dress in a box and when I look at it from adult eyes I suppose it was a cheap rather tacky dress. It was made of this powder blue shiny material, nylon probably, and it had this huge skirt which was trimmed in lace like a kind of crinoline. I just thought it was wonderful and because it was my birthday and I was having this small party – five or six children from our local young Christian group – my mother let me wear it. I felt like a princess, I can still feel the way that skirt felt when I turned round quickly, I can still remember the sound of it rustling as I moved. And I remember this boy – Stephen something – telling me I looked very pretty and it was the first time anyone had said anything like that . . .'

'Did he kiss you?' Rob asked gently.

'No, no it was nothing like that. It was just that my mother always had my hair cut very short, in a crop and she dressed me in very plain, dull clothes. She used to say that "vanity was a mortal sin" and we only had one small mirror in our house – in the bathroom, presumably so that my father could see to shave himself. That day stands out because it was the first time it had occurred to me that I could be something other than the person my mother had decided I would be. I could be like Auntie Julie, I could be pretty . . .'

'What happened to the dress?' he asked.

'I don't know. I only wore it the once. I think my mother must have hidden it away or given it away or thrown it out because I never saw it after I took it off when I went to bed that night.'

'I don't think you could ever look prettier than you do today,' Rob said reaching out and touching my pashmina.

'I don't think I have ever felt prettier – not even then in that dress – than I do today,' I said leaning forward to kiss him again.

There were moments, too, that afternoon when we became like children ourselves, doing the foolish things that you do when you are intoxicated by each other's presence. We climbed the same trees that Rob had climbed, he claimed, as a child, we did some naked arm-wrestling and we paddled and splashed in the stream.

We were so caught up in each other that we didn't notice the time until the sun went down. Rob had another reason for taking me to the New Forest that day. He had told Paul and Anna that we were back together and they had invited us, albeit, I suspected, reluctantly, to dinner that night.

By the time we had got dressed, cleared up the picnic and got back to the van it was nearly seven-fifteen. I felt a little uncomfortable about going straight to Paul and Anna's house. Not just because I was uncertain of my welcome – I could still remember the words of the angry letter Anna had written me when Rob found out about Goran – but also because I suspected that the two of us smelled of sex.

We stopped at a little pub on the way and I went into the loo to try to make myself look more ravishing and less ravished. My hair, which was now so long it reached below my shoulders, was matted and filled with burrs, bits of grass and decaying leaves. My clothes were creased and grass-stained and my face, arms and neck were flushed and red from the sudden unprotected exposure to the sun. My lips were sore from all the kissing and my mascara had smudged all around my eyes. I did the best I could but I still felt awkward and nervous about being scrutinised by Anna.

Perhaps my memory has painted a rather idealised picture of that day, but everything, even supper with Paul and Anna, did seem perfect. I knew that to a woman like Anna the whole turkeybasting business would be totally incomprehensible. I didn't expect any warmth or forgiveness from her. And at first she was a little stiff and silent. But I think there was probably something a little invincible about Rob and me that day and somehow, by the end of the meal, Anna became less distant.

I think she had always known that my affection for the twins was genuine and when I asked if I might just look round their bedroom door to see them sleeping, she jumped up from the table and led me upstairs.

'They are beautiful, Anna,' I said as I looked down on Camilla and George and inhaled that sweet smell of small children.

'When they are sleeping they are, Chrissie, but my God when they are awake they are trouble. Twins at two are doubly difficult.'

'But they were always so sweet-natured,' I said making direct eye contact with Anna for the first time that evening.

'Oh, they still are, it's just that they work as a team which makes them twice as naughty and twice as dangerous. I left them with Paul the other day and while he was doing something in the kitchen they managed to get a chair and carry it to the front door and open it. Thank God nothing happened to them in the time it took him to notice they had gone,' she said as we left the twins' room and moved down the hall into her bedroom.

'Sam is sitting up now, he's very strong and very determined. I sit him in the middle of his mat surrounded by toys and then he leans too far forward to pick something up and he tips over. Then of course he cries because he is cross and humiliated and shocked and I'm laughing which only makes things worse,' I said, the mere thought of my lovely baby making me suddenly miss him and prompting me to add, with a quick glance at Anna, something about discovering 'true love'.

'Rob has told us he wants you to be a family. I can't say that I was very supportive of him or keen for him to resume his relationship with you. You are a very lucky woman, Chrissie, much luckier than you deserve to be. You have got "true love" twice over. With Rob and with your baby,' she said in a censorious tone.

'I know,' I replied softly.

'Paul and I both want Rob to be happy but you should know that we don't approve of what you have done, how you hurt and misled him. And how you hurt and misled us too,' she said.

'I didn't mean to mislead anyone,' I insisted.

'Ohhh pleeaase, Chrissie,' she said angrily.

'No, Anna, you must realise I loved Rob, I loved you and Paul, this house, Camilla, George the whole package so much that once the misunderstanding had occurred I was so frightened of losing it, losing you all, that I didn't dare tell you the truth.'

'I am not surprised. The whole story was so preposterous, so outrageous I am not at all surprised you were ashamed of telling us what had gone on. And I am still not sure whether I believe your latest twist on your sordid tale. When I think of the way in which you infiltrated yourself into the very heart of my family I could, I could do you some terrible damage, Chrissie,' she said.

'You don't know how much I wished – sometimes even let myself believe – that I was carrying Rob's baby, that my timing hadn't been so terrible. But I still can't regret what I did, Anna, because I have Sam. I cannot wish him away.'

Children, as they had the first time I had met Anna,

formed the bridge between us. After we had gone downstairs and begun the washing-up – Paul and Rob sitting together round the fire in the drawing room – we began to talk again about the bond between mother and child. And it was the strength of my love for my son that convinced Anna that she would give me a second chance.

'But I will warn you here and now, Chrissie, that although I will forgive you now I still have my doubts and I will never, never forgive you if you do anything to hurt Rob again. In fact I might even kill you,' she said with a Mary Poppins with malice smile.

When she had finished her little speech, she took off her Marigold gloves, untied her apron, smoothed down her pleated Jaegar skirt and then embraced me. I remember thinking, when I had dried up the pots and pans and stored them away, that although Paul and Anna's traditional domestic arrangement might, on the surface, look a little like the set-up at Goran and Carole's home, it was very, very different. Anna might have cooked the meal, waited on the men and cleared away whilst they sat chatting and drinking but she was very much Paul's equal. Anna might wear clothes that covered most of her body and would never attract the unwanted attention of another man, but, rather like her decision to stay at home and bring up her children – she had trained as a solicitor – she did so by choice.

That evening with Rob, Paul and Anna was as important a part of that day as the love-making at our picnic. Rob had always been very close to his brother and his sister-in-law and I know it meant a lot to him to see us all together that night, talking and laughing as if the mistakes of the past had finally been forgotten. Rob and

I had already decided that we wanted to get our own place close to his old home. Our previous fanciful plans of living in a Romany caravan had turned into more realistic dreams of a tumble-down rose covered cottage in which we could live and love and raise a family. And before we left that night – like Cinderella I had to be home by midnight – Paul and Anna suggested that we should move into Rob's old bedroom and live with them until we found a suitable property. The idea that I could, as soon as I could practically organise things, move out of Goran and Carole's home had the same effect on my mental state as a shot of morphine might have to an injured man. On the long journey back to London – Rob was so sweet that he was driving me all the way back to East Acton station and then driving all the way back to Hampshire – we worked out that in a little over a week we could be together, forever.

We had talked a lot about my giving up work, Rob knew I wanted to be a full-time mother, and since property prices were so much cheaper outside London my dream was now an attainable reality. I know it's stupid to assume that Rob and I would live happily ever after because so few people actually do. But that night I felt blessed, I felt as if, in the end everything had worked out for the best. Our love, I was absolutely certain, would last an eternity.

Halfway back to London there was a terrific thunder storm which was almost biblical in its proportions, flashes of lightning briefly illuminating our faces as we travelled through the night. It was still raining when we approached East Acton station and Rob took the risk of driving me all the way home. I like to pretend that Rob's dropping me off in Milton Avenue, within sight of the house, had nothing to do with what subsequently happened. But I know now that of all the mistakes I made it was the most potentially fatal.

Chapter 25

❧

Sometimes I think that the cruellest part of the whole thing was that I didn't know it had happened and that I had no sense, no intuition, that Rob was in danger.

I didn't hear about what had happened until ten the following morning when I came out of the tube at Green Park and turned on my mobile to discover a series of frightening messages. Although my brain couldn't process what I had heard my body reacted immediately to the news. Rather in the way that people who find bodies in movies are overtaken by the urgent need to vomit, I felt the bile rise from my stomach and make its way, unmistakably, up through my throat and out of my mouth. I retched onto the crowded pavement, while oblivious strangers pushed past me.

The first message had been sent by Paul at about five that morning. 'Chrissie, something terrible has happened. Rob's been in an accident, call me as soon as possible'. The second had gone through to my retrieval service an hour later. 'Chrissie, I don't know whether you have got my message but you have to contact me. Rob needs you. I don't know how else to get to you. Please call me'. The third and fourth messages, telling me that Rob was in a coma and was in intensive care at the Charing Cross hospital must have followed at hourly intervals after that.

Eventually the nausea subsided and fear took over. I didn't have Paul's mobile number and when I rang the number at Glebe House it just rang and rang. I thought of ringing through to the Charing Cross but in the end I just hailed a cab, vaguely aware of the distaste of the driver at the sight of my vomit-stained clothing, and asked him to take me straight to the hospital.

Those places, in big cities, are confusing enough when you are visiting them for nothing more worrying than a routine x-ray. But in a state of high anxiety they are like medical mazes, with every signpost pointing in the wrong direction and no one around capable of helping you find your destination.

I think I knew from the moment that I saw the woman at reception react to Rob's name that I was too late. But it wasn't until I was shown into a waiting room and found Paul sitting with his face held in his hands that I really began to panic.

'He's gone, Chrissie,' he said without seeming to have noticed my arrival in the room.

It's funny how the mind conspires to make you concentrate on things like the grain of the wood on a table or the leaves of a plant on the window sill when you know you have to face bad news. I can remember making mental patterns out of the surface of the table in an effort, I suppose, to deflect or delay what I was about to hear. I even began to trace those patterns, nervously, with a finger.

'No,' I said eventually.

Paul still didn't move, still didn't take his hands from his face. I think now that he was trying hard not to cry, or at any rate not to let anyone see his distress.

'No, Paul,' I cried again after a moment or two.

It took the arrival of Anna, her face swollen and red raw with her pain, to bring the three of us together in grief. I flew into her arms and she held me and we cried together. Later it occurred to me that Anna, and of course Paul, could well have blamed me for what had happened to Rob. If it hadn't been for me he would not have been driving back the night before and he might still be alive. In so many different ways they could have held me accountable for his accident, but they didn't. I think my own distress, my own sense of loss was displayed so transparently in my face that they knew it was equal to their own. And our common sorrow, our joint distress, somehow bound us together.

There was no question but that I should travel back with them to Glebe House. I rang Joanna and somehow managed to tell her something of what had happened – although at that point I didn't know the details of what had happened to Rob – and she, for the first time in ages, took charge of my life, insisting on packing me a case of clothes and bringing Sam to me at the hospital so that I could travel back with them from the hospital when Paul had sorted out the awful practicalities that must be dealt with in such circumstances.

I am not sure when exactly Paul managed to tell me what happened on the night Rob died. At some stage, the initial shock must have been replaced by curiosity and I found myself wanting to know more.

'Chrissie, it's difficult for any of us to know what happened, there wasn't anyone else involved,' Paul said carefully.

'He was fine when we parted. Although there had been this terrific storm,' I recalled.

'His van somehow skidded off the road. The weather

conditions were terrible, it was the early hours of the morning and visibility was down to zero. The police think he was going too fast and he lost control of the van.'

'But he was such a careful driver, Paul,' I said.

'He had been drinking, Chrissie,' Paul replied solemnly. I don't think there was any suggestion in this statement that he thought I had in any way contributed to the accident but I nonetheless wanted to establish that we had, in fact, consumed very little alcohol on that day. We hadn't needed it and Paul knew himself that Rob hadn't drunk much during supper – he had made a point of refusing another glass of red wine because he had to drive me home.

'But we didn't drink more than a glass of champagne during the day – I accidentally knocked the bottle over during our picnic. And he only had a glass or two over supper. He can't have been over the limit on that.'

'Two and a half times over the limit, Chrissie,' Paul said.

'Surely not. We stopped at a pub on the way to you but even if he had a beer it wouldn't,' I said but Paul, who clearly found the subject difficult, interrupted me a little impatiently.

'It wasn't just alcohol, Chrissie. The brakes on the van were worn through – I kept saying to him that we ought to get it serviced. The funny thing is that I could have sworn he'd told me he'd had it checked at one of those Kwik-fit places a couple of weeks back. But apparently he didn't.'

I was so shocked and so destroyed by my loss that I didn't question the details of what Paul was telling me. I just accepted that what he said – what he had been told by the investigating officers and what would be concluded at the subsequent inquest – was an unchangeable, immutable fact. I went along with everyone else's view – that it was an accident, fuelled by alcohol and bad weather conditions that had been waiting to happen.

I like to think that to some extent I helped them get over the horror of that time in rather the way that they helped me. In amongst the tears that we shed during that period there was, in the day to day routine of the children, a shocking reminder that life has to go on. It was my open love for George and Camilla that had brought about the first real bond between myself and Anna in the early days of my relationship with Rob and now the situation was neatly reversed. With every day she became more infatuated with Sam. Recognising, I like to think, that regardless of the curious and questionable way in which he had been conceived he was as precious to Rob as if he had been his own child.

It's easy to make too much of the behaviour of small babies but I felt sure, too, that my son sensed what he had lost, or at any rate what I had lost. In the middle of the night, twenty four hours after Rob had died, Sam woke up crying in a manner that he hadn't since he was a tiny infant. He was inconsolable and since I was no longer feeding him and I was concerned lest he wake the rest of the house, I carried him down to the kitchen to get him a bottle. It was difficult trying to calm him, boil a kettle, count out the spoonfuls of formula (I had, on Anna's advice, resisted putting him on cow's milk) and wait while the water cooled enough for him to drink. And as I was attempting all this, my own tears pouring from my eyes in tune with his own, Anna crept up behind me, wearing one of her crisp, white Victorian nighties, and took Sam from me.

'There, there, baby,' she said gently.

When I had the bottle ready she handed him back to me, marginally calmer than he had been, and she sat with me while he drank the milk.

'Rob loved him very much you know,' she said.

'I know he did,' I replied, the tears still falling from my eyes.

'And I can see why. He's a beautiful, beautiful boy,' she said, reaching a hand across to touch my son's plump pink cheek.

'He is, isn't he?' I said looking up and holding eye contact with Anna for a few moments.

'I want you to know that whatever may have happened in the past I regard Sam as Rob's son, as Rob himself did. As a Rider,' she said.

'Do you, Anna? Do you really?' I said, experiencing a brief respite from my grief, a moment of joyous recognition.

'Yes, Chrissie, I do. And Camilla and George love him, sense a kinship between him and them. You know, I probably won't ever have another child and now, well, it's even more important to me to feel that my family, their family, has grown. What I am trying to say is this is forever, Chrissie, you are part of us now.'

Sam had fallen into a peaceful sleep and I stood up and laid him in Anna's lap and knelt down beside her and awkwardly put my arms around her seated figure. She looked up at me and we exchanged a smile that confirmed our unity.

There were times, though, in the days running up to the funeral when each of us felt a strong sense of denial.

Part of me – quite a big part of me – just couldn't believe that Rob had gone. When someone young dies suddenly and tragically it is very difficult to accept and there were moments, moments of total madness I suppose, during those first days when I would suddenly refuse to believe that Rob was really dead.

I woke up on the third day after Rob's death convinced that it had all been a mistake. It was Anna's idea that I should confront what had happened. She realised, before I did, that the only way in which I was going to be able to accept the truth was if I were to see him. I am not a mawkish person. I found the public weeping and wailing that took place after Princess Diana's death disturbing and even distasteful. How could you possible mourn for someone that you didn't know, had never met? How could you compare the tears you spilt for a stranger to the awful grief you feel when you lose someone you truly loved?

A bit of me wanted to see Rob and a bit of me wanted to shut my eyes and carry on pretending that he was still alive somewhere, but I took Anna's advice. She came with me to the chapel of rest and held my hand while I looked at my poor, lost love.

There were no visible signs of injury. Rob just seemed to be sleeping. I got no comfort from touching and seeing him that day. It wasn't possible, as people sometimes say it is, to say goodbye to someone who has already gone. But I did finally acknowledge that Rob was dead.

The funeral was very simple and very dignified. One of the benefits of living in the same small village all your life is that you are known to an entire community. The little church was packed with people who had really cared about Rob and the vicar talked about him in such a touching and informed way that the ceremony really was a comfort. Anna had filled the vases between the pews with flowers picked from the garden and Paul had arranged the order of service with music he knew that Rob had loved. I took Sam with me and if there was any comfort to be taken on that day I took it from the manner in which all those people acknowledged my place, and the place of my son, in Rob's lost life.

Camilla and George were too old and yet still too young to be allowed to attend and so Sam, within the constraints of the ceremony in which we were involved, was able to take centre stage. At some point Paul turned to me and said that it was time he were baptised in this church in the Rider christening robe that he and Rob had both worn. I smiled at this suggestion and I daresay the lightening of my expression must have seemed, on that bleak, black afternoon, like a sudden flash of sunlight from a leaden winter sky.

We buried Rob in the churchyard not far from the spot in which his father and his mother were interred. I had never really thought very much about the manner in which the human body is dealt with after death. It is not, is it, something that you care to ponder on until you need to? – but it seemed right that Rob should be sunk into the earth in such a beautiful spot rather than consumed by fire in some awful, anonymous crematorium.

Afterwards we went back to the house and went through the nauseating charade of eating and drinking in rather the way you do when you celebrate the other important rites of human passage – christenings and weddings. Anna, with some small help from me, had prepared exactly the kind of feast that was proper in such circumstances – neat, simple sandwiches, discreet dips, trays of crudités. Every moment was hell and yet I didn't want that afternoon to end because I knew when it did I would have to return to London.

I felt as if all my hopes and all my dreams of happiness had died with Rob. I still had Sam and, once again, he became my only reason for living. The accident that night hadn't just shattered my lover's body, it had shattered all our plans for the future. How could I think of escaping from Goran's grasp by moving in with Paul and Anna now, close though we were? How could I imagine buying a rose-covered cottage in Hampshire now that my reason for being there had gone? How could I give up work and be a full-time mother without Rob in the role of father?

As I prepared for our return to London I felt so overcome by grief and depression that I began to wish, more and more, that my son and I had been caught up in the accident that had taken Rob from us.

Chapter 26

In a curious way, Joanna and I now reversed roles. I became the hopeless, braindead depressive and she became the strong, resilient dependable friend. I don't dare to think of what might have happened had Joanna not been there for me.

She looked after Sam, she comforted me and she kept the rest of the world away from me. I daresay her old strength had begun to come back anyway now that she was off all the anti-depressants and back with her children. But I also believe that my needing her, my really, really needing her, gave her back that sense of her own worth that had been missing for so long.

Anyway she rose to the challenge of organising our lives brilliantly – she cooked, she cleaned, she dealt with all the bills and she even managed to extend my compassionate leave at work, which was a surprise because compassion, generally, had been somewhat missing in my workplace.

At first Joanna gave me no indication that she had anything other than my own grief on her mind. It was some time before she began to, very gently and with enormous subtlety, reveal what was preoccupying her – the circumstances of Rob's death.

She began by asking me, when she thought I could take it, odd questions about the accident. Or rather by making statements that raised questions in my mind about the accident.

'You know, Chrissie – and please stop me if you don't want to discuss this now – I can't believe that Rob would ever have knowingly driven when he was drunk. He was always so careful, wasn't he, on the occasions when he ate with us here? I don't remember seeing him have more than one glass of wine or one can of lager, do you? But then of course I didn't know him in anything like the same way you did,' she said one evening over a supper that, for the first time in a while, was accompanied by a chilled bottle of white wine.

'I don't think I ever did see Rob drunk. I know I drank more than I should from time to time. The first night we met a combination of alcohol and some kind of bug rendered me quite senseless. But Rob was always so careful, so responsible. Oh, God, Jo, when I think of that first night it hurts so much I almost wish that it had never happened. That I never found him, never lost him,' I said laying down my glass and pushing my plate away from me.

'You don't mean that, Chrissie. Rob was the best thing that ever happened to you. You must never, never deny that fact. And you are right he was careful, he was responsible which is what makes what happened on that night even more odd. I mean, did he ever drive recklessly when *you* were with him?' she said, gently trying to lead me back to the accident.

'No, it was a bit of a joke between us. I had always been out with the kind of men who somehow thought that there was a connection between their masculinity and their motor. Having a car with a massive engine was about more than material status, it was about their sexual superiority. But Rob was so different, I used to say he drove like a woman and regarded his car, well his van, as women are more likely to do, as a means of getting from A to B. Rob didn't need to prove himself by being the first off at the lights or cutting up some man in a fast car, it just wasn't him,' I said.

'And that other business – was it like Rob to drive with bald tyres and failing brakes?' she continued.

'Well, that is odd because Paul mentioned that he thought that Rob had had the brake pads changed a couple of weeks before the accident and when I come to think about it, I do remember a day when he couldn't pick me up from somewhere because he didn't have the van. What's all this leading up to, Joanna?' I said, my clogged brain eventually making contact, like the keys in the ignition of a car, with what she was attempting to tell me.

'Look, Chrissie, I know I was guilty of overreacting to Goran in the past but the thing is, this is different. I think that what prompted me to go over the edge so easily before was some kind of instinct about him. It might sound fanciful – spooky even – but I think that when I was pregnant something in me was trying to warn me about him. I sensed that he wasn't what he had always seemed.'

'Haven't we been through all this before, Joanna?' I said wearily.

'We went through my suspicions and what everyone assumed was my paranoia, but we never really looked at the facts. And it wasn't until Rob died – so strangely, so suddenly – that it occurred to me that if Goran could prove that I was deranged, I could probably prove the same of him. And I have, Chrissie, I have,' she said with a delicious, malicious smile that was, even in my distressed state, positively contagious.

'What exactly do you mean?' I said throwing her grin back at her like a mirror.

'Well, it started out with me trying to find something that would link him to what happened to me. I wanted valedation for myself. And so one day when Carole was out with the kids and he was at work I sneaked in there and began to look around. That first day I found two things that turned into significant clues. I found Rob's address in Hampshire written on a scrap of paper and I found a Post-it with the name and phone number of my next-door neighbour. A nosy man, key to our Neighbourhood Watch, whom I had long suspected of disliking me.'

'And how are these things clues?' I said cautiously.

'They didn't really emerge as clues until my next sneak visit. That time I found Rob's van registration number noted on the family's big day to day wall diary – written on the very day of the accident – and then I found a stash of the same sleeping pills that had been found by my bedside when I was committed . . .'

'SO?'

'SO? Can't you see, he isn't just guilty of destabilising me – not perhaps that difficult or terrible a thing – I think he's guilty of something much, much worse.'

'What are you saying, Joanna?'

'What do you think I am saying?' she replied. 'I haven't told you before but that night Rob died – quite a long time after you had come home and gone to bed – I was woken by the sound of doors slamming in the drive. I probably would just have drifted back to sleep if I hadn't heard these voices shouting – male voices. Anyway I got out of bed to get some water and I looked out of the window and saw Vedo and Goran having this heated argument. I couldn't understand what they were saying but I could tell that Vedo was frightened and Goran was trying to calm him down. When I got back to bed, I looked at my clock and it was three forty-five in the morning. It all fits, Chrissie, they must have had something to do with what happened to Rob.'

I fought the truth at first. Didn't, couldn't believe that Goran could have been involved in what had happened that night. But several things had been worrying me about the crash. I knew that sometimes the level of alcohol recorded in a body during a postmortem was irregular, but there was no way that Rob, on that day, had consumed more than the equivalent of three glasses of wine. Even accounting for chemical changes after his death there is no way that his alcohol level could have been so high. He had told me, when we parted, that he was going straight home – a journey that would have taken no more than two hours – but the accident happened four hours later just outside London. There was no doubt that something had happened to Rob during the missing hours. He must have met someone, consumed more alcohol and then blundered, drunkenly towards home, which was totally, totally, out of character.

And even when I took into account Joanna's obsession with Goran, I had to admit that if there was a man with a motive it had to be him. It didn't take Joanna long to turn my vague doubts into a growing suspicion. Maybe Goran had seen Rob drop me off and he had somehow followed and stopped him? Heavens, maybe he or Vedo had followed us the whole of that day. It wouldn't have been the first time that Goran had attempted to get Rob out of my life by foul means. But even if Goran had found out that Rob was back in my life – and the clues Joanna had found pointed towards that fact – it was a huge leap of imagination to think that he might have actually plotted his death. Joanna, though, had taken that leap. Decided that it was even possible that he or Vedo had cut through the brakes on the white van. I acknowledged that Goran was a domineering bully but I just couldn't see him as, well, a murderer. And there was no evidence, anyway, that Rob's crash was anything other than an accident. All we really had was a series of strange coincidences that, combined with our fear and distrust of Goran, had prompted us to question what had happened on that night.

But it was enough to galvanise us, to force us to come up with a plan that would allow us to take back control of our lives. We couldn't, we decided, exist like this any longer. We had allowed ourselves to be victims for too long, it was time to fight back.

Chapter 27

❧

We worked the whole thing out so carefully that I don't think Goran had any idea what was on our minds. Several weeks after Rob's accident, the social services finally agreed that Emma and Tom could be returned to Joanna's care. The only condition they imposed after Goran had raised an objection to the ruling was that for the first three months Joanna should remain living in number 12 Milton Avenue.

And although Joanna gave the impression that staying under Goran's roof was a high price to pay it did, in fact, give her the perfect cover for the first part of our plan. Which was to win Carole back onto our side.

By now both Joanna and I saw Carole more as a victim than an enemy. We knew that her relationship with Goran was abusive – hadn't we heard her being subjected to at least one savage attack? It was obvious that he had an unnatural control over his wife – how else could he have effected such a dramatic change in her personality and appearance? He had a sinister and disturbing hold over her and as her friends it was our duty to do something.

Helping her to make up her mind to leave her husband was not mean-spirited on our part, it wasn't just an act of revenge against Goran, it was an act of charity. At least so we reasoned at the time.

Before we put things in motion, we decided that we ought to give Carole one last chance to talk to us. I suggested that we have a meal together in rather the way we had in the days before we had become the odd dysfunctional family we now were. She said she would have to check with Goran but when I pointed out that it needn't involve him babysitting because we were, after all, living in the same house, she tentatively agreed to come.

We were aware that our approach to her would have to be very subtle, that we couldn't openly criticise her husband, not only because we didn't want to alienate her, but also because we didn't want to alert him.

Joanna cooked a fish pie, I contributed a bottle of wine and when all the children were in bed, Carole came down. I was aware, as soon as she entered the flat, that she was secretly pleased to be with us. She was even wearing a dress that, I felt sure, had come from her old wardrobe, a black fitted jersey dress that made her look a little more like the Carole we used to know.

'This is just like the old days,' she said a little ruefully as she sat down at our little table.

'Why did we ever stop doing this?' Joanna said.

'Because life got in the way,' I replied.

'Let's toast the future and put the past behind us,' Joanna said handing Carole a glass of wine.

'Oh, but you know I don't drink now,' Carole said quickly.

'You can't refuse a little toast, darling, just sip it and leave the rest. Goran will never know,' I said and, as if she were some naughty girl who risked being caught playing truant from school, she raised the glass to her lips.

'To the three of us, to friendship, to love, to some kind of future,' I said, trying my best not to cry (the tears were never very far away at that point of my life).

'To the family,' said Carole with a smile.

During the meal, I surreptitiously kept filling her glass and within a very short while she relaxed and drank. This, I later realised, was a mistake because it had been so long since she had consumed any alcohol that in no time at all her speech became slurred and her thought processes confused.

'Carole,' I said when I reasoned the moment was right, 'didn't we always say that we would never let a man come between us?'

'We did, and no man ever has,' she said smiling inanely at me.

'That isn't entirely true, is it, Carole?' Joanna said quickly.

'Well, I can't think of a man who's come between us, except that man of yours, Chrissie,' she said, her words becoming more and more difficult to decipher.

'What man?' I said appalled and yet somehow compelled to make her go on, make her mention Rob's name.

'Rob, he wanted to destroy ush all. Wanted to take you away, Chrissie, split up the children, end what we have fought so hard to get,' she replied.

'Oh come on, Carole, that's nonsense,' Joanna said, instantly alert to how I would react to such a statement.

'WHAT did you just say, Carole?' I said in cold, controlled tones that belied the colour that, I knew, was blazing from my face.

'I said the only man who's come between us was that man,' Carole said with such a stupid expression on her face that I had to fight back the urge to slap her.

'And Goran? Don't you think that he has come between us? Don't you think he, more than anyone else, has contrived to turn us against each other?' Joanna said.

'If you knew what Goran had done to keep us all together you wouldn't say things like that,' Carole said.

'What has he done, Carole? Sent me nearly mad and neatly disposed of the one man that Chrissie has ever loved? It isn't Rob that was responsible for pushing us apart it was Goran.'

'How dare you criticise my husband! He looks after me in a way you wouldn't understand. He took you both in when you were desperate, he has done everything he can to hold us all together. What did that Rob do? Nothing. He was no match for a man like Goran. Goran loves me, he is everything to me and it's about time you learned to respect him as you should,' she said getting up from the table and knocking over her glass of wine in the process.

I think I might have blown the whole thing if Joanna hadn't suddenly grabbed back control of the situation and calmed Carole down. She realised that we had to sober her up before she returned upstairs and that we had to reassure her that, whatever we might have said this evening, we did respect Goran. Joanna made coffee and soothing conversation designed to allay Carole's suspicions.

When she had gone, apparently unaware of our true motives, we sat down and came to the conclusion that we had no alternative now but to go through with our plan. We couldn't work out if Carole was in denial or genuinely so in fear and awe of her husband that she believed everything he told her. But we knew that in order to regain control over our own lives and our own futures we needed to have her on our side. Whatever it took we would have to shock her out of her state of denial.

It had been Joanna who had come up with the original idea. I was so out of it I just went along with whatever she suggested. And in a way, because part of the plan involved my acting out a role, it helped me get through that dreadful period of my life.

Joanna had impressed on me that Goran must never know that we were suspicious of him. Rather he should believe that we had accepted our fate – and his haunting presence in our lives. We should be as sweet and compliant as would be believable (sweet and compliant did not come naturally to me).

Phase one of our revenge would take place on Sam's first birthday, the following Sunday. Well, it had a symbolic ring to it.

Chapter 28

✆

It wasn't going to be a big celebration. In order for us to pull off our surprise attack on Goran we would have to keep it, well, in the family. Joanna, Carole, Goran, myself and our various children – nine of us in total – would mark Sam's birthday with a children's party followed by an evening meal for the adults.

Since space in our basement flat was so cramped – Sam and I shared the little back room now and Emma, Tom and Joanna had the bigger bedroom with the barred windows – it seemed sensible to hold the event in Carole and Goran's part of the house.

Carole embraced the idea with enthusiasm. She was never happier than when she was able to take on a truly matriarchal role in our lives and she set about organising a celebration for Sam that, I expect she imagined, would further draw us all together and set some kind of precedent for the future. She spent days in preparation, refusing to allow me to do much more than shop for balloons and presents for my baby. She made popsie-cakes, flapjacks, chocolate brownies and big cookies which she made to look – with hundreds and thousands, sweets and bits of angelica – like the faces of happy, smiling boys and girls. She made sandwiches shaped like boats, cars and cats. In a way, I thought as I watched her working on the Saturday before the fateful day, there was something rather childlike about Carole's behaviour nowadays. The trouble to which she went – not just for special occasions but on a day to day basis – to make things special for the children was touching but at the same time troubling. It was as if she had subsumed her whole life to her family, as if the Carole we had known had been replaced by some kind of comic pastiche of Old Mother Hubbard. She even, I noted, talked in a different tone nowadays. In the kind of sing-song and slightly patronising manner of a pre-school television presenter.

'Chrissie, wait until you see the cake. It's a bow-wow,' she said to me as she bustled round her kitchen.

'You mean a dog, Carole?' I said unable to prevent myself from forcing her to talk to me as a grown-up.

'Yes a dog, Chrissie. Surely you remember how much Sam loves doggies.'

'He's my son, Carole, please don't talk to me as if I don't know him,' I said tersely.

'Well you have to admit, Chrissie, that you have been pretty detached lately. It might be nice if you were more grateful for everything I have done for *your* son, rather than keep up this constant carping criticism,' she said in martyred tones.

'I'm sorry, Carole, it's just that sometimes you make me feel as if you are the parent and I am the part-time carer,' I said.

Carole put her arms round me then and held me to her ample bosom. I felt a little flutter of panic, a moment of doubt about the plan Joanna had concocted. I kept repeating in my head that it was for Carole's own good, her own good.

*　　*　　*

There were moments, on the day itself, when we all forgot the seriousness of our mission and actually enjoyed ourselves. Sam took such obvious pleasure in being the centre of attention. He wasn't yet walking but he sped across the floor on his bottom and could pull himself up on the furniture and although he couldn't comprehend that today was *his* day, he nonetheless behaved as if he understood that the badge pinned to his new babygro said 'Birthday Boy'.

'Look at him, he's showing off,' Joanna said as we sat the children round the table, placing Sam in the highchair at the head.

And when Carole brought in the cake with its single candle, which he blew out in a spray of chewed biscuits and spittle, he laughed so much that Goran lit it again to capture the moment on his camcorder.

There was, I thought, something rather fitting, about the way in which Goran viewed the whole of that afternoon through the lens of his video camera. I am still not sure what he actually felt for our children – that is for Tom and Sam – but that afternoon he appeared very comfortable, contented even, in the midst of our odd, extended family as long as he was behind the camera, recording rather than participating in events.

As I watched him, I suddenly remembered how Carole, in the early days of her relationship with Goran, had talked in awe about the way in which his ancestors had taken three or four wives but how he had told her that it was inconceivable to him to love any other woman but her. The concept of having children by three or four women was not, of course, strange to Goran. It was part of his cultural heritage. No wonder, I thought, he was so comfortable in our current situation. But would he, I wondered, still be true to that old promise – that he would never love, or even lust, after any other woman but Carole?

At about seven, Joanna took Sam, Tom and Emma downstairs and put them to bed whilst I helped Carole prepare the evening meal. When Joanna came back up she looked more beautiful than I can ever remember seeing her – her pale blonde hair loose around her shoulders, her blue eyes glowing, her full mouth accentuated by a soft pink lip-gloss.

The thing about Joanna, as I've mentioned before, is that she never used her looks. She hardly ever wore make-up and most of the time her hair was scraped back in a pony-tail. Nor was she body conscious – I don't think I had ever seen her wearing anything tight or revealing.

But this evening was different. In fact this evening it was almost as if Carole and Joanna had swapped places. Because now it was Carole whose face was bare of make-up, whose hair was pulled back and whose body was camouflaged beneath a long, loose unflattering frock. And, in dramatic contrast, it was Joanna who was wearing a Wonderbra, a tight Lycra top, a skirt with a split up each side and a pair of stilettos (Joanna only ever wore flat shoes).

I knew that she was only wearing them as props, a costume really, for her role in our master plan. We had spent the previous evening going through my wardrobe (she borrowed everything from me) and dressing her in different ways. The two of us screaming with laughter as she posed as the femme fatale in front of the mirror.

Carole was a little surprised to see Joanna dressed up – my worry about the whole plan was that she would realise how absolutely out of character Joanna's appearance was that evening and that she would be immediately suspicious of her motives.

'My goodness, Joanna, you have made a bit of an effort,' she said rubbing her hands on her hideous overall as if she was slightly ashamed of the way she looked. 'Maybe I should go up and change . . .'

'You look fine,' Goran said dismissively looking not at his wife but at Joanna.

Did it upset Carole to see her friend looking so absolutely stunning? Did she experience a tinge of jealousy when she saw her husband obviously admiring Joanna? I can't say for sure but she certainly became quieter and quieter as the evening progressed.

My own role in the events of that night was as best supporting actress. I had to ensure that Joanna had the maximum amount of time possible alone with Goran. To that end, I stayed in the kitchen helping Carole while Joanna sat talking, unusually intimately and flirtatiously, with him in the other room.

When the meal was ready, Goran sat at the head of the table and waited until Carole placed the leg of lamb in front of him. Then he stood up and said some sort of grace and began to carve.

I had always thought that Goran had never found Joanna attractive. But watching him being drawn under her spell that evening made me think that maybe he had hidden his feelings for her and that had influenced his behaviour; perhaps they had even prompted the whole bizarre turkeybasting scheme. It occurred to me, too, that revenge might not be Joanna's only motive that night. When she had put her plan to me I had regarded it as the ultimate self-sacrifice for her – overcoming her revulsion for both sex and Goran. But now I wondered if something else might have come into play. I had a momentary flashback to that very first day in Chiswick Park when we had jokingly assembled our 'Fantasy Fertility Leagues' of the men we thought most desirable. I remembered the look on Joanna's face when it was her turn to make her choice and she had nodded her head towards Goran.

Several times during that evening I questioned the wisdom of Joanna's plan and experienced a rush of compassion for Carole. At least four or five times I saw her watching Goran and Joanna with a look of undisguised jealousy on her flushed face. It was as if, I thought, Goran was unaware of anyone else at that table. He said nothing to me and his only exchanges with Carole were harsh commands or nagging criticism of the food and the long wait between courses. Joanna's behaviour became more and more daring, more and more provocative, and Goran's responses ever more obvious so that at one point – as I carried a dish out to the kitchen – Carole grabbed me and pulled me out of their earshot.

'What has got into Joanna, tonight, Chrissie?' she said more agitated than I can ever remember seeing her before.

'She's enjoying herself, Carole,' I said gently.

'She's throwing herself at Goran. I've never seen her dressed like that. I don't understand it,' she said, her eyes fixed through the open kitchen door on the lone couple sitting at the table.

'She's had a hard time, Carole. She's just relaxing a bit, letting her hair down. I think it's good to see her getting on so well with Goran,' I said feeling a little ashamed of the way in which I was firing Carole's jealousy.

'But just last week she was complaining about him,' Carole said.

'I think that Goran is the only man Joanna has ever

really liked,' I said meaningfully as I picked up the jug of cream for the pudding and went back to the table.

'Did anyone ever tell you that you have beautiful eyes,' Goran was saying to Joanna when I sat back down.

'Did anyone tell you,' she said punctuating the remark with a silly, girlish giggle.

'I always used to think that it was Carole who had the most beautiful eyes,' I said but neither Joanna nor Goran took any notice confirming, to Carole and me, that they only had eyes for each other that night.

The tension was, by now, almost tangible. Carole sat watching her husband and her friend with her hands gripping the table as if she were trying to diffuse a terrible pain within her.

What made Goran's behaviour so extraordinary was that our meal, as was usual now, had not been accompanied by alcohol. He was sober, intoxicated only by Joanna's side-long looks and, perhaps, the sight of her lean legs beneath the table. From time to time he would stretch across and whisper something in her ear in a manner that began to really alarm me. I had a growing feeling that it was all going to get hopelessly out of hand.

I could tell that Carole was becoming, with every passing moment, more and more tense. And when, on one of her many trips back and forth to the kitchen, she accidentally dropped a glass, Goran, who had barely taken his eyes off Joanna throughout the meal, barked at her as if she were a lower life form (which, to him, I suppose she was).

'For God's sake, Carole, why are you so clumsy,' he shouted.

'It was my fault,' I said quickly getting up and clearing away the mess.

'Nonsense, Carole should take more care,' he said giving Carole's retreating figure an ominous angry look.

By the time that she brought in the coffee, I had serious doubts that I would be able to carry out my part in the forthcoming drama.

The odd, ironic thing though was that in the end it was Carole who ensured that our plan would be put in motion that night. It was Carole who precipitated her own, and Goran's, downfall. As she was pouring the coffee I noticed that her hand was shaking and that small drops of the dark liquid were spilling onto the tablecloth.

'For God's sake, woman, there you go again! Why do you always make such a mess. What is wrong with you?' he shouted.

This only served to make her more nervous and her hands shake more.

'What is it with you, you useless woman,' he roared at her.

At first I didn't think that she was going to react – she was holding her head down in the submissive way that Jasmina did when she was in the presence of men. It wasn't until I saw the hot coffee flying through the air towards Joanna that I realised that Carole had cracked.

As the hot liquid made its way through her skirt and onto her flesh, Joanna began to scream. She got up from the table and ran out of the room, out of the door and down towards our flat.

Goran made as if to follow her and then, his face transformed by fury, came back grabbed Carole and struck her a blow across the face that knocked her to the floor. Then he went after Joanna.

I must have sat there for about ten minutes holding Carole in my arms and rocking her gently back and forth.

I couldn't make up my mind whether I should go on with our plot or just tell Carole everything. In the end a split second vision of Rob, lying next to me in the grass on our last day together, made me carry on.

In our original plan, Joanna had intended to excuse herself in order to go downstairs and check on the children. After fifteen or so minutes I was supposed to ask Goran to go and see what had happened to her, while Carole and I washed up.

The scalding coffee had changed the sequence of events but not necessarily the outcome. As I comforted Carole, I tried to work out exactly how long they had been gone and how long I should wait until I attempted to see if everything downstairs in the flat was going according to plan. Joanna and I had reckoned that it would take about twenty minutes for her to manoeuvre Goran into a compromising situation.

It wasn't a very sophisticated scenario. We had set things up so that, after an appropriate pause, I would go over and turn on the baby alarm which, until that moment had been switched off in the corner of Carole's kitchen.

'Let me make you some tea, you'll feel better then, darling,' I said gently leading her into the kitchen and sitting her down at the table.

'I shouldn't have done that, Chrissie, I shouldn't have reacted like that,' Carole said wringing her hands.

'Goran shouldn't have hit you. It was unforgivable,' I said as I put the kettle on.

'You don't understand our relationship, Chrissie. Goran loves me, that's why he gets so cross with me. He is a passionate man.'

'I got the general idea of that tonight. He certainly seemed passionate about Joanna,' I said.

'How dare you say something like that! I trust Goran with my life. Joanna was behaving like a slut tonight, like some cheap whore. If Goran responded it was just a male reflex. But he would never, never betray me,' Carole said angrily.

I poured her a cup of tea and walked over, as nonchalantly as I could, to the baby alarm.

'My God, Carole, the alarm's been off all night,' I said, flicking the switch down as Joanna and I had rehearsed the previous evening.

Suppressing my growing feeling of guilt, I turned my back to Carole so that she wouldn't notice me twist the volume knob up loud. It took perhaps thirty seconds for Carole to recognise the noises coming from the white sofa in the sitting room of the basement flat.

I didn't move, just stood there cringing at the unmistakable sound effects of sex – panting, sighing, the odd exclaimed expletive, the slap of flesh on flesh. Carole pulled herself up, pushed back her chair and made her way, quite slowly and apparently calmly, to the door. I suppose what motivated her to steal so silently down the stairs must have been the need to surprise her husband and her friend in the midst of their betrayal.

I let her go alone. I didn't want to be a witness to what might follow. But I left the alarm on. I heard the gasps of pleasure turn to those of shock. And then I heard Carole, in a surprisingly controlled voice – as if she, too, had planned this confrontation – address the adulterers.

She told Goran that she had known, all along, that the conception of the turkeybasting babies was madness. That she had always known that he had his own reasons for going along with the plan. It wasn't children, but sex. His dream had always been to have three wives, three sexually submissive servants – and now that dream had come true. She wanted to know how he managed to service Joanna and me, or were we so depraved that we did it together? Then she asked him when the fucking had started – was it right at the beginning, was the whole business with jam jars and sperm donations just a front for his infidelity?

When she had delivered this speech – which brought no response from either Joanna or Goran – the room below me went silent. I turned off the alarm and went back to the washing-up, deeply disturbed that Carole could believe that I had ever been sexually involved with her husband. She must have come back up the stairs, although I didn't hear her, and gone to her bedroom. I finished the last of the dishes and then made my way downstairs.

It never occurred to me that Goran and Joanna – as the final insult to Carole – would finish what they had started. The sight that greeted me when I walked into the sitting room was so startling that it rendered me speechless, which is doubtless why they didn't notice my arrival.

Joanna was furiously riding Goran who was squirming beneath her, his hands clutching at her breasts which were now perched at an alarming angle over the top of her Wonderbra. She was still wearing the stockings, suspenders and stilettos and her face, as she rode him to climax, was as wildly contorted as their bodies. 'Yes, yes, yes,' she was screaming. If she was faking an orgasm she was a far better actress than I had ever imagined.

Chapter 29

❧

I cannot ever really be sure of what Joanna had thought would happen later that night, but I know that the events that followed were a total shock to me. All I had wanted – and all I had assumed Joanna had wanted – was to get Carole on our side. As a unit of three I thought we would have the strength to finally stand up to Goran and eject him from our lives. I had always believed, quite rightly as it turned out, that the one thing that still bound Carole to her husband was their intense sexual bond. Carole had always been very passionate and jealous in her relationships and fidelity, I knew, was very important to her. The fact that it was now an abusive relationship only added to my conviction that Carole was in thrall to Goran, that she couldn't let go of the passion that they had shared in the past. Which was why she had allowed him to gradually dominate her. I believed, and I suppose Joanna shared that belief, that the only thing that would ultimately turn Carole against Goran was evidence of his sexual infidelity. I remembered incidents in past relationships when Carole, suspecting a lover of being unfaithful, had become like a possessed woman.

Perhaps I was naive – indeed in many ways I think that I was, oddly enough, the most naive of the three women – but I genuinely thought that our plan would liberate

Carole. In the end it did quite the opposite. When Goran had left, perhaps half an hour after I had walked in on the lovemaking, Joanna was positively gleeful.

'We did it, Chrissie, we did it,' she said throwing her arms around me.

'You did it, Joanna', I said, realising from the strong smell of mingled male and female sweat, that I was only ever intended for a walk-on role in Joanna's cleverly worked out drama.

'But I couldn't have done it without your help, Chrissie,' she said as if she were giving an acceptance speech at an awards ceremony.

'Did you have to go that far?' I said wearily.

'It wasn't a time for half measures. It had to be authentic, you do see that don't you, Chrissie?' she said.

I gave her a long cold look, sweeping my eyes slowly up her body taking in the tangled state of her underwear, her dishevelled hair, the smeared lipstick and the smudged mascara, and then I turned my back and went into the bathroom, slamming and locking the door behind me.

The curious thing is that on that night neither Joanna nor I heard any worrying sounds coming from the bedroom above. Perhaps after such an exhausting day we just slept more soundly, but anyway neither of us could recall hearing anything that might have indicated the life and death drama that had occurred.

Just after dawn, Sam woke up with a piercing yell, as if in pain. It's a curious thing, motherhood. Because although it loosens parts of your body, bits of you sagging where once they were taut and toned, it tightens up that section of your brain that was once laid-back and loose. So that instead of the slow waking up period that I used to enjoy pre-Sam, even on work days, I was now instantly alert, my mind sharply focused on what was ailing my son.

'Baby, baby what's wrong,' I said as I peered down into his cot.

He had been sick. I won't bore you with the details of the mess I cleared up except to comment that it has always amazed me how much waste material such a small body can produce. Sam was in such a state that I decided the only thing to do was bath him and in undressing him, I noticed that not only did he have a high temperature he also had a sprinkling of fine spots across his chest. I went into overdrive then.

There are few really fearful health threats left to the modern mother and that morning I found myself faced with one of them – meningitis. My mind went into such a spin, my brain focusing so much on the danger of the here and the now, that what had happened the previous evening temporarily disappeared from my memory.

My only thought then was to get Carole. She would know what to do. I ran up the stairs towards Carole and Goran's part of the house holding my grizzling, sickly baby in my arms.

It was only when Carole opened the door that I suddenly remembered the events of the previous night and experienced a moment of almost blinding guilt and recrimination. But my concern for my baby was such that I put aside my regrets.

'Carole, I don't know what to do. Sam's so ill. He's been sick and he's got a rash and I think it might be . . .'

Carole seemed completely calm and in control now, in total contrast to her behaviour the night before.

'Give him to me,' she said, reaching out for him and putting a hand across his brow to gauge his temperature, all the while gently crooning to him. After a few moments she got up and took a glass from the cupboard and laid it onto the little rash on his chest.

This was, I remember, the way of detecting meningitis – if the little spots don't disappear under the pressure of the glass then it is time to rush to Casualty. When they disappeared, Carole looked up and smiled at me.

'It's OK, he'll be all right. I think he must have eaten something that disagreed with him yesterday. He certainly made a pig of himself, didn't you, baby?' she said.

I was due back at work that day and having been given such a prolonged and generous leave of absence I was terrified of not turning up.

'I wish I didn't have to leave him, will he be all right? I could never forgive myself if anything happened to him . . .' I said.

'He'll be fine. You know I'll look after him. I love him so much now, Chrissie, it's as if he were almost mine. You get ready for work – leave him with me now and go and have a bath. When I've taken the older ones to nursery I'll drop Sam in at the surgery just to be sure, OK?'

'God, Carole, what would I do without you?' I said.

When I returned, dressed and made up for work, Sam already seemed a bit better.

'Carole, I know I sound like a neurotic first time mother – well I am a neurotic first time mother – but do you think Goran could just have a quick look at Sam for me?' I said.

It wasn't that I doubted her diagnosis – as I have said Carole was a wonderful natural, wise mother – but I wanted to be sure. I remember her reply so clearly, although the significance of it didn't hit me until much later.

'Goran has gone, Chrissie,' she said in a cold, resigned way.

I have gone over the events of that morning in my head so many times and I still cannot think of anything out of the ordinary about it. Sasha and Nino were dressed for the day and having their breakfast, Carole appeared perfectly calm and in control. There was no evidence of the previous day's party except for two helium birthday balloons stuck to the ceiling in the sitting room. In fact there was nothing untoward in the house that morning.

Although I didn't really want to go to work that day, I knew that there was no one in the world with whom I would rather leave Sam than Carole. She knew exactly what to do, she took some infant Dioralyte from her medicine cupboard and mixed it with a little cooled boiled water which she very gently fed him from a bottle.

When I went downstairs to get my coat and handbag, Joanna was up and fixing breakfast for Emma. We didn't talk, I could barely bring myself to make eye contact with her. By the time I got back upstairs to kiss Sam goodbye, Carole had him in his buggy and was ready to take the children, including a subdued Emma, off to school.

'Don't worry, Chrissie, I'll ring you at the office later and let you know how he is,' she said. 'Wave to Mummy, Sam, that's it bye-bye.'

'Thank you, Carole. And really I'm so sorry about what happened last night.'

'Not as sorry as I am,' she said with a resigned smile.

I didn't question too much what she meant by that because I could tell she wasn't in the mood to talk and anyway I had to get to work and she had to get the children to nursery and school – Nino now stayed till noon, leaving Carole with just Sam to care for in the mornings. Joanna, still not back in a proper working routine, looked after Tom.

I didn't think too much about what Carole had meant when she said Goran had 'gone', although I did wonder if she had meant that he had left for work or left, left. As in left her life. As it turned out he had left all our lives.

It was Joanna who found him, later that morning. I have no idea what she was doing prying around the house while Carole was taking Sam to the doctor's – perhaps she and Goran had planned another tryst – but she found him lying in a pool of coagulating blood in the middle of the matrimonial bed.

She couldn't see where the blood was coming from and she had watched enough episodes of *Casualty* and *ER* to know that she shouldn't move him to find out. Instead she checked for vital signs and found a faint pulse. She fled to the kitchen and made a call to the emergency services. By the time Carole returned from the surgery, the entrance to number 12 Milton Avenue was blocked by two ambulances and three police cars. Joanna said that even when she came into the house, Carole acted as if nothing had happened.

'What are you doing here?' she said coldly to Joanna as she took Sam out of the buggy, set him in front of the television and proceeded to give him a drink. Joanna's account of the events of that day were corroborated in court by the young PC who read out Carole's words as she came in. She had said, 'Thank goodness, Sam, we haven't missed *Teletubbies*'.

And when the air ambulance landed in the back garden she was more excited about Sam's reaction to the sight of a helicopter than anything else.

'Look, baby, look at the helicopter,' she said.

Even when the medics brought Goran through on a stretcher she looked at him as if he was a stranger and carried on with her commentary for Sam. Joanna said it was like listening to a very sinister and dark version of one of those early learning schemes, Carole repeating, in very simple language, what Sam was witnessing in the garden.

Whether she did that to distract him, or herself, is difficult to gauge. But the psychiatrist called to give evidence for the defence at her trial said that a very common reaction to a severe trauma was total disbelief and denial.

When they called me at the office my first thought was Sam. I think everyone has experienced, at some time or another, that mental confusion that occurs when you know you are being told something important and, instead of listening patiently, you rush to the wrong conclusion. Before my brain could process the words that were being spoken to me I had created visions, in my head, of rushing to Sam's bedside in hospital cursing, as I did so, my inability to trust my own instincts that morning.

It never, never occurred to me that anything terrible might have happened to Goran. And even when I accepted what I was hearing – that he had been rushed to hospital with stab wounds and had been pronounced dead on his arrival – it still didn't enter my head that Carole – or for that matter Joanna – might be involved.

They sent a car to take me to Acton Police Station where I was to spend the next five hours being interrogated, making statements, and attempting to work out in my own head exactly what must have gone on the night before.

I didn't see Joanna or Carole. I suppose at that stage we were all suspects.

Years and years ago, I remember seeing an old Agatha Christie movie on television. It was one of those whodunnits in which every character had a motive for murder so that you kept changing your mind as to who was the killer. You could believe it was the husband, or maybe the lover or perhaps even the nephew who stood to inherit the money. Everyone in it was a plausible murderer and that was the twist to the tale – each of them had administered one blow to the victim making them all culpable. And, really, it was like that with Goran. I mean I didn't plunge the sharp Sabatier knife into him and neither did Joanna, but we all 'did it'. We were all three guilty.

Although it was Carole who was charged – thankfully in the end only with manslaughter – and Carole who had to stand trial.

I think it was there – in Interview Room No. 3 at Acton Police Station – that I began to see how bizarre our family set-up seemed to other people. I mean obviously this wasn't a time for holding anything back and whilst, in this account, I have managed to justify certain aspects of our story it was quite different telling the bald facts to a – funnily enough balding – detective. It was rather like allowing some strange man to go through your dirty linen basket, it was intrusive and unsettling and – of course – shaming.

'So the deceased was the father of your child?'

'Yes,' I replied.

'And the father of Ms Horton's son as well?'

'Yes,' I said again.

'Isn't that something of a curious coincidence?' he asked, exchanging a baffled glance with the WPC sitting next to him.

'No, it wasn't a coincidence. It was planned,' I said.

'An interesting twist on what we used to call "family planning",' he said.

'Well the thing you have to understand is that we were all very close. There was this extraordinary bond between us. The three women that is and Goran, well in those days he seemed pretty much the perfect man . . .'

'Obviously,' the detective replied with an ironic little smile.

'But you also have to understand that there was never anything physical between us,' I said.

'Which brings us to the events of last night. Have you any idea what might have happened?'

I was sensible enough, shocked though I was, not to allude to the odd triangle of deception that Joanna and myself had constructed. My instincts told me that if, as seemed likely, Carole had stabbed Goran it would be better for her if the motivating factor was seen to be self-defence rather than jealousy. But I could tell, from my hesitation, that this man suspected there was more to the drama that had unfolded the previous night than mere domestic violence.

'I think,' I said tentatively, 'that she probably couldn't take any more from Goran.'

'Not the perfect man anymore?' he said.

'She never said anything to me but I knew that he was violent towards her. There was verbal abuse too. I think it was what you would call an abusive relationship,' I said.

I never, ever thought I would find myself in that situation and watching the expression on that man's face as he evaluated my evidence – and took in my carefully edited version of our story – makes me want to wince even now.

Relating certain moments in our history – how we had originally come up with the idea of Goran fathering our babies, for instance and the excruciating details of those Tiptree jam jars (and their forty-five minute fresh contents) – was just terrible. But in the end, whatever he might privately have thought, he seemed to accept that I was telling him the truth and I was finally allowed to leave at about six that evening.

The very worst thing about the whole experience was discovering that all the children – including Sam – had been put in temporary care. And although, the following day, Joanna and myself were reunited with our children, Carole was not so lucky.

Chapter 30

✦

One of the most frustrating things about the British judicial system is how long it takes for a case to come to court. And while it was only Carole who was kept in custody, in a sense all our lives were on hold during the time between her arrest and her eventual trial. Joanna and I couldn't face living in Milton Avenue with its terrible memories and bloodstained carpets and when Nino and Sasha were released into our care we moved back into her little cottage.

It was cramped with seven of us living in three tiny bedrooms but we felt safer there. I would like to say that Joanna and myself sorted out in our heads and our hearts what had really happened on the night Goran died. But for quite a long time afterwards I felt curiously repelled by her, unsure of what was in her head and yet so tied up with her in every aspect of my life that I felt unable to confront her with my suspicions. I think, though, that she did feel a great deal of guilt and remorse about her part in what went on that night. She withdrew into herself and took over Carole's role with the children while I went back to work. But there was an awkwardness in our relationship that had never been present before and only once, during the period leading up to Carole's trial, did we in any way confront what had happened.

I had returned one day from work to find Sasha crouching crying in the dark of the downstairs loo of the cottage. Joanna, clearly harassed by the ongoing responsibility of caring for five young children every day, had lost her temper with him because she had found him, earlier that afternoon, playing with some matches in the bedroom he shared with Emma and his little brother.

As I attempted to comfort him, I pulled on the light and stood, transfixed by the images that surrounded us. The scrapbook-screen effect that Joanna had created in this tiny room had always before struck me as beautiful and moving, covered as it was by hundreds of pictures taken from our adult lives. I must have been in the little loo since we returned to the cottage but the significance of the images plastered there had somehow not hit home to me as they did then, when I crouched down next to Sasha and followed his eyes as they focused on some of the photographs of his parents that were displayed on the walls.

'I come in here because Mummy and Daddy are here,' he said looking from a picture of Goran, young, moustached and cradling his infant son in his arms, back to me.

'Oh, darling,' I said putting my arms round him, 'I'm so sorry.'

We must have sat there, gently reminiscing about his early childhood, for about half an hour, the two of us entwined together, our tears mingling as we both gave in to our grief.

Much, much later that night, when I had settled him down and helped Joanna to sort out the mess of the day I told her a little of what he had said and she, too, was overcome by tears.

But it wasn't until the next day, when I came home from work to find the children already in bed and Joanna purposefully trying to rip down the pictures that lined the walls of the loo, that we finally talked or rather argued about the recent past.

'You can't do that, Joanna, this is Sasha's special place,' I shouted as I took in the piles of torn photographs that were strewn across the floor.

'But it's over, Chrissie, it's over and it's best he forgets. It's best we all forget,' she said angrily grabbing at a section of pictures that were glued so securely they would not budge.

'You can't do this, Joanna, you can't just wipe out the past.'

'It's the only way I can move forward, Chrissie, can't you see that,' she said through her tears.

'But we can't go forward until we have faced what happened,' I said.

'I can't face it,' she said simply.

'Why? Joanna, is there something I don't know or something I didn't understand about what we were trying to do that night?' I said.

She didn't reply, she just went on pulling pictures off the wall and weeping.

'Look Joanna, if you could turn back the clock, if you could go back and alter things would you do it?' I said desperately trying to make her talk.

'It was the only way, Chrissie, the only way,' she said but she wouldn't, couldn't stop crying.

We never talked about it again and the next day when I came home every picture had gone. If that little room had once been a shrine to our shared lives, it was now just an empty space. A black hole, Joanna said, in our hearts.

*   *   *

My life at that time was almost entirely divided between work and my responsibilities at home, Joanna and myself were almost like a married couple. There was no room for anything but the children and my work. I did maintain contact with Paul and Anna and occasionally I would take Sam down to see them. But time didn't seem to heal my wounds and I could never get used to being in their home, particularly when I slept in Rob's old bedroom, without him. In the end I stopped visiting them and limited our contact to phone calls and letters (Anna was a prodigious letter writer).

I visited Carole at least once a week but in the main our meetings were depressing and unsatisfactory. She had been so depressed and withdrawn in the immediate aftermath of Goran's death that she had been put on suicide watch. She told her lawyers that she had lost the will to live, that she deserved to be hung, that she wanted to die for what she had done. She even said, at one point, that she did not want a defence, that she wanted to plead guilty to murder even though the charge was manslaughter. It was the lawyers who insisted that I keep visiting her, despite the fact that she barely responded to my presence. I tried to get through to her but most of the time I just told her about the children, imagining that the more she thought of them the more eager she would be to mount a proper defence for what she had done. Once or twice I broke down and said that I was as responsible as she was for what happened that night, but she shook her head and said, quite matter of factly, that she was the only one who was guilty of murder.

Although I never said anything to the police about the real events of that night, and nor had Joanna, I did confess our plot to her lawyers. But they, rather as I had instinctively felt during my interrogation, insisted that her only defence should be self-defence. The problem was convincing her to give evidence in court.

I think the turning point came, about four weeks before she came to trial, when I took in some photographs we had taken at Emma's birthday party the previous weekend. When I had taken my place opposite her in the little room in which we met, I held out a particularly beautiful photograph of Sasha and Nino clowning for the camera in Joanna's little back garden.

'Oh look at them, Chrissie, look at them,' she said breaking down for the first time in my presence.

But she wasn't it turned out, weeping for her children, but for her husband.

'I miss him so much, Chrissie. Sometimes I wake up in the night, maybe disturbed by someone crying out in their sleep, and I think he is with me. And then I remember what happened, I remember Joanna and what they did together and the anger comes back.'

'It's not good thinking like that, Carole. You have got to put it behind you and concentrate on how you can get out of this situation and be there for your children,' I said.

'But you don't understand this loss I feel,' Carole said.

'Did you ever understand my loss? When Rob died I wished, I don't know how many times, that I had been with him, that I had died alongside him. I understand grief, Carole, what I don't understand is why you let Goran treat you as he did towards the end.'

'They wouldn't let me see him you know, Chrissie. When he died, when they told me he had died, all I wanted to do was hold him in my arms and say goodbye to him. But they wouldn't let me.'

I told her about my own experience with Rob in the horrid chapel of rest but I don't think she really heard me. All she could think about was her loss and her guilt and in the end I realised that the only way in which it would be possible to convince her to fight for her freedom was to do so through Goran. I made her look again at the picture of her two sons and I asked her what Goran would want for them now – that they should be denied their mother as well as their father – and she shook her head.

'He would want them to have the chance of some happiness, Carole. For their sakes, for the sake of their father, you have to defend yourself.'

She nodded. Once she agreed to co-operate, her lawyers managed to make the whole thing a pretty cut and dried case of domestic violence. The more curious aspects of our *ménage à quatre*, as some people ultimately saw it, were, if not entirely suppressed, then certainly sidelined.

The central issue was Goran's systematic mental and physical abuse of Carole. The question of premeditation was dismissed when, shortly after she was taken into custody, a doctor was called to examine Carole. It emerged that she wasn't wearing those long clothes purely to conform to Goran's rigid Moslem laws, she also wore them to cover the physical evidence of the batterings she suffered at his hands. The most recent injuries, inflicted on that last night, included a broken rib and internal bleeding that would prompt Carole several hours later to collapse and be admitted to hospital.

The catalogue of abuse read out by that doctor in court provided some of the most dramatic and convincing evidence for the defence. Joanna and myself, too, played our part in painting a bleak picture of Carole's hellish home life. Our account of the terrible rows we had overheard during the time we had lived in the basement flat was backed up by the tenant on the top floor, a nerdish little man who had the look of a serial killer himself. But I think that the most powerful witness was probably Jasmina who bravely testified to having seen Goran abuse Carole publicly and who also revealed the extent to which Carole, who had obviously found it easier to confide in Jasmina than in her two oldest friends, feared for her life.

It wasn't difficult, then, for her defence team to paint a picture of Carole as a frightened and oppressed woman and win the sympathy of the jury. Not least because, of course, Goran was a *foreigner* whose ways and customs doubtless seemed, to the twelve jurors, strange and therefore dangerous.

The only account I can give of what happened that night was the one that Carole gave in court. She was on the stand for an hour telling her anguished tale. How the relationship with her husband had changed after the birth of their second child, how their financial difficulties and her depression had altered the balance so that he became, she could see now, more and more dominant and demanding. It was as if, she said, he was no longer the man she had fallen in love with and married. He became increasingly critical and physically estranged from her so that they no longer even made love. The first time he had hit her, she said, she had almost been glad because, immediately afterwards he had been overcome with remorse and he had told her how much he loved and needed her. It had, she told a hushed court, brought them back together and made her feel important in his life again.

And so the pattern of abuse had begun. As the attacks

became more frequent and more violent she became more and more frightened and at the same time incapable of defending herself or finding a way out.

It was a bravura performance because, not once, did she mention the part that Joanna or myself played in her unfolding domestic drama.

When she finally came to recall the events of that last night she had effectively edited us out of the story – the betrayal that she had witnessed in the basement flat was never mentioned. Instead of jealousy or anger her only motive was fear. She had cooked a meal for Goran that night, she said under the gentle interrogation of her barrister, and he had been in such an aggressive and foul mood that he had thrown his plate to the floor in disgust. She had, as was usual, said nothing and meekly cleared up the mess. Then he began a terrible tirade against her that she knew would end – in their bedroom later that night – in a physical attack. For a full ten minutes he had listed her faults, telling her she was stupid, ugly, fat, useless and, as the final insult, 'not even fit for fucking'.

It was at this moment, as she reached the climax of her account, that she broke down and asked if she might stop for a moment. She sat with her hands covering her face for a while and then she somehow regained her composure and continued.

After his vicious verbal attack Goran had, Carole claimed, gone to bed. She stayed in the kitchen clearing up, hoping that by the time she got to their bedroom he would be asleep. Eventually, filled with fear, she had taken a knife from the kitchen drawer and crept quietly into the darkened room. Convinced he was asleep, she was in the act of slipping the knife beneath her pillow when he suddenly sat up in bed and gripped her hand.

She had never intended to use the knife – and she certainly couldn't recall any deliberate act of stabbing – but in the fight that followed somehow or other Goran had suffered a terrible injury.

There was never any doubt about her guilt but the jury – and more importantly, the presiding judge – were now on her side. When the sentence was announced – two years – I am not sure which of us was more relieved Carole, Joanna or me.

Epilogue

❧

I have been trying very hard to think where I should end our story. And although the narrative will, of course, go on and on I thought there was a sort of symmetry in ending it earlier this month – some two years after it all began – when Carole was released from prison having served only six months of her sentence.

If you recall, it all started with a picnic and it struck me as both symbolic and fitting to end at another picnic. It wasn't a perfectly beautiful day, rather it was one of those days – common in English summers – when big dirty-white clouds moved constantly across the sky so that when the sun did come out it was really hot and when, moments later, it slipped behind the edge of a cloud, it quickly became cool, and sometimes quite cold.

Joanna and I had meticulously prepared the food. Since it was a celebration it was more lavish than our usual meals – there were homemade cold pies, a whole salmon, a chicken, huge salads, bowls of fresh mayonnaise and about five different puddings. And since it was being held in the garden of our new home, we ate it at a long wooden table that we had covered with brightly coloured paper cloths. There were balloons and 'welcome home' banners and party novelties – hats, whistles, streamers.

We sat Carole at the head of the table and toasted her,

the adults with champagne, the children in fizzy fruit cocktails. As I lowered my glass and looked down the table I marvelled at how much we had all changed in such a relatively short space of time.

Carole, understandably, had suffered the most dramatic physical transformation. Her face was lined and her hair was no longer artificially streaked blonde, it was naturally highlighted by grey. She had returned to us two days previously and she was slowly adjusting to her new freedom. The light was beginning to come back to her eyes, the haunted look that had dominated her face in court and during her time in prison was starting to leave her. She had even begun to dress more like the Carole we remembered – she was wearing one of her old, bold dresses, although, I couldn't help but note, her body had lost its former luscious bloom and there was something a little stooped and diminished about her demeanour.

But there were moments during that meal, brilliant little interludes, when all three of us were almost able to recapture our old intimacy. Carole and Joanna, in the past six months, had managed to reach an uneasy truce achieved through prison visits and long, troubled letters. And on that day there was laughter, there was hope and there was even – at least from the children – joy.

I can't say that we didn't have regrets, of course we did. I know that even in my darkest moments – after Rob's death – I had never desired such a savage revenge against Goran. I know that Carole still mourned Goran, that she missed him as I missed Rob, and I am certain that Joanna still had periods of deep, deep remorse.

But what was important now was that we had survived and, in some ways, we had triumphed. Joanna seemed happier and more emotionally stable than I had ever known her. Living in the country suited her – well, all of us really. The children were stronger and healthier and happier and were afforded the kind of physical freedom that they could never have had in London. It had been a good move designed, mainly, to help us put our past behind us and allow us to face a shared future.

It was Carole who left the table first, prompted by the screams coming from the pram that was positioned beneath the trees at the edge of the garden. As she gently picked up the baby, cooing softly as she did so, her expression softened and relaxed.

After a while, still cradling the child, she came back to the table and stood over me as a sudden burst of brilliant, beautiful sunshine illuminated what was left of our feast. I thought then that although our lives had taken turns we would never have chosen, it was somehow right that we three women were still together.

Carole carefully laid Poppy on my chest and, smelling the milk or maybe just my familiar scent, she begun nuzzling against my cardigan searching for my breasts. That was the big change in me, you see – my beautiful baby daughter.

Sometimes I thought that the fact that Rob had managed to plant a seed with all his heart – but would never see it grow – was my punishment. But it was also my treasured reward. A baby, conceived in the old-fashioned way.

An unexpected gift that has shown us all that life, however it is brought into this world, goes on . . .